Puck Buddies

An unlikely love

Tara Brown

ISBN-13: 978-1535411219
ISBN-10: 153541121X

This book is dedicated to my wonderful editor, Andrea. This is me sucking up and essentially apologizing, because never has a book had more changes.

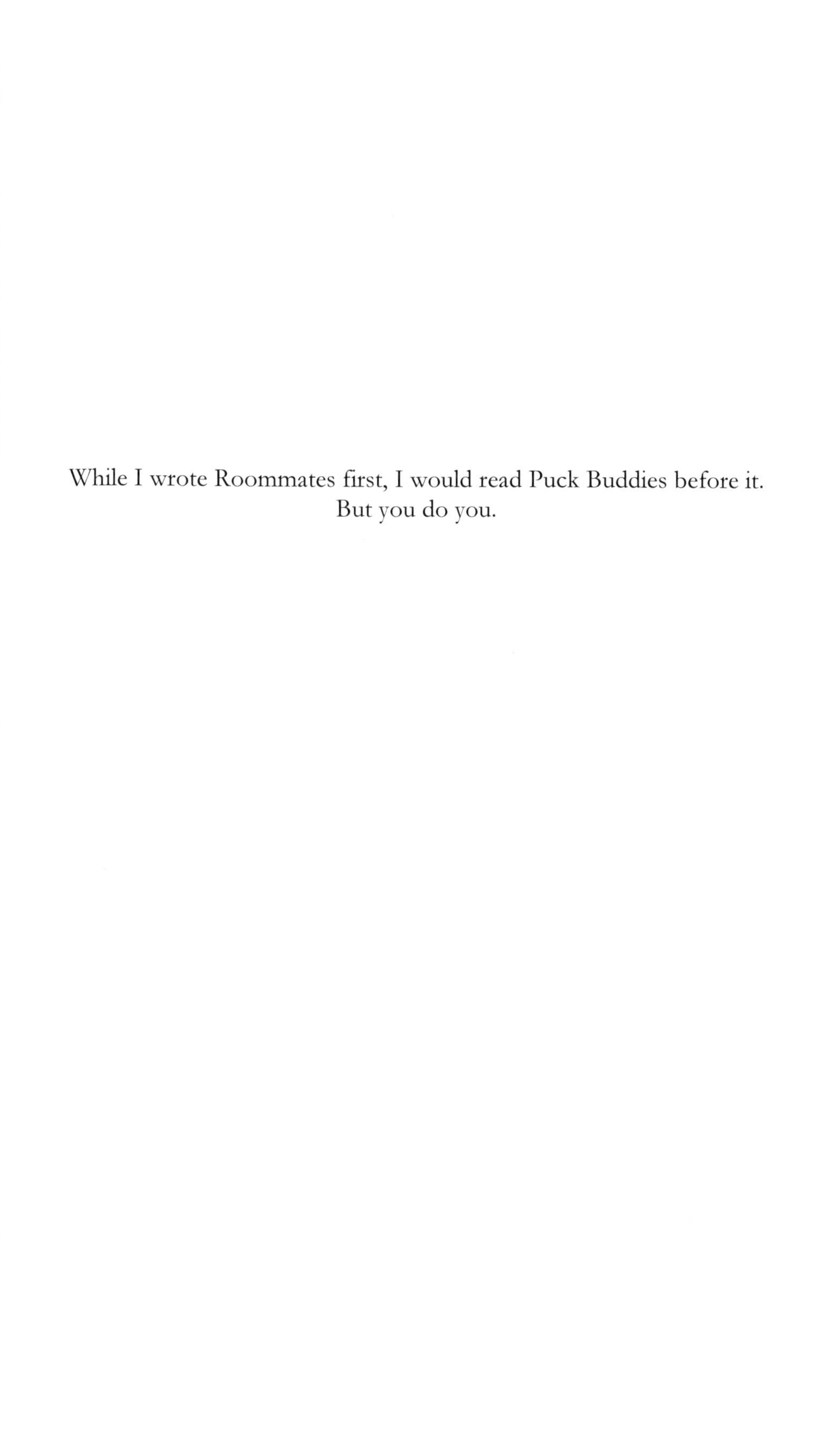

While I wrote Roommates first, I would read Puck Buddies before it.
But you do you.

The princess and the puck!

Prologue

Matt

February 28, 2015

I stumble down the stairs, leaning on my friend Brady and laughing.

We stagger along the path from my boathouse to the main house, both of us cooling off quickly in the frigid wind.

"Good game tonight, Brimstone." Fairfield nods at me as he passes us, leading some brunette back to the boathouse at the bottom of the property. She giggles and trips but he catches her, lifting her into the air and making noises like he's a car. He's such a douche.

I hate that Carson brought him to my house. We both dislike the asshole. But it's how society works. Had we slighted him on the invite there would have been parental issues. As in mine would have had a shit fit. It doesn't matter how old I get or removed from it I become, escaping this world is like getting out of Alcatraz.

But it doesn't mean I have to like it.

"Did you see that dipshit?" I point behind us when I know Fairfield can't hear me.

"The brunette with the big boobs?" Brady spins, confusedly.

"No, the dick with the brunette." I chuckle. "Of course you only saw the girl."

"What?" Brady scowls. "What does that mean?"

"Nothing."

"What about the dick?"

"He's dating this girl—not the brunette—another girl.

Anyway, he breaks up with her randomly so he can get with other girls. And then when he's done with them, he gets back with the girl afterward, so technically he didn't cheat."

"Bro." Brady lifts a swaying finger. "That's a legit play, bro. Don't hate the player, hate the game. That's a real way to get off scot-free. No drama."

"You're a moron."

"Whatever." He grabs his groin. "Men have needs." He laughs, leaving his hand there too long.

"You mean to tell me if you met the one—the girl who just did it for you—you'd cheat on her if you could get away with it?" He can't understand the way I do. He's never been in love. Brady doesn't believe in it.

"Naw, man. But that's a unicorn you're talking about. That girl doesn't exist. I'm never going to be dumb enough to fall in love. It's a pain in the ass. My brother used to be cool. Now he's whipped as hell." He loses the cocky grin. "But for real, if I ever did fall in love like how he is, and I didn't kill myself, I wouldn't cheat. Cheating is something scum does."

"Right. I enjoyed the kill yourself part though. You're an idiot." I steer us toward the house, fighting the breeze the whole way.

"Girls aren't part of the schedule. Finish my degree and get to the pros, that's it."

"Good luck with that schedule." I chuckle, remembering how I'd had one too. I used to have all kinds of rules.

"My dad never cheated. He was married for a pretty long time, and he never cheated before he died." He nods his head at the house casually, like he hasn't just dropped the dead-dad bomb. "I think I need to take a piss. This isn't the kind of house where you piss on the grass, is it?"

"No. My mom will kill you." I point to the large door at the far side of the courtyard. "Go through there and go to the first door on the right. I'll meet you upstairs."

"Roger that." He lifts a thumb in the air and staggers for the wrong door. We've been friends for years but he rarely comes here. There's a good chance of my mom hitting on him here.

"He's going to piss in your mom's planters."

Spinning around I come face to face with the girl I was just talking about. “He probably is.” I don’t even turn back to check on him. I don’t care and I can’t look away from her. I have a terrible suspicion she won’t be here if I do and this will be a drunk-induced hallucination.

Only she doesn’t appear the way I would imagine her in this moment. She’s different from everyone else at the party. She’s in jeans, a parka, and a wooly hat—something the Canadians would call a toque. “It’s a cabin fever party.” I point at her jeans. “Bathing suits and flowery shirts.” I glance down at my own bare legs and flip-flops.

“Yeah, I gathered.”

“How are you?” I ask too quickly, desperate for her. It’s the weirdest feeling, but I don't bother fighting it. I gave up on that the moment I lost her.

“Good. I just came to bring a bunch of your stuff.” She doesn't sound like she wants to hurt me, but her words and coldness toward me do. “I wouldn’t have stopped in if I’d known there was a party.”

“It’s in the boathouse. Everyone’s down there.” I shiver slightly from the cold air on my bare arms and legs but fight looking cold. “Wanna come in?” She came to this house to be rid of me and my things, knowing I never come here. She wanted to avoid me.

“No.” She says it breathy, in almost a whisper. Her face is filled with regret, but I don’t know which part she’s thinking about. Which acts she regrets. I suspect it’s all the moments I wouldn’t change, even if my life depended on it. They flash in the back of my mind, each one slicing me.

She bites her lip, maybe fighting saying something she’ll also regret, maybe just to avoid talking until she mutters, “It was a good game tonight.”

“I miss you.” I ignore her small talk and lay my heart out there for her to reject. I’m already exposed to the elements; I might as well be naked in every way. She’s the only person who has ever seen me vulnerable. Well, along with Charles and Benson, but they’re like parents so they don’t count. “I’m a fucking idiot.”

“I know.” Her expression changes for a second, possibly

a twitch, but she doesn't say anything. She waves and turns. "I have to go."

"Wait." I jog over and spin her around. "Wait." I say it softer the second time. "Don't go." I step in closer, brushing her hair away from her face. "Stay with me."

She lifts her gaze that hardens when her eyes meet mine. "Why?"

"Because I need you." I drop to my knees, in the snow. "Forgive me. I'm crazy about you and I fucked up."

Her lips toy with a smile but her eyes are flooded with emotions. She blinks, losing some of them down her cheeks. "Try not to get too drunk, Beast. You have a game in two days." She pulls out of my hands and turns away, leaving me there to freeze to death.

It's not the snow and the cold that will be the death of me.

It's my own stupidity.

Chapter One

Beer-soaked boobies

Sami

Oxford Circus, London
January 1, 2011
5:03 am

Walking past Banana Republic, I look at the blouse on the mannequin and then down at the beer-soaked dress I'm wearing, wishing I could say someone else dumped the pitcher on my chest.

I also wish I had the balls to just smash the window, take her clothes, and leave mine on her. A new outfit might offer a new perspective or even a new opportunity for an otherwise wasted night—wasted life.

Even with the night long gone and the morning here, cold and damp as usual, I don't feel any newness in the New Year.

I suspect it'll be the same crap year I just had, only this one I'm graduating. That is one bonus, a little more freedom from my parents.

I shiver as I stroll, hating that London and New York share the same wintery weather, and I can't say I like either version. Wrapping my arms around myself to stay warm, I want to regret staying in London the extra week but I can't. The South of France might have been a better spot to party with far better weather, but London taught me something I didn't know. An important life lesson: boyfriends are bullshit. Love is bullshit. People pretending to be in love is the biggest bullshit.

I'm glad I'm free of Drew, that moron. I can't believe I dated him for three months. It's my new record. Actually, the part I can't believe is that I made it past the first week. His being a Londoner likely helped. We didn't see much of each other.

My feet are killing me, so I pull off my Louboutin boots and slip on the Tieks I have in my purse. Luckily, I brought my hobo bag instead of a traditional New Year's clutch. I stuff the boots into the bag and sigh as the teal ballet flats bring me back to life. Pins and needles join the sensation of blood rushing back into my feet.

I look ridiculous in flats with my short midnight-colored cocktail dress, but the boots had run out of blocks left in them four streets back. The ballet flats can go all night, or all day rather.

As I continue down the dark street I glimpse my haggard reflection in a shadowy window and jump. I stop to stare at the mess I am and contemplate calling a car. But by the time the driver gets out of bed, into the car, and here, I could be home in bed.

I drum my nails against my lip, staring at my absurd ensemble in the glass, trying to recall when I saw a cab last.

Normally, Oxford Circus is flooded with them, but in the wee hours of the morning there's no one here.

The street gets chillier—no, creepier—as I do a full circle and see nothing and no one around me.

I'm alone, in London, in the dark. Like in one of those stupid movies Nat made me watch where the world ends and God forgot to tell the star of the show. She's alone in the city with her dog and zombies.

Being alone creeps me out more than anything, stuck with only the sound of my own voice and the empty echo of the wind.

I turn and rush past the shops, searching for the tube station. There's one around here somewhere. I map it on my phone, walking faster as I turn the corners, past the rounded edges of the old gray buildings.

While I've been to London more times than I can count,

I've only ridden the tube a handful of times. But it's five in the morning, I'm still a bit drunk, and not in the mood to wait, and it's doubtful I will happen upon a cab.

I hurry to the entrance to the underground, slightly smiling at the red circle with the blue stripe but losing the happy expression when I see it's not open. My shoulders slump as my plan crashes. It's exactly the end of the miserable night I should have seen coming.

I want to lift my head to the night sky and ask exactly what I did to deserve this, but I think I know the answer so I just stare at the closed doors.

"Shit. Is it closed?"

I jump, turning to find a guy close to my age with an American accent. "Yes," I say, trying to slow my breaths from the shock of meeting a stranger in the dark.

"Well, that sucks." He looks partied out, wearing a rumpled midnight-blue suit that almost matches my dress. His silvery white dress shirt is loose around his neck and the tie is gone, ripped off no doubt, evident in the way his stiff collar is sitting to one side. The lipstick on his cheek, noticeable in the faint glow of the streetlights, is smeared and too pink for his tanned skin tone, so I have to assume a lady friend tore off his tie and wrinkled his suit.

Dry humping will do that every time.

His eyes trail my dress and then his suit. "We look like we planned our outfits."

"Yeah." I bite my lip, recognizing him from somewhere and hoping it isn't some nasty one-night stand. I hate the awkwardness of "I've seen you naked and not at your finest, but now we're at a café with other people so let's pretend we've never met."

"Well, this is bullshit," he mutters but I'm stuck staring at his clothes. His calfskin wingtip dress shoes with their burnt reddish hue are exactly the shoes I would have picked for that suit. But he doesn't seem like the metro type who would know haute couture from a sale at Bloomingdale's.

Did the lipstick dress him? Did she force the suit and tie?

"Well, shit. For a city known for its cabs, I haven't seen a black cab in an hour."

"Are you for real?" I tilt my head.

"What?" He gives me a lazy grin, the kind that normally ends with my skirt up around my waist.

"You can't say black cab. That's racist." I scoff at him. "And most of the cabbies here are white."

"Seriously?" He laughs. "This your first time here?"

"No."

"Whatever." He jerks his head to the right. "I'm headed this way. You wanna walk and see if we can't find a cab? It might not be safe for you to walk alone."

"No. I'll call a car." I lift my phone and groan, "Never mind. My phone's dying at this very moment, because why not?" The swirling image hits the screen just before it goes dark. "Shit."

"Mine died hours ago. Not that I would recall the number to my car. I don't even know my own phone number." He yawns. "Look, it's like fifty degrees out. I'm freezing. Let's just walk. You shouldn't be out at this time of night anyway. Where are you going?"

"Hyde Park."

"Me too." He sounds tired. "Come on." He takes his jacket off and puts it around my shoulders, offering me his arm.

"Thanks." He's a gentleman. I should be leery of the stranger-danger thing, but he's American, and I can't help but trust one polite American over the possibility of meeting a group of random guys in an alley while I have no cell phone.

"No prob." He takes in a deep inhale and smiles. "I love London at night. There's no traffic."

"I've never seen London this early."

"Or late." He's chipper for the hour.

"No."

We walk past the old buildings while he natters on about random things, and I focus on not noticing how sexy he is. The lipstick is like garlic to a vampire for me so it's easy to avoid flirting, although I can't help but appreciate the work of art he is.

The dim streetlights are just bright enough to note his

perfect suit body. Not only is he big and tall, but the pants are clearly tailored to show it off. The way his ass sort of lifts the pants draws my gaze. He doesn't have a big ass but he's got a fit one—perky maybe.

In the dress shirt, his shoulders and arms are massive, stretching the material just slightly. It's a good look, apart from the lipstick on his cheek and shirt showing he's already had a ride tonight. He's actually got another girl on him, at this moment, which for me is up there with cologne I don't like.

But who am I to criticize?

At least he hasn't got half a brewery on him.

"So where are you from?" He lifts a hand, halting me. "Wait—let me guess—I think I'm good at this. I noticed a bit of a New York accent there, only the refined side of the city. You're an Upper East Side, Hamptons brat, aren't you? A debutante or something like that." His eyes dazzle and I love the fact he has no idea who I am.

"Something like that."

"I'm kind of from Kentucky, but I've been living in the North longer than I ever lived in the South."

"Cool."

He's stupid hot. How is it when I've had the worst night ever, the beer-soaked clothes prove it, I run into the hottest guy in London?

God hates me, that's why.

The way this guy talks and walks reeks of polite confidence, my kryptonite. Not just cute boys though. I like cute boys who know they're cute, and despite being covered in kiss marks, they have enough manners and poise to say and do whatever they want while not being a dick. Not because they can't be a dick but because they choose not to be. Like a billionaire who chooses to fight crime at night. It's a fine line to be cool, confident, and forward without being a bossy jerk.

"I'm—" He offers a hand.

"Let's not," I cut him off, not wanting him to know my name. All this relaxed walking and me staring will end. He'll know me straightaway. And then it'll be him staring and me feeling awkward. Not to mention, he'll see the outfit and sell the story, and I'll be in for another stint of rag magazine rehab, the only kind that counts in my world. No one cares that I've never set foot in a rehab clinic. They care that the magazines and gossip say I have.

"Not what?"

"Not introduce. Let's just let this be a random London meet up. Two lost Americans needing someone to walk with while they wait for a damned cab." I roll my eyes. "Black cab, no less."

"It's a thing." He chuckles. "The black cabs are a traditional British cab called a hackney carriage. They're custom-made even, just for the cab companies. I got the spiel from my driver. I swear, it's a thing."

"If you say so." I lift my deadened phone into the air. "I'm googling it when I get home."

"Do it." He gives me that cheeky grin again. "So what brings you to London on New Year's?"

"My dad insisted we spend Christmas as a family, and he had to be in London so we all came here. Of course. And then I met up with an old friend and my boyfriend and we ended up going to a party."

"You don't sound happy about it."

"I'm not."

"Is that why you looked lost?"

"What?" I give him a sideways glance.

"When I saw you back there, at the tube station, you looked lost but maybe more than that." Something about the way he says it makes the moment real, not small and friendly, so I am real back.

"Yeah. I just don't understand how I fall for the stupid stuff guys do every time. They do little things in the beginning that make me think they're something they're not and they trick me, but I fall for it every time."

"Like what?"

"Like guys who kiss the top of girls' heads, hovering there for a moment like they're breathing us in. We're suckers for that shit. And the worst part is, I see them for who they are when they date my friends. But I end up with blinders on when it comes to me. Like I forget the guys who say the right things at the right moments are the ones who have practiced it a lot. The Mr. Collinses of the world. I need to date a guy who says all the wrong things because he's clearly never tricked a girl into being in love with him."

His confused face tells me he doesn't get my Jane Austen reference, but he stays with the general topic of conversation. "Is that how your New Year's fell apart? A guy who says all the right things?"

"Yeah. It's like a magic trick and I fell for it again. Anyway, what brought you here?" I don't want to talk about my New Year's Eve, at all.

"Hockey."

"Weird. Is hockey a big thing in England? Do they even have ice here? I thought it was all soccer and rugby."

"Hockey's bigger than you think." He grins. "I mean, it's not huge–it's not like it is in Canada or something, but they have a couple of teams that are all right."

"And you play?" The question is laden with disbelief. He said driver a minute ago and now he plays hockey? The driver, the beautiful suit, and the shoe ensemble would all suggest otherwise. But his body does scream athlete, especially the way his arms stretch his sleeves even when he's relaxed.

"Yeah." I like the way he smiles when he says it.

"Are you any good?"

He looks as though he might answer but then he laughs. "I thought we weren't getting to know each other. Just a random passing."

That makes me grin back. "You're right."

"Can I at least ask why you're soaked in beer?" He raises one of his eyebrows.

"How do you know it's beer?" His question makes me uneasy. He might have been there and followed me.

"You reek of it. I could smell it across the road when I crossed for the tube. I thought it was either a homeless person or a brewery."

"Oh." I laugh. "It was for five hundred dollars." I press my lips together, totally ashamed.

"I have to hear this story."

"I was partying and my boyfriend turned out to be a complete ass face so I left and ended up at a pub, the Prince of Wales, over near Kensington Palace. Anyway, there was an impromptu wet tee shirt contest." I cut the story there. "I won." I almost smile but the memory of pulling down my strapless dress and pouring beer on my bare boobs to win isn't something I want to share. I still can't believe I did it. I don't even know why I did.

No, that's not true.

I do know why and the look on his face still makes it worthwhile.

"That's hilarious. Your handbag costs over five grand, but you soaked your boobs in beer for five hundred bucks. Didn't see that coming. Not in a blue dress anyway. Shouldn't it be white?"

"I guess." I laugh with him. "I didn't see it happening either. It was a spur of the drunken moment. It was a stupid end to a bullshit night at the end of a week of bullshit nights, at the end of a bullshit year."

"Well, I hope this is part of the perfect start of a new year." He says it in a way that suggests he might be hitting on me.

"Do you know where we are?" I don't want him to hit on me. I mean I do, but not right this moment. I am covered in beer and sweat and God knows what else.

He lifts his gaze from me to the buildings around us. "No."

"Great." I shiver as a black car comes around the corner.

"A black cab!" he shouts like an excited little kid and rushes forward, lifting his hand and whistling loud.

The cab stops in the middle of the road as he hurries to it. He gets the door and grins at the cabbie. "You need to tell her this is called a black cab and I'm not a racist."

I climb in to find a well-dressed English gentleman and a spacious backseat.

"I cannot say whether you're a racist, but you're quite right about the name of the car, sir. Black cab. Now where to?" The cabbie has a thick accent, the kind that Jon Snow has in *Game of Thrones.*

"One Hyde Park." I fight the urge to ask him to say, "You know nothing, Jon Snow."

"I'm not going to say I told you so. Because the man said it for me."

"Whatever." I get comfortable in the chair, excited to be sitting in warmth.

We drive past the Marble Arch and turn toward my apartment and I have the strangest sensation. We've laughed and joked, and I told him something I've never said aloud before. And I don't even know who he is, but I swear we've met before.

I turn to suggest we exchange names now that the night is over and we probably will never see each other again, but by the look in his eyes, he's beaten me to it.

"I have to, I'm sorry," he says as he frowns and raises his hands to my cheeks, lifting my face gently with only his fingertips, but he doesn't move in. He stays here, close in proximity but not enough. Our breath dances in front of our faces for a heartbeat before he finally bends forward slightly, brushing a trace of a kiss on me.

He parts my lips with his, slipping his tongue against mine. His hands slide down my arms and pull me into him, into the kiss and the passion that was slowly building and has now burst.

My hands lift to his hair, hauling him down to me, smothering me with him. He wraps around me as his hands roam my back.

The cab stops, jerking us both forward, and he pulls back, taking all the warmth and magic with him.

It takes a second for me to get my breath or open my eyes.

When I do he grins and winks. "Nice not meeting you, Deb." He gets out of the car and walks down the road like none of this ever happened.

I lift my gaze to the driver. "What do I owe you?"

"The gentleman already paid." He winks too. "That's some kiss huh, miss?"

My cheeks flush and I climb out of the car. "Some kiss." I

watch him walk down the road, hoping he'll look back. I still have his jacket. But he doesn't hesitate. He rounds the corner and he's gone.

Deb?

Why did he think my name was Deb?

A strange sadness aches inside me as I walk up to the apartment, but it's replaced with something else, delight.

I press the elevator and nod at the steel doors. "Perfect start to a new year."

The hint of his kiss still on my mouth, mixed with the ache of knowing I won't ever see him again, is the perfect aftertaste for the theme of the entire trip.

Especially as my phone goes nuts and the picture of me with the pitcher of beer pouring over my boobs flashes in Messenger.

Chapter Two

Friends off

Sami

Manhattan
August, 2011

The hem of my shirt is caught on a button, exposing my entire side but since we're at the door to the club and surrounded by paparazzi, I can't fix it. I don't like to fidget in public where photos can be taken. If you're doing anything but soft smiling, you are depicted as if you've just had a seizure or injected a hit of heroin.

Not that it matters. I don't need to fix the shirt.

Wearing it this way will set a new trend.

In a week everyone who identifies themselves as female from fourteen to forty will be wearing their shirt slightly higher on one side, showing off a fake tattoo. Or God forbid, a real tat they get because I have this one.

Mine's a fake clover because I need a bit of luck—fake luck—any luck.

The beefy bouncer leers and I almost grin back, almost.

My mother's reminder that resting bitch face is important when this many people are taking photos flits about my head every time I see cameras. One wrong smile and suddenly there's a photo in the papers of me crying or wasted. Being Sami Ford is a job—one I inherited, not one I interviewed for.

And we all hate it when we see a picture of my scrunched-up face with a headline announcing how hooked on drugs I am. If I were a crackhead, fine, but I haven't been high in years. I haven't even been drunk since the first of January. I was on house arrest, technically. Being in Greenwich is almost a form of jail. At least I had Nat though.

But now my dad has decided it's time for me to be back in society. Under the agreement that I'll be drinking exclusively in places where photos aren't allowed. It's the only way for me not to end up in trouble.

Mainly because, according to the trashy rag papers, I'm a drunken slut. But the stories are lies. Mostly.

Not that anyone believes my side of it. I was tried in the court of public opinion, the worst court ever.

The last time I ended up in the papers was the worst, New Year's Eve.

I made one reckless choice when I was going through a hard time and they crucified me for it.

And the other two times I made the mistake of being in the wrong place at the wrong time. I wasn't even drinking. The first time, I just walked past a known rehab clinic, clinging to my stomach as a bad burrito tried to assassinate me. And the second time, I was laughing and staggering because Natalie, my best friend in the whole world, told me some crazy joke when my heel hit a crack in the cement.

Everything I've ever done has been stuff any normal girl might do at my age.

But I'm not normal.

And I don't have leeway, I have a trust fund.

So my shirt stays halfway up my torso on one side, revealing far more skin than I had anticipated and what appears to be a new tattoo.

Nat gives me a sideways glance, clearly annoyed from the stairs where she's no doubt blinded from the flash. "Why can't you sneak in the back entrance like the regular celebs?"

"I'm only here to make an appearance for my dad. I'm still sort of in trouble since the whole London thing. Dad wants good publicity."

"Well duh, you flashed your mommas in a random pub when you were seventeen. You got that poor pub in shit.

Underage drinking and nudity aren't cool, even in Britain."

"Thanks, dick," I snarl.

"Seriously though, if my parents see these pictures, I'm dead." She offers her version of resting bitch, but it's always with a nervous quality. On her perfect little face, unsettled nerves are obvious. She has no poker façade at all.

"Your mom won't recognize you and she never watches *TMZ.* You're fine." I wink and drag her in. "My dad made me promise I would come down, but we don't have to stay. Maybe like an hour. Do a bit of dancing and leave."

The club is bouncing, which means Nat might want to stay. She loves dancing almost as much as she loves protesting. But she has to get in the mood. Thinking about her mom is the opposite of getting in the mood.

"What DJ is it?" Nat hurries behind our escort to my new private table.

"I don't know. I think it's one of the European guys that dated Katy Perry or someone like that." I slide into the booth next to her, giving her the look. "Let's just have fun and when we're done, we'll go home. Your parents won't know we even came into the city. I swear. Vincenzo will have us back to Greenwich before they even finish lunch."

"You can't promise that. My mom lives by the society pages. If she sees us here, I'm dead."

"Oh my God. I have yet to see a nightclub in the society pages. You need to calm down, for reals. Nadia did your makeup super intense. I barely recognize you. You're fine." I can't fight the eye roll. "Try to remember you're an adult now. You're legal to vote for God's sake. Stop letting your mom treat you like a child. Besides, I need you to focus on something way more important than your mom's latest hissy fit." I smile wide, flashing my teeth at her.

"You're fine," she groans.

"I had spinach in my pasta. Look closer. I can't walk around here looking like I haven't brushed in years."

"This better not come back to bite me in the ass." Nat scans the room, still uneasy. She lives and dies by her mother's opinion, which in my opinion is crap. Her mom has some weird ideas about how to belong to the upper crust of society. As a member of the upper crust, I can tell you, her ideas are whack.

"Seriously. Are my teeth cool or not?"

"You're fine, just stop. It doesn't matter anyway. You could wear spinach in your teeth and spinach teeth would become cool. Girls have been flashing their boobs and doing wet tee shirt contests for months."

"I know. That's why I'm here. Making good publicity for the family."

"You're still only eighteen and in a club in New York. I don't see how this is better PR for the family." Nat nods at the dance floor when she sees the look on my face. "A couple of dances and then we go before I get caught for sneaking into the city?"

"Fine"—I lean forward, gripping her hands—"but I still think you need to remember you're in an exclusive club where no one is taking pictures. You're totally safe." What I want to say is woman up, but I can't. Natalie Banks is my best, and maybe only, friend.

Which means I have to tolerate her inability to tell her mom to suck it. Mrs. Banks was a mean bitch as a teacher, and she's even worse as a parent. She puts the mother in smother. And Mr. Banks is the ultimate doormat. "Yes, dear" is a catchphrase at their house.

And because of it, Nat is the ultimate goody-goody.

We're polar opposites.

I smoke. She turns on a fan.

I drink. She gets the barf bag and holds my hair.

I skip school. She takes notes.

She's a huge dork.

I've spent the last couple of years trying to undo everything her mom does so I can break her out of her shell. She's fun when she lets loose.

But most of the time she tries too hard to be what her mom expects.

Normally, she wouldn't fit in with the rest of us rich kids but she's beautiful. And beauty forces the world to forgive a variety of sins and flaws.

And she's gorgeous. She looks like a fairy or a tiny

angel. Fragile is the word for her. But only in appearance; physically she's a savage. You can't fight with her, not even playing around. She's wiry and cheats. She bites and pulls hair. There's no actual winning with her. She's scrappy and fast to my lazy and out of shape.

The only way to overpower her is to turn on a video game. Then she goes into an ADHD coma and hyperfocuses on the game.

Needless to say, gaming with her isn't fun.

With her, not much is fun in the traditional sense of the word, but I still love it. It's an escape from my life, sort of how being with me is an escape for her.

She does the weirdest things for fun.

When we were little I rented a cruise ship for a birthday party, whereas her birthdays were small and homemade.

I took us shopping around the world, and she made us read Sweet Valley Highs together, some old books her mom had. Then we had to play Sweet Valley High with our Barbies. She always got to be the nerdy sister and I was the slutty one.

It mirrored our real lives.

Not that we could have ever passed for twins.

I'm her opposite, with my tawny hair, dark-green eyes, and tanned skin. Not to mention, I'm way taller than she is.

"So why are we at this club, like whose is it?"

"My dad's friend's son just opened it not too long ago. He asked if I would show up and be visible to entice others to come."

"I can't believe the rest of the world believes we'd just hang out here, clubbing. We just graduated high school for God's sake." She laughs. "My mom would hate this place. Hate me being in this place. Hate me."

"She hates everything. Your mom is being a dictator lately so who cares what she hates? Her cockblocking on us being at college together is bullshit. She and I are friends off right now. I don't understand why my dad can't just pay for you to go to Columbia with me?"

"Trust me, you and my mother were never friends on, and I never even applied to Columbia." Her cheeks flush.

"Don't even say it. You can't buy my way in and pay my way in life. This isn't *Pretty Woman,* I'm not your hooker."

"Yeah, you are."

"Whatever." She laughs. "That's just not how it's done, not in the real world. Besides, I want to stay home for a few more years. My dad needs me to run interference. Imagine him all alone with her?"

She's lying but this isn't the moment to fight about it, again. I've been hounding her all summer over her mother making her stay home and go to community college for her graphic art degree. Her entire future is currently at risk. But I refuse to allow this to be how it plays out.

I have plans for her. Thinking about them I almost do the villain finger pyramid and laugh maniacally. Almost.

"So what's up with Colin?" Her eyes dart to my phone.

"I sent the breakup text."

"Classy. A text. I thought you'd call at least, call him out on the Tinder thing."

"He doesn't answer his phone. The Tinder thing is gross but the relationship never would have worked anyway. He's a pothead and boring as hell. We've been seeing each other for a couple of months now, and the few times we hung out, he played *Halo* with you more than he spoke to me."

"Don't diss *Halo."*

"I just don't understand recreational drug use if it makes you more boring. He's a slug. Good luck to the Tinder girls. Maybe he'll find a nice stoner to chill with."

"Did you guys even have sex?"

"I had sex a couple of times while we were dating but not with him. I think the weed has killed his sex drive. Waste of talent and time. What nineteen-year-old boy doesn't like sex?"

"Speaking of wasting time, we should just go dance and pretend like we're having fun. Your dad's son's dog's boss would want that. Plus, then we can leave sooner." She glances at the dance floor with a look of annoyance, but it only lasts a flash before her eyes perk up. "Oh my God."

I don't even have to turn my head or ask who she sees.

And there's only one guy who can evoke the look on her

face or the excitement in her voice.

William "Douche Nozzle" Fairfield.

I almost sneer and tell her we can go home like she wants, but when I glance in his direction he's too close for us to fight it. He's already walking our way.

"Oh good," I add, wishing there was a drink in my hand I could spill on myself and force us out of here. Except spilling drinks on myself has been officially boycotted since New Year's. It's been added to the list, along with dating celebrities, forcing the staff to play Cards Against Humanity with me, and wearing workout clothes in public.

A server comes by as if reading my mind and offers me my drink, a gin and tonic with double limes. She hands Nat a crisp green appletini and saunters off, without a single word.

"We've never been here before but she knows our drinks?" Nat cocks an eyebrow.

"I guess someone here knows us."

"Seriously though, what if William ordered them?"

"He didn't." I want to say he's not gentlemanly enough but putting him down only hurts her feelings. It's like reverse, reverse psychology; I insult him and she likes him more.

"He's so hot," she mumbles as she raises the drink to her lips.

"And he knows it."

He's also a bit older than we are, which with him translates somehow into superiority and adds a wonderful accompaniment to the completely narcissistic way he already carries himself. In comparison, he makes my entire family appear as if we don't even share a single hair of conceit amongst us. Which is saying a lot. My dad reminds me of Sir Walter Elliot from *Persuasion,* another one of the movies Nat made me watch. I didn't tell her I loved it and have watched it several times since. My favorite is the one with Rupert Penry-Jones. He's hot as hell.

"What?" Nat turns, giving me a sour frown.

"What?" Maybe I mumbled something about hot guys of Austin.

"You said something."

"It was nothing. Oh God, he's coming over," I groan.

"I know." Her face lights up, gushing pathetic crush all over us both. "Do I look okay? Is my makeup too much?"

"Better than he deserves," I mutter.

"What?" She leans in again. "Why are you talking so low?"

"I said you look beautiful."

Her gaze narrows, but he's at the table before she can question me.

Her bright-blue eyes and pale blonde hair give her a sweet girl-next-door look that science says guys like William should fall for, but she's naive on how to work it, and him. So he works her instead. It's been going on since we were twelve, and I don't know how much more I can take.

He's an idiot.

He doesn't deserve to wipe the shit from her shoe, but she's so beaten down by her mom she doesn't see it.

I have nightmares about the day she tells me they're getting married and he only hits her because he loves her.

I hate him. He's an asshat.

But I love her so I tolerate him. Until I can have him killed off, which is my ultimate plan.

"Ladies, how are you this evening?" William approaches with a grin, speaking directly to me because Nat's so into him. He does it all the time, like he enjoys being chased by her, which is super not manly.

"Great," I sneer.

"Where's Colin?" He scans the bar for my boy du jour.

"He's home. Reading the breakup text I just sent before we left the house." I don't even blink as I say it.

"A text? Harsh, Sami." William laughs.

"I received an anonymous email with a link to his Tinder account. His *active* Tinder account. Nat made a fake profile and asked him to meet up, and of course he agreed to." I keep the part where I'm glad I never had sex with him to myself. Him or Drew. Disgusting asshats.

"Holy shit! Tinder! Damn. What an idiot. The guy's high all the time. You're better off," he adds, like he's not also an idiot.

"Yeah, whatever." I shrug.

My eyes drift behind William to the guy he's introducing to Nat, "This is a friend of mine, Carson Bellevue."

"Sami and I are well acquainted with one another." Carson gives me a knowing grin as if a memory has flashed in his mind. Likely it involves me sitting on his lap while he drives his dad's Porsche with the top down. We were top down times three.

"This is my friend Natalie Banks. She went to the academy with me." I distract him with Natalie so he'll stop making that face and thinking about me with no shirt on.

Everyone has seen me with no shirt on. It's not even a big deal anymore.

"Hello, Natalie."

"Hey." Natalie nods at Carson but bats her long thick lashes at William the D-bag.

"Natalie. How are you?" William tries his usual bullshit where he pretends they're vague acquaintances.

"Great." She hardly even flinches at the way he acts.

It's pathetic.

And the meaner I am to him the angrier she gets with me, not him. Even when the flaws are so obvious.

She is the truest example of love being blind.

Sometimes I cry about the hopelessness of the situation in the shower when I'm alone, or just sob on the inside like a winner when we have to hang out with him.

Like right now.

Carson's eyes leave mine and dart back to Nat's, which is an inevitable outcome. Nat is gorgeous and she doesn't know it, the perfect toy for boys like Carson and William. "Lovely to meet you." He offers her a hand, taking hers and pressing a kiss into it.

William raises his eyebrows when Nat blushes. "All right, Bellevue, don't slobber on her." He glances down at our drinks and turns his head toward the bar. "I'll go get us something better to drink." He turns and leaves.

Carson takes the opportunity to slide into the booth next to Nat. "So are you going to Columbia with us?"

Us?

He's going to Columbia too?

He never mentioned that was where he wanted to go.

"No." Nat shakes her head, averting her eyes. "I'm going closer to home."

"Oh, in Greenwich. Which school?" His lips twist into a wry grin.

I open my mouth to defend her right to go to a random community college when something catches my eye. I want to say it's just a cute face because I am a sucker for a cute boy. But that's not the reason I'm staring.

It's him.

Black-cab guy.

My heart races and my mouth dries, thinking about the kiss. The whole event has chapters in my journal, diary thingy, dedicated to it.

It's still the single greatest ending of any night, ever.

And now he's here . . . in New York.

In the same bar as I am.

And I look hot this time.

And I smell good, not like old beer.

Blood leaves my entire top half when I realize he's strolling over, with perfect swagger. He smiles wide and I wonder if he saw me across the bar or even better—he came here because he heard I was here.

That would be how it works out in my journal, something romantic like that.

But his eyes don't meet mine; they brighten as he slaps Carson on the back. "Bellevue!"

Carson turns, his face lighting up the moment he sees the gorgeous creation next to him. "Brimstone! Holy shit, bro. I haven't seen you in ages." Carson jumps up and shakes hands with the guy beaming at him and ignoring me—*me*—the person black-cab guy shared the greatest kiss in the history of kisses with. "Are you in the city to play or *play?"*

"Just hang out. Maybe soon I'll be playing here though. I'm still in Michigan for now. Gotta finish school so the old man doesn't have a stroke." Black-cab guy answers him so casually, not darting a single glance my way. Is he avoiding me or does he not even recognize me?

Was I that unmemorable?

"So still with the hockey?"

"Yeah."

"To your father's dislike, I'm sure! Still the black sheep then?"

"You know it." He shrugs. His casual indifference contrasts well with Carson's obvious man crush. Not that I blame Carson. I'm crushing from over here in the cheap seats, fully eavesdropping.

Black-cab guy looks different here, better.

No suit.

No lipstick.

Just a tee shirt and some old worn jeans. The ensemble looks soft over his hard body, better than the suit did. He's more in his element like this, I think. Like he could pump gas into his truck and not worry about spilling any of it. He's drinking beer from the bottle for God's sake. I didn't even know you could buy a bottle of beer here.

He's completely casual and relaxed and underdressed, and yet the club let him in, which can only mean he's someone who can underdress. And even weirder, he knows Carson.

He doesn't come across as somebody Carson would even flick dirt at. Nonetheless, he's practically gushing all over him. So whoever black-cab guy is, he has to be someone of importance. Carson is a bigger snob than William the Douche.

But even weirder than all of that is the fact that if he knows Carson, he must know me too.

Which means he pretended not to know me.

Who the hell is he?

I recognize him from somewhere but I have no clue where.

My gaze drifts to his hands gripping the beer.

I shiver, just slightly, or a lot, recalling the moment those hands cupped my face so delicately, while he pretended not to know me. Just as he's doing now. Only now it hurts more because he's also pretending he didn't kiss me.

But he did.

And I have relived the moment for six long months. I

didn't date for months after Drew because of that kiss.

So much so that some days it was the highlight of my entire day. I would fall asleep wondering where he was and if he was thinking about me too. Apparently, the answer to that question is no. No, he wasn't.

I want to call him out on it, but I can't be the one to remember him when he clearly doesn't remember me. Not a chance. I don't do desperate with boys. I might be dumb when it comes to guys, but I am not needy. Not out loud.

My self-esteem, which has been known to take a beating here and there, crashes as I wonder at my being as memorable as he was.

My eyes lower to my drink as my heart cracks in disappointment, just a small piece of it. I had visions of how this moment would go. I'd made a list:

We would meet up in some foreign country, just like last time, both blown away at the randomness of the second meeting.

We would go for a walk filled with awkward tension and our hands would accidentally brush against each other but not actually touch.

We would laugh about running into one another and recommend the sights of the foreign city we both liked.

It would start to rain and we would duck into a doorway.

The pounding rain would quell the noise of the city, and in that moment, he would confess he hadn't stopped thinking about that kiss.

He would tell me that he hadn't stopped thinking about me.

And we would kiss again.

"Sami Ford. Of course you know who she is."

I lift my eyes at my name, losing the daydream. "What?"

"Hi." Black-cab guy nods casually as we have a moment. It's the kind you hear about but never have, where your eyes lock and there's no one else in the room.

But he ends it.

He blinks, forcing me to blink too and it's over.

"And this is her lovely friend Natalie Banks. They're from Greenwich." Carson points his thumb at Brimstone. "Ladies, this is my bro, Matt Brimst—Brimley—we call him Brimstone. It's a long story."

Matt.

His name is Matt. It's a disappointing name. I wanted it to be something better. Captain Wentworth perhaps.

But Brimley sounds familiar.

I give Matt my best indifferent look. I don't know what he's thinking, but I definitely won't be the one to admit I remember him.

Whatever.

Forget him.

Matt smiles politely. "Ladies, nice to meet you." He doesn't linger a moment before his eyes dart back to Carson's. "So how's your sister?" He nudges and grins wider.

I've been dismissed for Carson's stupid sister.

I don't even have a response to that.

"You better not even think about my sister, man. Keep your ginormous hands off." Carson shoves him. They both laugh and I fight not to notice the way he smiles and how his eyes squint just the right amount and his teeth are so straight and white.

He's perfect.

It's unfortunate I will have to hate him for the rest of my life.

My self-esteem might have weak moments but my inner bitch doesn't.

He wants to slight me?

He wants to pretend he doesn't remember the cab?

He wants to ruin the best kiss I ever had?

Fine.

Good.

Screw him.

There are millions of boys in the world who kiss just as magically. It probably wasn't even that magical; he was just the first nice person all night.

"Wanna dance?" Nat nudges me out of my silent argument that plotting revenge sex with strangers to slight a boy who doesn't even know I exist is not a solid plan.

"What? Sure." I suck back my drink and let her drag me from the booth.

"William's still at the bar," she mutters. "So much for getting us drinks."

"He gets sidetracked easily." I glance over, grimacing at the way he's leaned in talking intimately with some brunette in a tight minidress. "Ignore him, it works wonders. Boys try to play us by doing grumpy guy at the bar or barely acknowledging us. Trust me, we fall for it every time. We want them to be happy. It's some bullshit leftover in our DNA from the last five hundred years." At least that's what my shrink says.

My eyes dart back to the guy at our table, Matt.

His indifference to me might as well have come coated in chocolate syrup, but I know better than to get a spoon.

"We need to reverse that shit on them. Be uninterested and act like you don't care. It will drive him insane." I plan to follow my own advice as I pull her to the middle of the crowded floor when the song changes to something we both love.

She perks up a bit as we dance, throwing her arms in the air and laughing when someone falls in sky-high heels.

We dance and every couple of minutes I notice my gaze has wandered back to Matt.

Sweet Jesus!

Why does he have to be so friggin' hot? It's not even fair.

"Thinking about attacking Carson again?" Nat nudges me and shouts over the music.

"No." I almost shudder at the thought. It was like making out with a girl, only with whiskers. Actually, the two girls I've made out with were better. "He needs to just come out of that closet he's in."

"He's not in a closet, he's flexible. He's into everyone. He's omnisexual." She laughs.

"I guess," I mutter, still preoccupied.

"What are you looking at then if it's not Carson? Oh, are you checking out that Matt guy?"

"No!" I scoff. "Pshhhh. I am so not into peasants anymore. That was last season. He's just random. He's dressed like he might go to a frat party, but he's friends with Carson and knows everyone? I just never see Carson slumming it like that. Trust me, that's it. No interest at all."

"Doth the lady protest the beefy gentleman a little too much, maybe?" Her smile makes me smile.

"Not at all. He just looks like dirty sex, okay? You know how I have a hard time passing it up. Blue collar is the forbidden fruit of the Upper East Sider. We all have the fantasy about the mechanic and the gardener and carpenter. There's just something about their dirty hands on our pristine bodies; we can't fight the attraction." All I can do is hope rolling my eyes shows how little I think of him. A lie neither of us buys.

"Whatever. I hate to break it to you, but your body isn't so pristine. Just go talk to him. At least one of us can have some fun. Unless you wanna just go?" she teases but I can't imagine talking to him. And while I wish we could leave the bar altogether, I refuse to slink out depressed over a guy.

"No. Let's pretend we're the most fun girls in this bar. It'll get William." I wink and contemplate hooking her up with Carson for a night.

If she weren't a virgin I totally would, but no one should lose their virginity trashed. I speak from experience on that one. I don't even remember it and I hate that. But worse still would be losing it to Carson. He's known for inviting other people into the party. Something I can't imagine Nat would ever do.

The plan goes back to getting her drunk, so I drag her to the bar for some shots and then back to the dance floor to tear it up.

Chapter Three

Reality Bites

Matt

"So she's not still seeing Colin?" Carson asks William as his eyes drift to the dance floor where Sami Ford is laughing and dancing her heart out. She's even more beautiful than the last time I saw her. It's a problem for me. Not her beauty, the fact I find her irresistible.

"I don't know. She was. I never thought it would last as long as it has. I heard it was suggested they date to try to do some damage control. She hasn't been out at all except in Greenwich. My brother saw her at a couple of luncheons and some of those parentally planned, mandatory dates." Will rolls his eyes like he's better than the societal curse, yet we both know he's neck deep in it. His parents are horrible people. I should know, mine hang with them all the time. "I heard after she was seeing that British guy who took the video of her pouring beer on her tits, her dad told her to simmer down. I think they like that Colin's a pretty chill guy."

"Pothead. The word is pothead," I blurt, trying hard not to focus on the fact Drew made the video. It makes me want to kill him.

Carson laughs. "That's right, you know him, don't you?"

"Yeah." I don't like to dwell on it. Every time Sami dates someone, it's one of my friends. It's annoying as hell. My entire life revolves around my one regret: not being the guy who got to the Sami Ford line first.

But that ship's sailed and she's forever on the list of things I can't have.

Of course adding her to the list only makes me want her

more.

It's a vicious cycle which involves more self-hatred than any other subject.

Luckily, most of the time I'm out of town for hockey so I don't have to suffer in silence much.

Running into her in London was a complete kick in the balls. Being a friend of Drew's I shouldn't have kissed her in the black cab, but I couldn't resist. Now I'm glad I did. "So Drew took the video?" Rage and evil thoughts start to build in me.

"Yeah, man. She caught him cheating on her or some shit so she goes into the pub and wins the wet tee shirt contest, and he said he filmed and uploaded the video."

"Talk about being a little bitch about getting dumped." Carson looks as pissed as I am.

"Well, it's Drew. He's always been a little bitch. She only dated him because her dad told her to."

Knowing that's how her night went kills me inside.

In all my life I'd never seen a more beautiful preoccupied gaze than the one she wore, staring at the entrance to the tube. She might have been drunk but it had worn off, and she was stuck with the shame of whatever she had done. It was refreshing to see at the time. Most of the empty-headed heiresses we know don't regret anything. Everything is YOLO. It's annoying. No consequences because someone will fix it or buy people off or lie to the papers.

But not her. She was filled with regret that morning. I saw it clear as day.

A storm of emotions sailed across her eyes as she talked about her mistakes and guys.

I wanted to see behind the curtain—to know everything about her. Not the regular stuff everyone else knows, but the tiny details she keeps to herself. The ones she hides because they make her different than the other snobby girls. I wanted to heal all the places she'd been wounded by other guys, by my friends.

But I couldn't.

It would have broken the one rule I have about girls and my friends, my hard limit. The one thing I believe sets me apart from who I used to be and who I am now.

And as a result, half a year has been spent envisioning how differently that night could have been, had I just ignored my rules and gone up to her apartment at One Hyde Park, instead of going around the block to cool off before going to my place. Had I known Drew had done that to her, I would have gone up with her.

What are the odds she'd be here?

I blink and rejoin the conversation between Fairfield and Carson, coming back at just the wrong moment.

"Sami's a stone-cold fox. I don't care what you heard, Sami-fuckin'-Ford doesn't date people because her dad tells her to. She does what she wants. I'm still jerking it to the video of her pouring beer on her tits. Drew might be a twat for filming it, but she's fine." Carson laughs and his comment makes me want to choke him out. Not kill him but maybe knock him unconscious. Just for a moment. Right after I kick the shit out of Drew.

Scowling, I glance back at her and the lucky clover tat she's flashing. I'm Irish. My cock takes it as a sign, permission to forget all the rules.

I need to find something else to do with my time, and my hands. They're twitching with demands watching her dance, lifting her shirt in the air every time her arms go up with the beat.

In my weak moments I consider going over and asking if she wants to go for a walk, just to get her alone so I can tell her I haven't stopped thinking about that kiss since it happened. Or the fact she's infected me these last eight months with a constant stream of memories and regrets and possibilities.

"Dude!"

"What?" I snap my head around to Will and Carson gawking at me.

"This place is lame. You wanna go to that new bar over across from the pasta place we went to last time?" Will asks as Carson gives me a weird look, his eyes drifting to where I was staring.

"No. I'm going back to my place. I'm pretty bagged. The

guys I came with are leaving soon." I point at the three Rangers who invited me up to hang out for the weekend. "The team has been trying hard to get me to sign a contract, but my agreement with my father has always been that my first degree will happen before the NHL. So I come up and train with them and get courted. It's a lot like dating. They take us out and show us a good time, hoping we dig the team and choose to play for them."

"They show you a good time, that's funny. They don't realize you invented a good time." Carson laughs.

"Yeah."

"Clearly, they haven't been to the cabin fever party at your house." Will scoffs and glances back at Sami.

"Right, exactly." I roll my eyes at Carson who snickers. "And now thankfully they've all paired off so we can kill the night early and I can get some sleep." The thing I actually want when I come to the city. Coming to Manhattan is like a little retreat from college for me. I sleep in and play video games. There's no pressure to party or have fun if no one knows I'm here. But being with the Rangers is different. It's go time non-stop.

"You pucks. I thought most of you were into each other." Will laughs. "Circle jerks and all."

"Ask Carson's sister how much she likes our circle jerks." I take a drink of beer, laughing.

"Whatever, asshole! She wouldn't even flick a cig at you," Carson snarls. His overprotectiveness of his sister has always made tormenting him enjoyable.

"You sure you don't wanna come?"

"No, I'm cool here. I'm bagged. You guys have fun. I'll let ya know when I'm in town again."

"Maybe we can show those hockey players what a real good time is." Carson waggles his eyebrows.

"They wouldn't be able to keep up. See ya." We shake hands and I head back to my group. They're surrounded by girls, of course.

Three unmarried hockey players don't have to look for ass, it falls into their laps. Hell, even the married ones are beating it off with a stick. Well, some of them. A lot of them have a little slice on the side.

Scanning the club, I pause on the set of eyes staring at me. Sami narrows her gaze like she hates me and goes back to dancing.

"Brimstone, this is Minky."

"What?" I turn toward Laramie and realize he's talking to me.

"What's with you tonight, man? You are in space, brother. Come back to earth and meet Minky. She's from South Africa. Minky, this is Brimstone. He plays for Michigan." Laramie, one of the Rangers I'm friends with, cocks a grin. "Minky likes hockey players, long walks on the beach, and whatever else hot girls like." He laughs. It couldn't have been a cheesier moment if he'd tried.

"Hi, Brimstone." Minky, a gorgeous brunette with sharp green eyes, gives me a wry smile. She inhales, lifting her already perky tits. "How are you?"

"Hi. Nice to meet you." I try to be polite but PFs aren't my jam. Hockey and girls are two different aspects of my life that I don't like touching each other.

When they do, there's a good chance that more than one guy in the locker room has had my girl. Which isn't appealing to me. I don't like sharing. Not with friends and not with teammates.

There's nothing more disgusting than a guy telling me what an amazing bang a chick was as he hands me her number, like I need to experience what he has. We call them pass-along girls or puck fucks, and I don't participate. When I was younger for sure, but I got burned and it stopped being fun.

When I do eventually decide to be with someone, one day, I want her to be mine.

Thinking the word "mine" drags my gaze back to Sami. She staggers and stumbles, falling on the dance floor with her friend. When she gets to her table she slams back another drink. "Jesus." I wince.

"What?" Minky smiles blankly.

"Nothing."

"Oh, okay. Anyway, like I was saying—" She rattles on

while I watch the shitshow going on in the corner. The little blonde falls and Sami bends down to help her up but falls down too. They both laugh, flashing more of themselves than I think they want.

A cell phone pops up, but as the pervert about to take the picture zooms in, a bouncer steps between him and Sami.

That's about as far as I can let it go.

"Excuse me," I cut Minky off mid-sentence, turn, and walk back to Sami's table to see if she's into going home or calling a car. Her driver needs to come and get her.

Sami tries to walk to the dance floor, but she shudders like she might get sick and instead leans on a table. Her eyes widen when she sees me, she even pauses. It's weird. Like she's uncertain of something, maybe me. It lasts a second before she's back to rocking the usual stone-cold-fox expression.

"Hey."

"Hey, Matt." She says my name with a hint of annoyance and leans against the table, swaying slightly as she grabs her drink. How the fuck she has another drink is beyond me. She's well past the point of not being served anymore and she's underage. We both are.

Her plump lips press against the cold rock glass, leaving a pink stain on the rim when she puts the glass back down.

"You want to go for a walk? Get a slice of pizza, maybe? Sober up? I can call your driver."

"What?" Her eyes dart to the little blonde she was with, the one who's in love with Fairfield. "A walk?" Sami pauses, bringing her eyes back to mine. "Like in the streets, outside?" She appears confused by the idea.

"Yeah, that's where the pizza is. You look like you need some food or your car or something." I can't help but grin.

"No." She shudders again. "I don't like that kind of pizza and I don't walk—" She appears as if she might say something else or she might get sick.

Trying to stop her from focusing too hard on puking I try to make her laugh. "Let me guess, I think I'm good at this. You have someone who does your walking for you. No wait, your pizza is always delivered? No—your chef makes you gourmet pizza, even at three in the morning?"

"You're a dick!" She laughs lazily.

"Maybe. But it's the truth, admit it."

"It's cheating. You already know that about me." Her eyes shine as she sways, making us both dizzy. "You know me, don't you?" Her eyes squint, losing the humor.

"I do."

"You're a liar." She shakes her head but she kinda laughs, bitterly. "Just so you know, I can walk fine just not in these shoes after dancing for hours. But I can and I've eaten pizza from a roadside vendor before, I just like gourmet better."

"I have no doubt."

"So," she says with attitude, but I don't know what she means by the "so," or what I should say next.

"We doing this or not?"

"Doing what?"

"Walking. Getting you pizza and sober. Calling your car. Getting you out of this bar."

"You seriously are asking me to go for a walk? Now? After you've acted like you—never mind." She looks pissed and not just drunk. "I'm here with a friend. Maybe next time you're in London you'll remember to actually show some interest in a girl before you just end up kissing. Instead of doing it and then ignoring her and pretending like that amazing kiss never happened. Or lying about knowing the girl." She hiccups as she staggers away, not making much sense but just enough that I see what's going on.

"Right." I turn. "Shit." She completely remembers me from London.

I don't know why I'm the one with the crappy feeling in my stomach when she's the one who had the boyfriend. She's pissed at me for not hitting on her when she was dating a friend? That doesn't even make sense. And she could have acted like she remembered when we met tonight, officially, but she didn't. I took my cue from her.

I'm about to just leave when I catch Minky staring at me. She's still at my table and giving me the look, the one suggesting we could be fucking right this second if I'm into it. But I'm not.

I contemplate what I'm going to say to let her down as I saunter back over. But I don't even get my lips apart to say I'm not into it before Minky has my hand in hers. She spins and struts off, pulling me with her but not saying anything.

Laramie laughs, lifting his drink into the air.

When we get to a dark corner she twirls, grinning and licking her lush lips. She hauls me in, but I put my hand on the wall, stopping her. "Can I ask you a question, as a girl?"

"You can do anything you want to me." She lifts her eyebrows. "Anything."

"Awesome." I want to wince at the awkward permission to play the back nine but avoid even acknowledging it. "If you were dating a guy and one of his friends kissed you on a random drunk night a long time ago, would you be pissed if the friend didn't show interest in you after that? Like this happened a long time ago, eight months."

"What?" Her shoulders slump and her sexy expression is replaced by disappointment.

"Like if I kissed—"

"No, I get the question. I'm not as dumb as I look. I mean, what does it have to do with this moment?" Her South African accent is gone. She sounds like she's from Detroit.

"Nothing." I pause. "I'm just confused. Besides, she isn't single; she's dating one of my friends. Last time I saw her, she was dating a friend. I couldn't show any interest without being a bad friend. And I have a rule. I don't date girls who have dated my friends. It's a thing for me. But she's pissed because I didn't say something. At least I think that's why she's pissed. I mean, we don't even know each other. We just kissed and then I left before I made a mistake—"

"So we aren't going to—"

"No." I shake my head.

"Want me to suck you off then?" The way she says it with her Detroit accent is undeniably hotter than if she were still faking the South African one.

"I don't." I laugh and step back. "I have a thing about love in the club too. Not really my scene." I nod my head once. "Have a nice evening."

"You have a lot of things. Maybe you need to pull that tampon out and stop being a little bitch." She steps into me, glaring. "If you kissed me and you meant it and you didn't show interest afterward, I'd be pissed. Boyfriend or not." She cocks a dark eyebrow, pausing for a moment and saunters off.

"Thanks," I mutter.

On the walk back over to tell Laramie I am spent and emasculated, I pass Sami swaying and tripping on the dance floor. I nearly pinch between my eyebrows as my years of Sami Ford fantasies are crushed. Seeing her like this makes me suspect the girl I saw in London was short-lived, or just a lie, and she is actually a ditzy heiress. She laughs and stumbles from the dance floor, gripping the little blonde friend. They lean against the table and slam another drink.

I scan the club, noting she's alone with the drunken blonde and no security, which is weird for a girl like her. But it was the same in London. So crazy. And now that Carson and Will are gone, they don't have any other friends here. This club isn't a place any of us have hung out at before. I wouldn't have come here if it weren't for the fact Laramie wanted to.

She trips and laughs, spilling drink on herself.

"Shit," I mumble and walk to the table. "Can I call your car for you?"

"No." Sami sounds like a child and shakes her head, pausing for a shudder. The third shudder always means vomit, in my research.

"Come with me. I'll get you a cab at least."

"I'm gonna puke. I don't need dat filmed by peeeze of shit cabbie." She is barely coherent.

Everything in me screams not to help her but for whatever reason, obvious insanity being a top possibility, I sigh. "Fine. I'll walk you home." There's no way I can call Charles and risk them puking in our car. He'll never forgive me.

"We can get dat pizzzza," she slurs. She's been slamming drinks nonstop for an hour.

"No. That ship has sailed. If you eat now, you're gonna barf. You are way drunker than I thought."

"Maybe I wanna barf. Let's go out da back." Sami nods her head that way, doing an odd half circle. "We needa hide from da paparazzzzi or my dadsss gonnabe pizzzzed." She blends her words into a jumbled mess.

"Don't go out the back. They'll be expecting that. We'll go out with my group of friends. They're a crowd of a dozen people. I'll hold you up and cover you."

"Okay." She shrugs.

"I donnnn feel so good." The blonde straightens her back, taking a breath.

"Here." I offer my arm. She hesitates for a second before linking her tiny hands around my bicep.

"Sssorry." I don't know what she's apologizing for.

"It's okay." I turn and offer my other arm to Sami. She doesn't appear sorry but she still comes in close. I wrap my arm around her back and try not to notice the fragrance, maybe jasmine or rose that wafts in the air around her. She smells almost exactly the way I remember, even a little boozy. While she's missing the ale all over her, it's gin now if I'm not mistaken.

"Ready?" I ask in a low tone as the hockey players all pass by the front door. Laramie glances my way, laughing when he sees Sami Ford on my arm with a cute blonde.

"Nice!" He gives me a grin as he strolls over. "You guys headed home?" He waggles his eyebrows.

"Oh yeah." Sami wraps her arm around my waist. "He's in sssome trouble." She winks and bites down on her shiny lip. She's a hot mess of confusion bordering on scary and incoherent. And it's not just because of the sweat stains on her silky tee shirt or the fact her mascara is starting to run. She also has that half-eyed stare going on, where anyone she looks at feels like she's looking through them.

"Lucky bastard." He nods at me like she might actually be something of a prize in the state she's in.

"It's not like that. I'm just making sure she gets home. I need some cover though," I speak low as I drag the two staggering girls to the door, holding them both upright. "Can you guys go as a herd and take the cameras with you?"

"We got you, dude." He gives me a thumbs up as the hockey players and girls head out into the warm night air. The reporters come to life and rush toward the crowd. Laramie is at the back of the group. He glances back at me. "Go right, we'll go left."

"Thanks, man."

I wait for a small group of laughing girls to leave the bar and swerve right in behind them, hugging the bricks of the side of the club.

"Oh shittttt." The little blonde trips, but she weighs about what my jeans might when they're soaking wet, so I scoop her up and carry her, while supporting Sami.

In the streetlights neither of them looks too hot. They're having problems keeping both eyes open at the same time. If the photographers got a picture of Sami like this, it might earn her another rehab stint. She's known for them. She got one after the last time we saw each other.

We make it around the next block with me essentially carrying them both, before I stop to check our status. "No one followed."

"I donn feel so good." Sami twitches like she might throw up and the blonde nods, signaling she's going to. I help her to an alcove where she leans on the wall and loses her dinner in a doorway.

"They're gonna be—hic—excited when dey show—hic—up for work tomorrow." Sami laughs, hiccups, and quivers.

We both step back from the barfing blonde, me with my hands in my pockets and Sami hugging herself. The wind isn't cold, but she's still sweaty and barely keeping her eyes open.

"Where's your hotel?" she asks after a moment of awkward silence. "We could go dere." She can barely keep her eyes open.

"My place is next to the Four Seasons on Fifty-Seventh." I pull my hands out and stifle a yawn. "And no, we can't. You need to go home. You're too drunk even for pizza."

"Did your friends putchu up?"

"To what?"

"In a hotel." I can't tell if she's joking or not. "Do you work in a fffactory? Your hands are rough." She reaches over and takes one of my hands in hers. "See?" She rubs my palm.

"No. Are you being serious right now?"

"Whaa?" She's already forgotten her question.

"My friends didn't put me up—and no, I don't work in a factory. Maybe you should call Colin to come and get you."

"Where?"

"Here. Do you want me to call your dad?"

"No, fffuckim!" she slurs and I have a terrible suspicion she is exactly who I always thought she was. That regretful and emotional state she was in before was probably just due to some heartburn. She's an idiotic heiress, the only flavor they come in. The main reason I hate the world we belong to.

"Whatever." Annoyed, I turn and check on the blonde. "You all right?"

"Yeah." She stands up straight, wiping her mouth. "Ssssorry."

"It's fine." Exhaling heavily, I lift her into my arms and give Sami a look. "Where to?"

"Just off Fifffth." Sami points in the wrong direction. "Do you even know where Fifth Ave is, peasant?"

"Come on." I take her hand and drag her the opposite way she's pointing.

The illusions I had about the infamous Sami Ford die for real that night.

In fact, I kinda hate who she is.

I realize it later when I catch a glimpse of my reflection in the elevator on the way down from her place.

There's lip gloss coating my collar and cheeks.

My shirt is sweat stained from carrying her friend for blocks.

The same friend's throw up is caked to my back.

And the number to Nordstrom's is slightly hanging out of my pocket.

Fuck Sami Ford!

And not in the literal sense.

Chapter Four

Boy toy

Sami

“What happened?” Nat moans, covering her eyes.

“I don't know. I think God hates us.” I tremble from the overwhelming urge to vomit. The daylight creeping in the edges of the shades blinds me and my whole body has a heartbeat pulsating through it.

“I hate us.” She sits up slowly, leaning against the bed frame.

“Me too.” I don't dare try to get up. Instead, I reach for my phone and send a single text.

“Did we have fun at least?” She glances my way, shivering like she might get sick and smelling like she already has.

“We must have.” I swear I’m whispering but the words are echoing off the walls.

The doors burst open, filling me with hope that we’ll feel better any second.

“Nadia?” I turn, cringing when I see a scowling face instead. “Daddy.”

“You girls have some nerve showing up at three in the morning. Do you have any idea what that looked like? That young man holding you up?” He glares at me. “And carrying your unconscious body?” His stare softens for Nat. “This is not why you came to the city. I thought we were done with these shenanigans, Sami. You promised no more crazy nights. I asked you for one little favor and this is where it goes? Every single time, huh, kid? And here I thought you’d grown up since London. I don't care if you have fun, but you're bloody well going to be ladies while you do it!" He turns and storms from the room, slamming the doors.

We both flinch, lifting our trembling hands to our ears.

"Oh my God, he's so mad."

"No. That was all show." I shake my head slowly, trying not to spin the room worse. "He's just doing his due diligence. He has to get angry or he isn't parenting."

The doors open again but this time I'm excited to see the person coming in. "Nadia, thank God. You have to revive us." I offer her one of my arms for the IV.

"Uh, you know how I feel about needles." Nat looks like she might forgo the rehydration, anti-nausea, and Advil cocktail Nadia is famous for.

"It's that or suffer."

"Fine." She lies back and holds her arm out after a moment. Her dislike of needles is nothing compared to the misery we're both suffering.

The cold IV fluids feel remarkable within minutes. It's a magical serum.

"Who's the young man your dad was talking about?" Nat asks after a while. "I don't remember anyone. Was it William? Jesus, did he get us home?"

"I don't know—oh wait." Memories slip into my hazy brain and a guy is there. "Someone walked us home. You threw up in a doorway and then all over him."

"Oh my God," Nat groans. "Was it William?"

"No, someone else. It was bad. He got us to the house. Were you there?" I ask Nadia because I can't recall it clearly.

"I was. I thought someone was breaking in so I came down to the door to find you—in a compromising situation. Your father came down after me. He was less than pleased." She's clearly uncomfortable talking about it.

"What happened?"

"It was terribly embarrassing, Miss Sami." Her eyes widen with worry.

"Nadia, this isn't the moment for you to be a pillar of discretion. I need details, specifics. What happened? Don't spare my feelings. Just say the facts as they happened.

Think police report."

Taking a deep breath, she pauses and then rehashes it for us, "You came in with the tall young man. He looked familiar. I believe he's been here before, but not with you. I think your dad and his are friends. Anyway, he was very large and strong. He carried you both home. When he laid Miss Natalie on the lounge chair in the foyer"—her cheeks redden—"you attacked him, kissing him. He tried to escape, but you told him you wanted to be—" She bites her lip.

"Spill it!" My head starts to hurt again.

"You wanted to be screwed by him since you met him in London because he was your blue-collar bitch, and you wanted his filthy rough hands on your pristine body."

"No!" I groan, shaking my head. "No! Oh shit! Oh my God." I close my eyes and let that digest before I wave my hand at her. "Okay. Fuck. What did he say to that? Did my dad see?"

"No. Your father wasn't downstairs yet. You stopped attacking the young man when Miss Natalie threw up in the planter." Nadia gives Nat a look before turning back to me. "Then he tried to leave. He said thank you for curing him of his feelings for you."

"His feelings? Oh my God!" I groan and recall small bits. "How the hell did any of this happen? What the shit were we drinking?"

"Oh, Sami, damn. He carried us all that way and then you gave him your weird peasant speech about the pristine body. You sounded like a Nazi freak." Nat speaks like she's clenching her teeth. I'm clenching mine.

"What happened next, Nadia?"

"You started laughing and told him what a disappointment he'd turned out to be. That he wasn't magical at all. You gave him your number and told him maybe it would be easier for him to find you this time."

"Oh my God." It just keeps getting worse.

"And then he called the number you gave him right in front of you, proving it wasn't your number. It was for Nordstrom. He was angry and told you he was disappointed in seeing you again and for thinking you were something you weren't." Her eyes softened. "I'm so sorry, Miss Samantha. You were so drunk, you couldn't have meant—"

"Oh my God! At what point did my dad come in?"

"From about the phone call. I think the Nordstrom after-hours message on speaker phone woke your dad up."

"What the hell?" Nat falls back on the bed. "I'm never going to be allowed to visit again."

I want to tell her to shut up and stop being a baby about her mom, but I can't. It might actually be my father who never lets us hang out again, and not because of Natalie, but because I'm corrupting her.

"At least it wasn't on *TMZ* or any of the news sites. Somehow they didn't see you last night." Nadia tries to make it better but this is a train wreck. "I searched the Internet for a new post about you but there was nothing."

"Close the blinds and let us sleep. Call the Banks and tell them we've got food poisoning. Nat will be coming home tomorrow," I bark as I pull my sleeping mask back down and lie back on my pillow, ready to pass out and never think of this again.

"That was mean. You shouldn't talk to her like that."

"I know," I groan. I feel bad and will make it up to her. Nadia is the best.

"Honestly, I have to go home."

I lift one side of the mask and glare. "You stink of vodka."

"Fine, one more night. But we're doing nothing but pizza and movies tonight," she snits.

"Don't mention food." I fight a gag.

I want to sleep but instead end up thinking, remembering things like me laughing when the sound of the Nordstrom after-hours machine filled the foyer from his cell phone.

Matt.

His name was Matt.

And he asked me to go for a walk, just like I wanted him to.

My heart burns and not from the bile sitting in my throat.

Chapter Five

Borrowed whores

Matt

Manhattan
August, 2014

The place looks the same. The minor renovations haven't changed it much.

I stroll out onto the deck and take in the view of the city. I've missed it. It's been eight months since I was here last. A long, hard eight months filled with school and hockey and training.

I'm mentally exhausted but the next part of the ride is about to start.

The card and bottle of scotch on the table next to the window make me smile.

The congratulations from my family are fake and the handwriting isn't even my dad's.

It's our butler Benson's.

He probably felt bad since they didn't even care that I was added to the roster for the New York Rangers. But Benson cares. He always has. I would know his traditional cursive anywhere. It's impressive to see someone master the art of calligraphy because he wanted to.

I don't think I've ever done anything because I wanted to, except play hockey. That is the one thing in my life I do because it brings me happiness. Most of the guys I play with are excited to be in the big league. For them their lives are being made by getting picked to play. That's not why I play. I have the luxury of playing because I love the sport.

Even if my family doesn't.

If anything, I'm risking a lot by being here. Hockey is a sacrifice.

"Mr. Brimley, you have a call. It's Mr. Bellevue." Benson walks in with my cell phone.

"Oh shit, I didn't realize I left my phone in the kitchen. Thanks." He nods, as I take the phone, and leaves the room. "Hey, Bellevue."

"Dude, I haven't physically called anyone in like a year. I forgot how to make a call. I texted you like eight times. You can't answer a text? Too high and mighty as a big bad Ranger? You guys circle jerking it at your place right now as an initiation rite?"

"Yeah, I just finished. Your mom was spectacular. What's up?"

"My mom isn't spectacular. Your mom told me what a dead lay she is."

We both laugh. Our moms are a running joke we've had since we were kids, and we don't know how to stop. That, and his sister, a girl I couldn't be attracted to if my life depended on it. She's another Sami Ford. The classification for bullshit snob in my mind.

"We on for tonight or what? Hot club near Chelsea Park on the corner of Tenth and West Twenty-Seventh. I sent the location in a text. It's pretty much invite only tonight, some special DJ is there. I got the owner to put your name on the list."

"Sounds good. I'll bring a friend, okay?"

"Girl or guy?"

"Guy. A friend of mine from Michigan might be coming up. Why, you interested?" Even though we never discuss it, I know about his bisexuality. As far as our world goes, he's still in the closet about it. But it's a walk-in with feather boas and *Gone with the Wind* posters. It's something he will never come out about. We all know what happens when someone like us comes out about being anything close to different. It's worse than eloping with a stripper. I am basically living that life by doing something so pedestrian as playing hockey.

"No, I don't want more competition for the ladies. For whatever reason, money doesn't bring the pussy the way hockey players do." He says it exactly the way a snobby rich kid should.

"Try having a personality. It'll get you further than your bank account. See ya tonight." I laugh and hang up, shaking my head.

My phone vibrates with several messages, escalating in disturbing content. The last message makes me wince.

Sami Ford will be there. Maybe she'll let you carry her home, like her little blue- collar bitch again.

He still torments me over being thrown up on and called blue collar. It's technically the worst insult Carson could be given. He doesn't know that in the real world it's not even an insult. Most of the guys I play hockey with come from blue-collar families. Their parents have sacrificed like mad to get them to where they are. Most of them are the nicest people I've ever met, until the money gets to their heads. Then they change and become more like the people I'm used to hanging with.

People like Sami Ford.

Snobs who can't get over themselves and abuse everyone they know.

My brain slingshots back to the night that has haunted me for years.

How on earth had I been so wrong about her being so cool?

She did me a solid that night though. She's out of my system for good, flushed by the stench of gin and vomit.

"Matthew!" My mother's shrill voice makes me jump and spin around.

"Yeah?"

"Don't say 'yeah,' darling. It's rude," she huffs. "Are you coming to brunch with us?"

"No. I didn't even know you guys were here."

"We aren't really here. Your father needed to come to town for a quick meeting, and now we're grabbing a bite to eat and then going home." Home being Southampton.

"I can't come. I'm heading over to the training center. We have some meetings with the coach to go over our own skill assess—"

"That's nice," she interrupts without lifting her gaze from her phone. "Well, if you change your mind, you know where to find us." She turns and leaves, clicking her way out the door in her Louboutins.

Change my mind?

Their lack of interest in my career is mind-boggling. Every other parent in the world would be excited that their kid made the NHL.

Benson gives me a look from the doorway where he followed her in. "Might I suggest a deep breath, sir?"

"And a shot of whiskey, or is that a bad idea before someone works me out for the next six hours?" I laugh.

"I would suggest the whiskey *after* the six hours, sir."

"Sound advice, as always." Taking his suggestion, I sigh a couple of times. "I better get going."

"I'll have one of your favorites waiting for you when you arrive back. Best of luck with your first practice. Charles is bringing the car out front." Benson gives me a loving smile and leaves me to my thoughts.

When I get downstairs to the street, Charles has the Bentley pulled around. I contemplated taking a cab like a normal human being, but I've got an hour until we start and it's a half-hour drive to Tarrytown.

"Good morning, sir." The older man sees my expression when I give the car a once over. "Your mother's suggestion, I'm afraid."

"I suspected."

He gets the door and I climb inside, fighting hard not to enjoy the smell of the car. It's my favorite in the world. Riding with my dad in the Bentley was a special treat. I grew up rich but my dad didn't. He was raised in Kentucky; his parents have a farm. But he worked hard and made something of himself and married rich. He prides himself on being a self-made man.

Something he wishes we shared.

Fortunately, he has my older brother to groom and focus on so I only get about twenty-five percent of his judgment. If it weren't for Tony, I would be forbidden to play hockey. But having him take over the family business distracts from my failures. Plus, my father believes this is a phase. Something I will do while I'm young, before I choose a real career.

"Are you excited for your first practice as a Ranger?" Charles asks softly, smiling at me in the rearview.

"I am, thank you for asking." What I mean is thank you for caring enough to ask.

"We are all quite proud of you, sir."

"Thanks." I pull on my headphones, not really in the mood to talk about it all.

It's a pleasant drive, one I enjoy. I've always liked Tarrytown and especially Sleepy Hollow. I read the book when I was eleven and forced Charles to bring me to the village. My mother had said it was a waste of time. So I convinced Charles to take me in secret, under the guise of going to the American Museum of Natural History. It bought us an afternoon to roam the graveyards and look at the village. He agreed, I think secretly enjoying sticking it to them.

When we get close I turn off my music and smile at the scenery. I love being out of the city.

"Do you recall that time we came to Sleepy Hollow and did the lantern tour through the cemeteries, sir?" Charles smiles wide.

"One of my favorite days. I won't ever forget it."

"Nor I. I feared I might lose my job every time we snuck off on one of those tours or trips to sightsee whenever you came to the city." He laughs, making me smile.

"You were a convincing liar, Charles. Mother never suspected a thing. The English accent and the gentlemanly nod wins her over every time."

He raises a bushy eyebrow. "The convincingly good liar was you, if you'll allow me the liberty to say so. For such a pleasant boy, you lie like a rug."

"I learned from the best."

The comment is offside so he doesn't agree, but he also doesn't disagree. Twenty-five years of working for my parents has shown him my comment may be rude, but it's accurate. My father has had a record number of mistresses and my mother has houses filled with clothes and shoes my dad doesn't know about. Neither one of them spends much time with the other, and yet they have a blissful marriage. Our life is perfect . . .

Charles pulls off the main road and turns into the parking lot of a nondescript training center. “It’s smart to have such a plain building house some of the country’s best athletic teams. No one would guess it’s the training center for the Knicks or Rangers,” he marvels.

“Yeah, I like it.”

Before I realize he shouldn't, Charles gets out and opens my door for me. “Here we are, sir.”

Assistant Coach Reynolds is standing on the sidewalk, talking to one of the female players for the New York Liberty. Both of their gazes drift my way as I climb out, looking like a visiting dignitary, not the new rookie.

“Your bag, sir.” Charles smiles and hands me the massive hockey bag loaded with more of my practice gear.

“Remember when I said we should lose the sir and you should call me Matt like everyone else?” I mutter, taking the bag.

His dark eyes narrow. “Remember when I told you English chauffeurs do not address anyone, not even the cockiest of boys, by their God-given names?”

“I think asking to be normal dudes around each other makes me not cocky.”

“Your cockiness makes you cocky.” His expression doesn't budge.

“Can we just agree that here, you’ll lose the sir? Just around the team?” I plead. “I will suffer harder if they think I’m a soft rich kid. Trust me.”

“They’ll see there’s nothing soft about you.” He tries but then concedes, “Fine.” He turns on his heel and heads for the car.

“Don't wait here for me, just go do something fun. Seriously.”

He gets in and drives to a parking spot and turns the car off, ignoring me completely.

Coach gives me a grim nod, obviously not prepared for the new guy to pull up this way. “Brimley.”

"Sir." I nod back, avoiding the dirty grin coming off the cute brunette.

"Better hustle and get ready." He turns back to the girl and continues his conversation.

"Yes, sir." I try to relax so I can enjoy every moment of this walk.

It's only the culmination of my entire life's work.

Each step into the building is important and I need to pay homage to it.

It's like walking the red carpet. Of course the journey, your life, flashes before your eyes.

Every hard moment and battle fought has brought me here.

It's something I've earned.

I didn't have to do it. I did it because I wanted it.

My father might not see it, but we're the same. I fight and work as hard as he does; we just had different dreams.

When I get inside the training center, I can't help but sigh at the smell in the air. I breathe it in deeper, savoring the scent of success.

The air here is made up of blood, sweat, and tears and it's everywhere, even in the foyer with the trophies.

I linger, staring and smiling like a moron.

In the hallway I meet up with several people I recognize from the New York Knicks. It's surreal. I don't normally feel short but as they pass by I'm the smallest man in the hall, at six foot three.

I head for the hockey locker rooms, which are something out of a fantasy.

Every guy I know on the team told me about the state-of-the-art center we had for training and the first time I saw it, back in a summer camp, I was more than impressed. I still am. It's the best facility I've had the honor of training in.

When I get to my locker, I grin at my name for longer than is cool but I don't care.

I'm here.

I've arrived.

A lifetime of personal goals are met in one turn of the locker room and seeing one name tag.

"Brimstone, buddy!" Laramie laughs. "I didn't know Rockefellers got starstruck. I thought you were the top of the food chain. But look at you. Did you pee a little?"

I lift a finger, my favorite one. "Shhhhh, you're wrecking it. Ignore the pee."

"It's just weird seeing you impressed." He comes and pulls me to sit on the bench next to him. "So, you ready to be ridden like a borrowed whore?"

"I don't normally double stuff the cookie, bro, so I don't even know what level of riding borrowed whores endure." I grin. "But if it's anything like the workout your mom gave me last night, I'm ready."

He rolls his eyes. "If you managed to get anything more than a Lysol wipe down from my mom, I owe you a drink. She was the only billet mom no one fucked, which was cool with me."

"I honestly have nothing to add to that." I chuckle.

"She's interesting. Anyway, what's going on tonight? Drinks with the team, after training obviously, but after that?"

"Some club with my friends. You in? I think my buddy Brady might try to make it up from Michigan."

"Brady Coldwell?"

"Yeah."

"Dude, I'm always in when you blue bloods are down to party, but adding Coldwell means I'm doubly in. Maybe Sami Ford and that hot blonde will be there again." He nudges me and waggles his blond eyebrows. No one has let me live down the night I took Sami Ford home. They all assume I had a threesome with two almost unconscious girls, which is fairly funny to them.

"It's safe to say we're too pedestrian for them." I use her own words against her.

He cocks an eyebrow. "Pedestrian? I don't even know what that means, man."

"She's interesting." I laugh and throw the words back at him.

"Well, whatever. Let's do this." He slaps me on the back. "I hope you had your Wheaties, eh. It's time to change."

The locker room comes to life as the doors burst open

and other players filter in, each offering me a handshake or a slap in the arm or back or even a hug. The captain offers a hug.

This is them coming back to work after summer break so everyone is pumped to see the team. I'm not the only new player so the welcomes are rolling off everyone's lips. Mostly it involves more spanking than I'm technically comfortable with. But it's hockey.

My adrenaline starts to build as we head out for the beating of a lifetime.

My first day training as a Ranger. Not a prospect. Not a junior. Not a college kid. A real NHL team member.

It's magical.

For about fifteen minutes.

Then it's painful.

On the tenth flight of bleacher sprints I learn exactly what a borrowed whore feels like. It's a bad feeling. I make a mental note never to borrow whores. They don't like it. No one does.

The excitement of being on the team has died, along with one of my lungs.

"COME ON, LADIES! GET THOSE KNEES HIGHER!" the assistant coach screams at us.

"WHO'S SORRY THEY SPENT THE SUMMER DRINKING BEER AND JERKING OFF?" Our fitness coach shouts and laughs at us as we all groan.

"I'm sorry," I whisper through a cough.

"It's gonna be a long day, bro," Laramie heaves. The flush in his face is gone and he goes pale. He takes a knee and blinks a few times until the color comes back. "I'm gonna barf."

"Yup!" I nod and try to get my breath as we wait our turn to take the next flight.

Long day doesn't describe the level of hell I'm in.

Not even close.

Chapter Six

Second chances

Sami

"Are we dancing this time or did we come just to get your sober face in the papers again? 'Cause seriously, I'm getting tired of going out for nothing. We go to these places for photo ops so your dad can pretend like he doesn't have shares in everything in the city and he's not using you to make money. Because that would be tacky and your father would never be tacky, out loud." Nat mocks me as we click our heels along the pavement from the limo to the club entrance. She's gotten so much easier about going to clubs now that we're almost of age to be drinking. She actually likes going out. But I don't. I dislike it even more now.

I don't glance at the huge lineup. I don't care who's here. I want in and out. "Face in the papers," I groan. "Dad told the owner I would come this weekend. We only have to stay an hour. Then we can sneak out the back and go eat carbs, drink wine, and watch a movie." I wink but she doesn't seem impressed.

"But I put on heels and makeup and I look pretty. Can we go to a fun club after this one?"

"You're the Paper Bag Princess. You look pretty in sweats. And this will be a fun club. My dad doesn't invest in anything that isn't a sure thing."

"You're his sure thing. And I texted William and told him we were coming here. He's in the city for a couple of nights.

If he comes I want to have fun. You promise to be fun, for me!" She gets that annoying whine in her voice, the one I want to slap the shit out of her for. Mostly when it's used with the name William.

Hearing his name makes me want to leave early even more. I had a bad feeling she might tell him we were coming out.

"Deal," I mutter as the cameramen and women shout at me to turn around.

I pose perfectly and spin, allowing exactly ten Mississippis before turning back to strut up the stairs, adding a little extra swagger for the cameras. "I have gone years with no bad PR, as of this summer. This is like an anniversary dinner."

"It's amazing how easy it is for you to win your father over by going to a club or restaurant he's an investor in. My mom wants nothing less than her first blue-blooded grandchild before she accepts me for who I am. Honestly, the only reason she's letting me get a degree in graphic art is because I'm dating *the* William Fairfield." She says it like it's a chore, but she and I both know she's so into him she has almost stopped existing on some levels. "She thinks I won't be working come next year when we grad. She's certain I'll be a stay-at-home mom and a homemaker, mixing William's drinks and rubbing his feet." She rolls her eyes but the vision isn't so off.

"My dad's so busy he doesn't have a moment to care what I do, so long as the pictures in the papers show a lady. Because, honestly, that's how he finds out what's happening in my life. This shoot tonight marks three years rehab-free." I wink.

Nat grins. "If he knew how dull you've become, he might actually miss Rehab Sami."

"Sometimes I wish I *had* been in rehab, just once. Then I could add it to the repertoire. Us Upper East Siders need more stories with edge. I'm tired of the same old bullshit. Party in Southern France, party in New York, party in LA, party in the right crowds with the right people who talk about the right shit. I'm tired of boating, skiing, shopping, and travel. And I'm even more tired of listening to people whisper about dating the wrong people while holding the hand of the right person. Rehab is at least dangerous and edgy. It might make me cooler than I am."

She laughs. "Only you would say that."

"Admit it, this club is filled with the two types of douche bags who exist in our world. There are the ones who want to tell you about their latest trip, pretending to be hipster chic and how they're saving the planet and deconstructing all their meals and beverages. Or there are the ones who don't pretend to care about the environment at all. They're jet-setting the world and their destinations are better than yours. The rest of the club is filled with the naive people who want to be in our world but have no idea the cost of being here."

"You sound like you're getting bitter from lack of sex. Your vag has to be filled with dust bunnies by now. What's it been, years?"

"No, dick. I had three one-night stands before I started seeing my therapist. She wants me to find worthy people and I haven't found anyone. It's hard for a girl to get laid and have respect for her vagina."

"I have nothing but respect for my vag."

"Right. The point is, I refuse to date someone who doesn't make me feel fluttery." I point at my stomach. "If I don't have that jittery nervous feeling in my stomach where I almost feel like I'm going to poo but I'm not, I'm not so much as having a drink with you. And I notice them the moment I meet a guy I like, or whatever. It's science." I still have never told her about Matt and the black cab.

"You and those nervous pains. You're a moron. The feelings you're getting are actual poo cramps. If you ate more greens you wouldn't have those stomach twinges. It has nothing to do with boys." She and I have disagreed about the way a girl's body reacts to certain men. For me that someone is a man I have never named and he was the last one I felt them with.

The fact she's never felt that way with Fairfield is hugely surprising . . . *not!*

"Stomach cramps won't matter when my parents get

their way and marry me off to the right kind of rich guy. My dad has been courting men already."

"You won't end up in an arranged marriage. You're Sami Ford. You are above that."

"We both know this is my fate."

"Oh my God, princess. No one feels sorry for you. Tell your dad to suck it and do whatever you want in life. He can't take away your trust fund. You'll always have money."

I turn and cock an eyebrow. "Really? You're going to go pots and kettles this early in the evening while we're still sober and William is on his way over?"

"Yes. Besides, I actually like William. I think one day we'll make awesome adults together." She laughs as we are seated at a table in VIP and drinks are brought. Mine's a red wine from France that Drew Barrymore had on Instagram. I've been drinking it for about three months. Nat's is a glass of red from the label she's stuck on from BC, Canada. The guy is from New York but lives in Canada and ages the wine in pyramids. It's weirdly cool. It's on the list of shit we need to see. Who even knew Canada had wine, let alone pyramids?

"It's nice in here." Nat nods approvingly. "I like the blue lights."

"You mean the same blue lights that are in every club? Admiring the decor doesn't mean I'll want to stay."

"No." She points at the blue lights strung up over the bar. "They look like jelly fish."

"Okay, those *are* cool."

"Right. This isn't the worst PR gig you've had. Not even close. Maybe we can stay and have some fun, and you can promise to be fun." She glances around the bar, waving after a second. "He's here."

"Great." I don't even bother to look in his direction. The shitty expression I have the moment she says it will only start something I always end up regretting. I have never told her I hate him. I've told her she's worth more. I've told her he's not that into her. I've forced her to watch *He's Just Not That Into You*, but she doesn't see it. Their off-and-on-again thing is annoying, and I had desperately hoped school would be enough to make her see there are other boys in the world, but she went to community college. There aren't other boys at community college.

No doubt part of the reason her mother agreed to it.

"I'm gonna go say hi." She gets up, leaving me alone.

"Whatever." I don't even lift my phone to pretend I'm not uncomfortable. I just sit in my discomfort and watch the club move like a wave. It's packed with all the usual suspects: The rich kids who act like they can't possibly wait to get out of here or to do their next line. I fit into that category. The people who are genuinely fun and like partying in clubs. And the hipsters with their expensive brand-name hippie-styled clothes and man buns.

Dear God, I hate the man bun. Except that one GIF of the guy putting his hair up into the man bun—that one was hot. But that beefy bro could have been hot doing just about anything.

The rest of the rat-faced male populace has used the man bun and beard to hide their hideousness.

At least the DJ is actually talented and the decor *is* perfect. You get the feeling you've entered another world. An underwater world. Even I can't hate on that.

"What are you doing all alone?" Carson gives me a cheeky grin.

"I'm not technically alone. Nat's over there"—I point—"with William."

"Cool." He leans in, speaking low, "You look hot."

"You look high."

He laughs. "I am. As fuck. Some hipster chick just slipped me something on the dance floor with a kiss. It was like a scene from an early DiCaprio movie." He slides into the seat next to me, coming too close for comfort. "And I have something to tell you." His eyes dart to Nat and William the Turd. "It's wrong but I can't stand knowing it alone. I saw him, Will, two weeks ago with some brunette. They were all over each other on a deck at a penthouse party."

"Two weeks ago?"

"Yeah." He nods. "I wouldn't normally betray bros before hos, but Nat's the nicest of us all. She deserves better than Fairfield."

"Agreed. However, two weeks ago they were broken up, had been for a while in fact. They got into a fight on a yacht and ended the relationship in June. I had hoped it was for real this time but now they're back on. Got back together last week."

"I wish she would see him for the dipshit he is." Carson wrinkles his nose. "I mean, he's a friend but he's an asshole."

"Oh, me too."

"You wanna dance?" He takes my wine and sips it.

"Sure." I shrug. "Why not?"

The song changes to a mix we both clearly love because we shoot up from our chairs and hurry to the dance floor. The DJ mixes Drake with Rihanna. It's weird and awesome. Closing my eyes and moving to the flow of the beat strips my worries away.

Carson is the best dancer I know.

Our arms go up at the same moment and then as the song breaks we both slow, moving like we might have taken a little Molly. I suspect that's what he got from kissing the hipster chick. I don't do Molly. I don't do drugs. I tried a couple of times but I get paranoid.

The DJ keeps us here, paused in the moments between the beat dropping.

When it does, the entire club comes to life, bursting like a wave swelling on the sea.

I love stoned people. They just dance better, they try harder.

When the song ends I forget I didn't want to be here and dance more. After a few songs Carson drags me to the bar to slam shots. I scan the room for Nat, stopping when I see she's having a serious moment in the corner with William.

"Oh shit." I suck back another shot and try to ignore the scrap going on.

"Looks like trouble in paradise again."

"The honeymoon period is getting shorter and shorter with them."

Carson lifts his hand. "Two more—"

"Bellevue!" A familiar voice shouting his name cuts him

off.

We both turn to find Matt-fucking-Brimstone looking about as hot as he possibly can. His dark-green eyes narrow when he sees me but it doesn't stop the butterflies in me, not even when he sneers. "Ms. Ford. I thought this place would be too pedestrian for you." He's such a jerk. A hot jerk.

"Brimstone." I roll my eyes and lift my fingers at the bartender. "And make that two more."

Carson laughs. "I was just getting bored. Shall I clear a space for the moment she calls you blue collar again?" He leans forward, chuckling harder.

"You know I don't hit girls." Matt's eyes blaze pure hatred at me, but I lift my favorite finger, flashing him a grin.

"I could take you," I mock him.

Carson nods. "I believe that. She would cheat and you would fight like a gentleman."

"Gentleman, my ass." I roll my eyes and give Carson a glare. "He's a big fat liar. How long would you say he's known me?"

"I don't know, years? His dad's a member of the Pine Valley Club with our dads. How long Brimstone, a decade? Longer?"

Matt's eyes fill with humor. "Longer."

"And that right there is the issue." Matt doesn't shy away from the obvious shade I'm throwing down. "I don't like liars."

"I never lied to you, Sami."

I ignore him until the shots arrive and then I drink all four back to back, pretending all the hate I harbor is because he lied to me and acted like he didn't know me. The reality has something to do with embarrassment I don't want to face either.

"Good to see you're still reckless."

"Well, I have full permission to get trashed now. I have my mule to carry me home." I wink back at his sardonic expression and slap him on his thick arm.

"My days as your mule are over, Highness." He speaks through a clenched jaw.

"This is getting good. Call him a blue-collar bitch and then we can all go dance." Carson steals the next shot that arrives.

"Blue collar is a compliment for what he actually is." I look right into Matt's eyes when I say it.

"Sort of like being called "lady" is for you." He bows slightly before walking away.

My jaw drops.

"You've gotten worse in the years since you've been near each other. Have you seen him or is your grudge-holding skill really at ninja?" Carson hands me another drink.

"I haven't seen him." I don't say that I've watched him get drafted to New York on TV. I've never watched a moment of hockey, but I found myself strangely curious about the fact he was moving here to play.

"When did he lie to you? 'Cause it seems to me you're just being a bitch. I mean, he fucking carried both of you home and you insulted him in front of your dad while Nat puked on him. Did he kill your dog when he dropped you off?"

"I just don't like him," I snarl at Carson.

"Oh snap." He lifts his hand to his lips, laughing at me. "You're embarrassed and can't apologize like a big girl. So now what? He's dead to you? Mature, Sami," Carson scolds and leaves me there at the bar alone.

"Hey, are you Sami Ford?" a guy next to me asks the moment I'm alone.

"No." I shake my head.

"Dude, you look so much like her." He grins and blinks lazily, drunk as hell.

"I get that a lot." I turn and risk strolling over to Nat.

William gets his smug grin on his face when I'm near them. "Hey, how's it going? How's Columbia?"

"Great." I don't ask him about school because I honestly don't have a single shit to give about him.

"Is your family headed for Martha's for the Labor Day weekend?"

"Of course," I reply blankly.

"I guess I'll see you there."

"Us." I nod my head at Nat who's upset about something. "Nat's my plus one."

"I thought you couldn't come?" He turns his head to her.

"You didn't ask me." She's annoyed about something other than Martha's Vineyard.

"I think our moms spoke about it. Your mom said you were busy." He tries to still be casual about it, regardless of how douchie it looks that his mom continues to arrange his playdates, and he can't just man up and ask his girlfriend out on his own.

"Oh. She didn't tell me you wanted me to go. Maybe that was when we were broken up." She says it pointedly. "But Sami's right, I'm going to the party with her." Nat gestures toward the bar. "Can we go get a drink?"

"I can get it," William offers, likely because I'm here.

"No, that's cool." I grab Nat's arm and pull her away from him. When we're at the middle of the bar I lean in close to her ear. "What's wrong?"

"He's got something going on the weekend in September we were supposed to go away. We've been planning it for months and now he's busy. He said when we broke up last time he assumed all plans were canceled." She sighs. "I guess that's fair. I never thought about it like that."

Fire burns inside me. I square off to just lambaste her with the truth—the ugly horrid truth—that I fucking hate him and he's a tool. But the moment I part my lips Carson comes over, nudging her.

"Nat, come dance with me. Sami's being a whore."

"What?" I glare.

"You're being mean to poor Brimstone for no reason. That's whorish behavior. And I want to dance."

"Brimstone? Who's that?" Nat questions.

"Nat, you must recall that poor guy you barfed on years ago." Carson's eyes glow with mischief.

"He's here?" Nat's jaw drops as Carson nods. "Oh my God. That guy who carried us home? You saw him?" She turns around to search the crowded club. "Where?"

"There." Carson points.

"We have to go apologize. I still don't get why you were so mean to him. His parents are super rich and his mom is like royalty, and you treated him as if he was some slob on the streets and I puked on him." Nat drags me with her. I try to pull back, but she's scrappy for such a tiny thing. She drags me right to the crowd of beefy guys Matt's with where he's leaning against a table chatting with a herd of women. She pushes past the girls, earning us sneers, and goes directly to Matt. "Hey, we've never formally been introduced."

"I remember you just fine." He sounds as excited to see her as he was to see me.

"We want to apologize. And thank you." She glances back at me. "We were assholes and you were so nice to walk us home."

"Carry." He smiles back, losing the attitude. No doubt succumbing to her beautiful blonde angel act. Only with her it isn't an act. She's genuinely sweet. "And it was my pleasure." His eyes don't even flicker in my direction.

"Right, of course. *Carry.* I'm so ashamed. I can't believe I got that drunk. And you kept us out of the papers. You saved my life. You don't even know." She lets go of me and puts her hand forward. "Anyway, I'm Natalie Banks."

"Matt Brimley." He takes it and shakes her hand.

"Lovely to meet you."

"You as well." His eyes dart to mine after a moment. His smug grin comes back and my stomach tightens. He looks like he's waiting for something.

But I don't offer anything. If he thinks I'm kissing his boots after he lied when he pretended not to know me, he's nuts. He's an ass who owed me more than just getting me home.

"Apologize." Nat glares at me.

"Absolutely not. You might be fooled by this, but I'm not." I point a long finger in his face. "I see you."

I turn to walk away, but he grabs my hand and turns me around. "Just say sorry and we can be friends. Honestly, what's your problem?"

Carson and the guys with them all laugh and make a face like Matt better watch himself with me.

"You!" I jerk free. Nat calls me from the crowd behind us but I keep walking. I need more shots.

Chapter Seven

Third chance

Matt

She sucks back another shot and shudders, yet again. She has to be the worst drinker I've ever seen. She always shudders like she might puke.

But she's easily the hottest one too. Even making that weird face from the taste of the booze, she is sexy.

Watching her makes me think things. What I need to remember is the way she acted, like a typical rich asshole. Or better yet, keeps acting. Had she apologized, everything would be different. But she is so stubborn.

Rich girls are such bitches and she is the queen bee.

And hot or not, twenty years from now she'll be my mother, and hers. Stuck up and living this bullshit existence where they can't see just how fake it all is. She'll be married to whoever her dad feels is the right choice for the family. She'll have affairs and take trips, and he'll work nonstop but in secret be banging the girl he loved when he was seventeen.

"I don't think I've ever seen her hate anyone, except Will." Carson pulls me from my silent rant. "But no one who's honest with themselves likes Will. He's kind of a twat." He continues to rattle on next to me, "Sami usually gets along with everyone. You my friend, are special. She's one of those girls who just does what she does, not giving much thought to other people. For her to focus actual hate is crazy."

Sami leans on the bar, laughing with the guy next to her and turning her back on us. She places a hand on her hip, pushing her ass out a bit. In her outfit I can easily imagine exactly how she looks all the way up the back of her body. Thanks to the YouTube video Drew made of her pouring beer on her boobs, I can imagine the front too.

She's fucking perfect.

Well, if she had a filter and some manners she would be.

"Dude."

I glance at Carson. "What?"

"What's with you two? Did you do something to her? She hates you and you stare every time you see her."

"What do you mean?" I don't know the answer to the question. I'm not sure I ever did anything to her.

"There's something there, and I'm not an idiot. What happened?"

"We kissed once a million years ago. It was whatever. Nothing that deserves her always being pissed at me. Or not apologizing for being a complete bitch. The blonde apologized. I'm totally over it. But Sami was wrong and she can't own that."

"You kissed Sami Ford?"

"What, it's not a club."

"It kinda is a club."

"Not one I want in." Again my eyes wander over her way.

"Too late, you're in now. Card-carrying member. Too bad she hates you more than she hates anyone, maybe even Fairfield."

"The dislike between us is mutual. I think she's a snob and she thinks I'm an ass. End of file."

"And yet you still want her." He's wrong.

"No. Trust me there's nothing but contempt."

"Okay," Carson mocks. "Maybe try selling that when you've managed to stop giving her that look." He pats me on the arm and strolls into the crowd just as Laramie comes over and sits next to me.

"Hey, man. Where's Brady?"

"He didn't make it. He's got some MILF on the line and couldn't pass up the opportunity to introduce her to Mr. Clinton."

"He's nasty." We laugh but I can't tell if Laramie thinks

it's gross or not. I know I do. But Brady has his thing.

"He really is."

"Whatcha staring at?"

"Nothing."

His eyes follow mine because as much as I hate it, Carson's right. I can't stop staring at her. "Ohhh, Sami Ford again. She's hot, eh?" He nods his head. "I was gonna ask you if you mind introducing us, since you already rode that train, but I'm starting to think you didn't get off at the station. You have a thing for her, eh?" He cracks a grin and I want to punch off his face.

"We don't have a thing. She just owes me an apology, that's all."

"Well, go get it, brother. She owes you. You clearly need closure on this subject. Sometimes closure is just a dirty session of hate fucking, don't rule that out." Laramie laughs and slaps me on the back but he doesn't move. He's waiting for me to go demand my apology.

And why shouldn't I get one?

It would fix all the awkward tension between us.

She acted crazy.

Fuck her.

I finish my beer and walk her way, cutting right in where the other guy is standing. "Hi." I give the grin, the one that always makes her sigh.

"Excuse me." The guy who was chatting her up tries to tap me on the shoulder.

"What?" I turn and glare at him. He lifts his hands and struts off. "Not worth it."

"What do you want?" she snarls as I glance back at her.

Seeing that rage, I can't help but crack a bigger smile. "I just came to see if you wanna apologize in private, it's easier. I know how proud you are, so I thought I'd be the bigger man here and give you a mulligan."

"A mulligan?" Her jaw drops. "Are you fucking kidding me? You pretended not to know me in London, you kissed me, and then when I saw you again you pretended like we'd never met. You're some head-gaming psycho and I want no part in that."

"You were dating Drew. He's a friend. I knew you were dating him when we kissed. It wasn't a head game. It was me being a bad friend and feeling guilty for it."

"He's your friend? He's an asshole. Now I have a bigger reason not to like you."

"Okay, that's fair. I will give you that one. He's a moron. But in London, you're the one who said you didn't want us to say each other's names. If anyone was playing games it was you. And when we met again in the bar you also ignored me. That was hurtful."

"You ignored me first. And in London you were drunk and had lipstick from some other girl on your suit and cheek. What was I supposed to do, look past that? Of course I didn't want your name, you still smelled like the other girl. It was gross."

"Says the girl who was covered in ale from flashing her tits. Like you're so much classier."

"I never pretended to be something I wasn't. *Ass.* But you asked me where I was from and made fun of me being from the East Coast on purpose because you knew me. And then you pretended my name was Deb. You're a weirdo and you might have the others fooled, but I see it."

"Deb is short for debutante, Highness. You are a deb. We both know that. I was at your cotillion, I was an escort that year."

"OH MY GOD! I KNEW IT! I KNEW I KNEW YOU!" she bursts, slapping me on the chest hard with both hands. "I knew I knew you! You escorted Elinda, that chick whose parents got a divorce and the dad came out that he was actually gay and her mom has been his beard all these years. Her family's a hot mess. I couldn't believe you escorted her after all that. I can't believe I didn't recognize you because I seriously remember her hideous dress clear as a bell."

"Jesus." I don't fight the look on my face. "You really are exactly who you pretend to be."

"What?" Her voice gets high-pitched. "And that means what exactly? Who did I pretend to be? Is this because I didn't remember you? You're that pathetic? I meet a lot of people and checking out other girls' dates isn't exactly my style." She almost spits in my face she's so angry. She leans right in, her breath becoming my air.

"You think I care that you didn't remember me?" The conversation is going backward. We aren't fixing it. We're making it worse, and I'm not helping at all by hovering over her, even if she doesn't back down. She's so small compared to me, but she might as well be ten feet tall for the ferocity in her eyes. "I couldn't care less that you didn't know me. And I should be asking you the same question: why are you so pissed? Is it because we kissed and I pretended we didn't know each other or is it because I didn't fall all over you? Huh? You're so used to having guys fall at your feet that you can't handle one not giving you the time of day? I'm so sorry, Highness. I'll remember to bow next time I'm in your presence."

"Fuck you!" Her eyes widen but she doesn't match me with venom. She turns and storms off, leaving me there regretting every single fucking word. I hate being the last one to say something mean. It's always what both people think about from then on. She's the victim and I'm the asshole because I spoke last.

"Fuck!" I signal the bartender. "Two shots of bourbon."

He brings them over and I knock one back before my body wins and I head in the direction she's gone. Fortunately, she's storming to the back in heels and my legs are longer.

I'm almost caught up when she hurries past the bathrooms to the very back of the club and out the doors to the alley. She is huffing and muttering when she glances back to find me hot on her trail. "Go away!"

"This isn't over! You have things you wanna say, so say them!"

"I have nothing to say to you." Again, we lean in on each other threateningly.

"You know, I can't believe I EVER thought you were different than all the other spoiled little girls in this world. I gave you the benefit of the doubt, when in reality you're the worst of them all. You think your looks and money should let you get away with treating people like shit? Well, that's not how the world works, little girl." I point my finger right in her face.

"ARE YOU REALLY SO SAD THAT YOU NEED AN APOLOGY, CAVEMAN? FINE! I ACTED LIKE A DICK! I CALLED YOU BLUE COLLAR! I'M SORRY! I DIDN'T REMEMBER YOU! I'M SORRY! I PUKED ON YOU, IT WAS WRONG! I'M SORRY! I WAS DRUNK AS HELL! AT LEAST I HAVE THAT AS AN EXCUSE! WHAT'S YOURS FOR PREYING ON A DRUNK GIRL IN LONDON AND CHARMING HER WITH ALL THE THINGS YOU KNEW? ARE YOU HAPPY NOW? YOU GOT YOUR APOLOGY, BEAST?" Her eyes burn as she unleashes all her rage.

"No!" I step in closer, maintaining my cool. "I don't think anything you could possibly say would make me happy. You don't care about anyone but yourself, and your apology was pathetic." We are close enough that I feel her growled exhales on my face again, and I'm certain she can feel mine.

"Oh, I'm sorry, Matt"—she takes a deep breath and her eyes get to that crazy place where only girls can go—"I'm sorry I ever met you!"

"Oh really, are you?" I mock her.

"I am. I wouldn't care if you were the last person on earth, I still couldn't care less than I do about you." She leers at me and if looks could kill, this one would have me on fire.

I lean in even more, roaring my sentence back, "I feel exactly the same way, Highness!"

Maybe it's the bourbon. Or the beer. Or the raw passion seething out of both of us. Or just the fact our faces are inches apart and I'm breathing her in.

Whatever it is, a switch clicks on in me.

My hands are on her arms and my lips crash down on hers as I lift her up into me. She kisses back, moaning softly, "I hate you!"

"I know, baby. I hate you too. But you feel so good." I suck her lip, letting her breath become my air.

We were screaming and ranting and my body is still vibrating with hate, but I don't want to stop.

I contemplate pulling back but her hands almost rip the

hair right off my head as she slams me with force against the door we've just come out of.

We explode on each other in a dirty alley against a concrete wall.

She climbs my body while I grab a lot of ass and haul her into the air, cupping her perfect butt as she wraps around me.

Her nails dig into the back of my neck making it all hurt so good.

She fits in my arms the way I imagined she would. We kiss and I can't stand the thought of fucking Sami Ford in an alley.

I carry her and walk to the corner, away from the club. I lift my phone out of my pocket with great difficulty as I plant kisses on her neck and she makes attempts at eating me. I send a text asking Charles to track my phone and bring the limo with the partition closed and music high.

He knows what it means, but he doesn't know what this moment means to me.

Chapter Eight

Third Time's a Charm

Sami

His hands are huge with thick, strong fingers. Them cupping my ass is one thing, but I can't wait to see them on my body, or in it.

Our kissing isn't like our first time; it's not soft or passionate. It's desperate and savage. There's biting and viciousness. Hate fuels every movement, every taste, but I don't care. I want more. He makes my stomach tense in a way I can't stand, but I don't want it to stop.

Matt sucks my bottom lip in, dragging his teeth along it. I wiggle out of his arms as he lowers himself into my neck and kisses and bites softly, even pulling my shirt off to the side so he can get to my shoulder.

I'm mid gasp when a car pulls up.

He shoves me back with his chest against mine, directing me like we're dancing until we get to a limo. He presses me against the side of it as he fumbles with the door. When he gets it open he pulls me to him, he kisses once more before pushing me inside. I sit, trying to get my breath and find the reason I am here.

He climbs in across from me and we stare at one another. I don't know if he's freaking out but I am.

We're alone and not touching and all the feelings that were so real in the bar and the alley are gone, replaced by inexplicable lust.

I hate him, but I don't want to get out, not until I think about the fact the car is here. All the plays in his book come to life the moment I pause and look around me. "You were texting while we were kissing? You texted your car?" I drum my nails on the leather seat as we drive off. "Smart." *Shit.*

"Yeah." His eyes burn through me.

Music turns on as if by magic, but it's his driver setting the mood for him. It sort of kills the mood for me. Matt's done this before, a lot. It's too fluid and too predictable. It makes me feel predictable and cheap. I hate this feeling. I don't even like one-night stands anymore. I like one-night make outs where we both leave feeling disappointed.

Linda's voice rings in my head, reminding me that the only way someone is going to see my worth is if I show them how I am to be treated.

Letting a dirty hockey player fuck me in his limo, like he does all the other girls, might not be the signal I want to send.

"We doing this or what?" He narrows his dark-green gaze.

"Uhhh—" I vaguely recall him saying that to me previously. "What?" I can't remember what I said to him before.

"You look like you're having second thoughts."

"There's just so much left unsaid between us, and I left Nat at the bar. I can't do this. I shouldn't." I need to get out of here before I ring a bell I can't unring. He's hot but my feelings for him are fairly set. I can't be in this limo, staring at the way his shirtsleeves cling to his biceps. I can't be thinking about that kiss. I have to remember I hate him.

"She's with her boyfriend. She's fine."

"They're fighting and she's drunk. I have to get back."

"You want to leave because you hate me?"

"And you hate me." I wish I could be mean again but the kiss is so much of why I'm in this car, like he's the pied piper of the butterflies inside me.

"I don't hate you. I couldn't even if I wanted to. Believe me, I have tried."

I almost bite a hole in my lip staring at his. The tension in the car could be cut and served on fine bone china.

"Stay with me." He whispers it with a hint of pleading. His

eyes bore through me and I let myself consider staying.

How bad is it really to let a dirty hockey player fuck me in a limo? Really? In the grand scheme of things, it's not that bad. Sometimes a girl just needs to get laid, whether Linda agrees or not.

Exhaling all of my will to leave, I sit back in the leather seat, unsure of where this is going to start or how. He looks like he's ready to attack and I worry I need to brace for two hundred and forty pounds of six-foot-three man beast.

But he doesn't.

Instead, he sits back like me, giving me that lazy grin, the one he gave me the first time we met. I tense.

"Am I going to fuck you until you can't see straight or not?"

I exhale twice more before I nod. "Yup." My answer takes up all the space between us.

Space we remain frozen in.

Maybe he doesn't know what to do with the consent. I know I don't. I've said it, but I don't know where to go from here. I can't make the first move. I won't.

We stare at each other, waiting for the other person to do something.

He opens his mouth like he might speak, but instead holds his breath for ten Mississippis before he comes forward, hesitantly, dropping to his knees. He slides across the space between us, lithely for such a large person, past the answer I gave to his dirty question.

He pauses at my legs, his warm hands touching them cautiously. He rubs my knees, digging his fingertips in, before he deliberately spreads them open as wide as my skirt will go. His fingers crawl up my bare thighs, sending shivers through me. The warmth of his rough hands leaves a fiery trail on the inside of my thighs.

When he gets to my plain white underwear he grins. "Laundry day?"

"No." I blush even though I have always defended a woman's right to wear tighty whities. "I just really like white cotton underwear." I laugh. "And I honestly didn't think I was staying out longer than an hour, maybe two."

"You weren't planning on going home with anyone?" He brushes a finger over the middle of the underwear and nods when I gasp.

I shake my head; my mouth is pressed shut.

"But you've thought about this, even if you hate me. You've thought about me fucking you." He softly drags his wide thumb up and down the thin fabric.

"No," I gasp again as he moves in a light circular motion, staring straight at me.

"Yes, you have. I have too. I've thought about you for a long time."

I can't take the intensity of his stare mixed with the admission, so I close my eyes and let my head fall back as my breaths fill with subtle moans. He almost tickles as he moves to the side of the underwear, slipping his finger beneath the cloth. He slows again, running the length of my slit as my body becomes like a pincushion. Every tiny nerve is lit inside me.

He pauses after a moment, forcing me to open my eyes and glance down just as he drags my underwear to the side, exposing me. "You have a beautiful pussy." He traces my lips with his wide thumb again, staring for a heartbeat before he lowers his face between my legs. I spread farther to accommodate his body, but he lifts my calves onto his shoulders and buries himself in me.

I can't fight crying out when his warm mouth lands on me, covering me in heat as he flicks and sucks until he's right—I can't see straight.

My hips move against his face, grinding in a circle as everything builds. He slides one of those meaty fingers into me, gently at first and then building in speed until his fist is bumping against my ass and his tongue is flicking me.

Everything peaks and maintains at exactly the right spot. My hands grip the leather seats and I make more noise than I want to.

His finger pumping in and out jerks me, cutting off each moan with a grunt.

He increases his pace, building up to a proper fucking.

My body tenses and tightens around him, quivering as

he presses down hard on my clit with his thumb but keeps his finger thrusting. My back arches and my toes curl, and I nearly snap a nail off on the leather seat as the orgasm rocks me from every direction.

I don't get the break I might need.

The moment I'm done, he's up and pulling a condom on his already bobbing cock. I don't really get to see it and am uncertain of the size or girth when he puts my feet on his shoulders and grins. “Ready for the finale?”

I bite my lip and nod.

He rubs himself against me for a second before pushing in. I clench down at the wrong moment and his girth stretches me.

“Relax,” he reassures me. “I'll go slow.” He gets the head in first, slowly dipping it in and pulling out, allowing my body to adjust to the difference between his finger and his cock.

Working us both, he groans when his hips hit my ass. His huge hands knead my thighs as he uses my legs as his grip bars, pulling me into him and meeting me with a steady pace.

He doesn't rush.

He savors the entire trip in and out of me, which is my favorite. I hate being banged unless it's from behind.

His eyes meet mine in an awkward moment of thrusting and groaning, but our stare stays on one another. I can't look away. He's inside me, pressing down on me, and somehow he finds his way into my mind as well.

My exhales slow with the pace, adjusting for moaning as we move like a ship on the waves, rocking and groaning.

The pained expression, the trouble in his stormy dark-green eyes, consumes me. I almost experience what it's like being inside me, his eyes are so expressive. He's in blissful agony as he reaches down, letting my legs fall wide to the sides. He pulls me to him and scoops me up, sitting back at the same time so I can ride him.

Before we were sort of banging, just enjoying it more than a real pounding. But now something else is happening. There's savoring where there should be using. The hate has melted away; it can't take the heat of this. I barely can.

My fingers drape over his head, clinging to him. His hands grip my ass, lifting me up and down on his cock at the same pace I ride him, but his arms encase me in him. We're sweating and pressing into each other's faces, breathing each other's exhales and sweat. His teeth find my shoulder again, gently nibbling as he trails my neck to my cheek. He reaches up, swallowing one of my boobs in his hand, massaging and grinding into me and me him.

His shaft is long and thick and the ride up and down rubs all the good spots inside me.

I move a little faster. Being on top I control the one place I really want him to get to. I don't need his whole cock for it so I bob.

"No." His eyes shut for a second as he shakes his head. "I'm gonna come, stop."

Ignoring him, I quicken my pace, also about to climax. His hands grip and try to pull me all the way down and hold me still but my orgasm is here. I force the movements for us both, whimpering into his ear and gripping his head as a second wave of everything hits me.

He realizes what's happening and moves with me, doing exactly what I want. But the moment I exhale through the last of my orgasm, he's done. He wants to fuck, or rather make me fuck him. I'm forced to bounce on his balls while he thrusts like a warrior. It's *Game of Thrones* but the Upper East Side version. He holds me so tight I'm sure I'll have bruises on my hips as he jerks into me repeatedly.

When he's completely done, we clench each other, neither of us moving except to tremble and shudder with delight.

I don't know what to say because I don't know which version of us is the truth. One moment we were screaming and then we were oddly and uncomfortably civil and now we're this.

I insulted him and told him I hated him and now he's inside me in every way, and I have a feeling I'm inside of him.

I want to go back to oddly civil but I don't know how.

As I cling to him I feel like I might be forbidding him to move because I don't want to face him. We didn't just fuck. We did something else that I'm not comfortable with: we admitted something big to each other with a stare. It's as if he knows all my secrets. My eyes betrayed me when they whispered them all to him. The way we gaped at each other, got lost in each other, erases all the petty hate. It explains the intense way I felt about him, good and bad. The passion is there between us, whether we use it for good or bad, it's there just like I knew it would be. When we kissed in the cab two and a half years ago, I suspected this is what this would be like and now we're here.

"Sami?"

My eyes widen and I'm still panicking but I whisper, "Yeah?"

"I'm gonna lose that condom inside you if I don't pull out. Can you move?"

That's the first thing he says?

I barely realize we're still on planet Earth, I can't think straight just like he promised me, and that's all he has to say?

A harsh realization hits me.

This is the kiss all over again.

I'm reading too much into the pleasure and passion.

He's good at kissing and good at fucking, and I haven't ever had that before so I'm a stage four virgin clinging to him.

He's like this with everyone.

I'm making this all mean more than it does. I'm just another girl in his limo to him, and he's the best at everything to me.

Shit.

It's a one-night stand and I'm leaving dissatisfied, but for the first time, it's for the wrong reason. You can't have a one-night stand with someone you've had fantasies about dating. This was a huge mistake.

"Yup," I reply too chipper and weird as I sit back and pound on the partition between the driver and us. The car stops and I do the strangest thing I've ever done—okay, not the strangest but not the smartest either. I grab my underwear, that I didn't even realize he had taken off, and open the door, stepping out, half naked like a baby deer walking for the first time.

"Sami?" he mutters, still getting onto the seat behind him and doing up his pants as I walk along the road without another word. Feeling exactly as trashy as I look, I struggle roadside in some random industrial section of the city to get my underwear back where they belong. They're drenched in some of him and some of me and all the awkwardness one can fit into underwear. "Get back in the car." He throws the used condom on the road and I gag a little bit.

"No thanks." I walk over and try to slam the door, but he stops it with his beast hands. I suspect he could tear it off the hinges if made angry enough. "I'm good. Thanks for the fun night." I smile politely and wave as I walk, pulling out my phone and pressing the number for my car. "Hey, Vincenzo. Can you track my phone and come and get me?"

I don't know where I am. I don't think I recognize it. I'm unfortunately back on planet Earth.

"What are you doing?" Matt strides to me, leaving the door open. "I'll give you a ride back to the club."

"I feel like you already gave me a ride. We don't need to make this awkward. We can just pretend this didn't happen." The words are so hard to speak, my voice almost cracks.

"But it did happen. And I want to give you a ride home."

"No, you want to be a gentleman." I nod at the car. "But I don't need you to be a gentleman after that." I point at the car and the condom. "I'm not drunk. I have my own limo. You don't have to worry about me. We aren't friends, Matt. We don't even like each other. I don't know what that was but it's over."

"Get in the fucking car!" He's being super serious so I take a step back because I'm that girl who has to color outside the line you just told me not to.

"No. You can't tell me what to do."

He takes a step forward but I step back. "I swear to God, I'm going to pick you up and put you in the car if you don't."

"Whatever, Beast!" I laugh in his face, not daring him to

pick me up, but because we have arrived right back to where we were before the orgasms, fighting.

"I mean it!" He moves toward me fast, lifting me up over his shoulder and carrying me kicking to the car.

"Put me down!"

"NO!" he shouts back for the first time and instead of listening I struggle harder.

"Put me down!"

He does as I say but he pulls me to the car and slams the door. He sticks one of his meaty fingers in my face. "This is the wrong neighborhood to leave you alone in a skirt and silly shoes! We can wait here until Vincenzo gets here!" He's huffing his breath and looks like he might murder someone. His nostrils are dangerously flared.

"You're a dick."

"No, I'm not. I had a hard workout today, like I threw up a couple of times. I'm not in the mood to get beaten up by some carjackers because you have to make this weird. It wasn't weird until you got out of the car. People have sex all the time; it's no big deal. We fucked. Get over it, Highness!"

"Oh, don't worry, Beast, I was over it the moment it ended." My eyes lower to my phone as I send a text telling Vincenzo he needs to hurry or I will be going to jail for killing a man.

"Why do you have to do that? Why are you so bent on hating me?" He leans in, his lips twisting into a sneer.

"I'm not bent on feeling anything for you. In fact, I'm glad this happened. You have just proven to me you are exactly the guy I thought you were."

"Holy fuck." He rolls his eyes and sits back.

The silence is awkward but the agonizing reality of him being who I thought he was is much worse.

My mind taunts me with the way I imagined him, the things I daydreamed about.

All of them were the fantasies of a naive girl.

We stare out opposite windows as I wish I could have the fantasy version of him back.

Chapter Nine

More borrowed whores

Matt

The drive home is conflicting.

I hate myself for breaking the one rule I never break.

But even worse is the way the ice queen has gotten into my veins. The kind of gotten in where I'm scared I won't be able to sleep.

I want to slap myself in the forehead a couple of times for being so stupid and weak.

She's a girl, nothing more, and yet she seems to have weaseled her way into my head.

She acted so crazy, proving she is the nutjob drama queen I assumed she would be, but the feeling of holding her will haunt me for the rest of my life. We fit, we matched. She makes me nuts.

Shit!

Usually the thought of being with someone my friends have been with makes me sick, but I can't make myself regret it. I want to watch her orgasm over and over. I never want to watch another girl orgasm unless it's Sami Ford. Sami-fucking-Ford. Satan herself.

I don't know how to feel about that but I think it should be bad.

Desperate to talk it out and hoping to make some sense of it all, I press the button for the intercom. "Can you pull over so I can come sit in the front?"

"You know what I think about you sitting in the front of the limo." Charles sighs into the speaker.

"Come on."

The car stops and I hop out before he even has his door open.

When I get in the front seat he gives me the look, the one where I know he knows and he knows I know, but he doesn't want to talk about what he knows.

But I don't care. "So, she was interesting. Some display back there on the road. She acted like a child." He's quiet so I force the answers from him, "What do you think?"

"She's Sami Ford. I don't know what you think you've bitten off, but let me assure you, you will not be able to chew it." He turns onto our road.

"Oh, dude, I agree. She's going to be the death of me. Which might be for the best since she's dated like three guys I know already, and you know how I have that thing with that."

"Young man, do you want my honest opinion?" He sounds tired. I wish I were.

"I do."

"I don't know how to break it to you politely, but telling your body and heart someone is off limits because they have dated someone else is not only immature, but it's also dangerous. Men like the hunt. When someone tells us we can't have something we want it more. I'm afraid you've set yourself up for failure here." He laughs softly, shaking his head.

"Well, it doesn't matter now. She hates me again. So there's no point in worrying about her being off limits." I glance out the window at the city, muttering, "I thought we worked out our issues and then *bam,* right back to hating each other."

"How did you work them out exactly?"

"We screamed at each other, she gave me the worst apology I've ever heard, and then we had sex. It was fairly amazing."

"Okay. But there was little to no rational conversation, which means there was no closure on the issues you had before. I'm not up to speed on your problems with her so I'm afraid I can't be of much help."

"She hated me and thought I was an asshole, and I thought she was a snobby psycho." I don't want to get into the whole backstory.

"That doesn't explain much, but I will go out on a limb and suggest that the moment you told her that fucking her was no big deal was the one that sealed your fate." He chuckles and I wince. I don't know why but hearing Charles say "fuck" is almost like getting an extra cookie and kicked in the balls at the same time.

"You heard that part?"

"I did unfortunately. I had the symphony playing quite loudly until I stopped the car and then I turned it off, hoping to get directions as to where we were off to next. I dare say though, she won't be giving you another chance to change her mind about you. So your problem with girls your friends have dated is solved." He mocks me.

"I don't even know why I said it. She was just being so weird and I was trying to smooth things over. She was hot and then she was icy cold. And something happened from the moment it ended to the moment she shut down, and I don't know what." I try to shrug it off but all I want to do is scream, loudly.

He laughs. "My dear, young man. She is a woman. It's her prerogative to be angry with you. Especially, postcoital in a car."

"I think I *coitaled* quite well. I thought she was happy."

"Until she wasn't." He chuckles harder. "Being a heterosexual man has few advantages in life. Loving women is not always one of them."

"Tell me about it," I groan and stare out the window until we pull up to the front of the building. The doorman grins as he gets the car door and tips his hat at me. "Good evening, sir."

"Almost morning, Mick." I slap him on the shoulder as I climb out and wave at Charles. "See ya tomorrow." I head for the elevator, bummed out. I contemplate a late night workout to kill my twitching, but I'm still aching from the beating the physical trainers gave us.

When I get upstairs I pace in the dark, restless and

regretful.

Having the huge apartment all to myself makes the longing in my chest worse.

I slap my hand against the back of my phone repeatedly and walk back and forth in the shadows on the floor while I consider whether or not to get her number from Carson. But then I'll have to explain. Do I want to explain? And where do I start? The story is getting convoluted.

No, phoning her is out of the question.

She's my hard limit. I need to see this as a sign I shouldn't have done it.

Instead, I kick around the idea of getting a cab to her house, in spite of my need for sleep. We have an afternoon training session that involves sprinting on the ice treadmill with resting periods spent on the super slide boards. It'll be grueling. And going to her place will involve fighting and then fucking and then maybe more fighting. She seems to be one of those girls who want the drama.

Do I want drama?

No.

Going to her house is out of the question.

I drop my face into my hands and groan as I lean on the marble kitchen island and consider eating something.

She's in my head.

I'm night eating and stressing out like a woman.

Fuck.

I grab my phone and leave the kitchen. No crazy girl is going to ruin my first week at Rangers camp with her magical vagina and crazy temper tantrums. I'm stronger than that.

And if I'm not, I'll fake it till I make it.

But the shower doesn't make it better.

Cleaning myself and remembering her body against mine gets me hard again, but jerking off, even with the soap, just isn't the same.

Stuck with a sad boner and a desperate urge to run to her place if need be, I go to bed.

But I don't sleep.

I replay every moment from her sitting back and me

spreading her legs. Everything was great then. She was happy, I was happy. Then we banged. That made me happier.

Then she was huffing her breaths and I was huffing mine and the condom started to slip off, and I don't need babies, not even Sami Ford babies.

The moment I told her the condom was slipping, she was upset. I felt it. She tensed and climbed out of the car.

I grab my phone and call Beverly, my sex guru cousin in Kentucky.

"Someone better be dead or I'm going to kill you myself." She says it *keel.*

"I need help."

"Mattie, it's three in the morning. Don't you have some puck business to attend to?" She sounds like she's smoked a pack of cigarettes.

"It's wicked serious. Like life and death."

"Oh my God, it's a girl, isn't it?" she growls.

"Sami Ford." I close my eyes as I say it, knowing the beating I'm about to take.

"Fine, you have three minutes." She doesn't mock me, which is weird. No Southerner lets a moment like this one pass her up but she does.

"So we were fighting at this bar, me and Sami. And then we ended up making out and instead of being smart and shutting it down, I messaged Charles to come to me and he did and then we got in the car."

"What did I say about calling Charles to drive you around while you screw girls?"

"I know. That part of the story is sort of irrelevant though."

"Is she mad at you?"

"Yeah." I pause.

"Well, it's not irrelevant if she's pissed. You drove around with one of the richest girls y'all know in the backseat of your limo and fucked her like a borrowed whore."

"Why is borrowed whore the new thing? Is everyone saying that? Am I the last to know we have a new insult? And how is a borrowed whore a bad thing? 'Cause if you can't pay aren't you the lame one—"

"Mattie! Two minutes," she snaps.

"So we're screwing and she comes and I come and we finish, and she's sort of clinging to me and the condom is slipping off, and I say that it is, and she tenses up and freaks and leaves the car—"

"You're an idiot," she interrupts me again. "The first words out of your fool mouth, after you bang her like you paid her for it, is that the condom is slipping off? No 'That was amazing'? No 'God your tits are perky'? Not even a 'Fuck you, Sami Ford'? Just the cold, hard fact that the condom is slipping?" She groans. "If you can't figure this one out, I can't help you. Even God ain't gonna touch this one, moron." She ends the call before my three minutes are over.

"Ohhhhhhh." I put the phone down and close my eyes. "Shit!"

There's only one way to make this horrible pain end. I get up in the dark and stalk across the room to my violin. I lift it from the stand, tighten the bow, and position it. Closing my eyes, I begin.

Beethoven is the only thing that will let me kill this annoyance at three am.

I give up after half an hour and pull on clothes to leave the house quietly. I don't call for a car. I walk in the dark to her place. The sun is coming up soon but I don't care.

I don't care that she dated dudes I know, I don't care that she hates me.

I care that I fucked up.

Unlike her, I can apologize.

When I get to her building the doorman nods at me as he gets the door. In New York I am my mother's son so he doesn't bat an eyelash at my being here. I don't know how the hell these guys know who's who in New York, but they always know me.

They have remarkable memories.

In the elevator my hands start sweating.

What will I say?

Besides obviously what an idiot I am.

When I get to her door I lift my hand to knock but I stop

when I hear it.

I step into the alcove for the stairs and listen as the elevator makes its way to the floor. She stumbles out, laughing and clinging to the blonde.

They're drunk and giggling. "Shhhhh." She holds a long finger to her lips.

The blonde staggers, barefoot and holding her shoes.

When they slam their way into the apartment I slump against the wall, wishing I'd just done the right thing the first time.

I wait three minutes and then knock.

The blonde answers, cocking an eyebrow. "Hi."

"Hi. Can you get Sami?"

She nods, her expression is a confused one, but she closes the door.

A second later the door opens. Sami gives me a disgusted look. "What?"

"I'm sorry."

"Oh me too." She slams the door.

I lift my hand to pound on it, but pause, certain that would be another mistake.

Chapter Ten

Sighting 2,000,017

Sami

Manhattan
December, 2014

"Sami, he's here," Nat whispers and glances over at the scarf rack in Bloomingdale's.

"Who?"

"The only person you ever avoid in Manhattan since he randomly showed up at your place that night in the summer." She rolls her eyes.

"Oh, come on. Is he following us?" I tighten everywhere to the point my hands are shaking, and turn in the opposite direction of where she's looking.

"Man, we see him a lot."

"That's it, I'm moving as soon as I grad. I'll just move to Europe and we'll leave it at that. Then I'll never see him again."

"Oh my God, stop. He doesn't even see us. Don't move and he'll walk by and you can go back to shopping." She grabs my shoulders and continues to watch. "You're being a baby about him anyway. Maybe it's time to confront the fact you guys have a thing you never speak of."

"I told you we don't have a thing. And besides, I'd like the South of France or Italy. I can't keep running into him and hiding because I don't want to see him."

"If you just talked to him or stopped hating him, you'd

never see him. This is God trying to force your hand to deal with things like a big girl."

"I don't want to see him or talk to him," I snap.

The thought of him makes me sick.

Not because he's disgusting, which he is.

Not because the way he treated me was disgusting, which it was.

No.

Even the image of the condom slapping onto the cold cement isn't why.

The reason I loathe him is that I am still desperately attracted to him. He treated me like shit, and I still spend all my time watching his stupid games on TV or noticing the cut of his jacket against his big arms when he does interviews after the games.

And those hands.

Dear sweet baby Jesus, those hands.

It's not at all like being attracted normally.

No.

It's more along the lines of gut-wrenching sadness when I see him because I won't experience that bliss ever again.

It's some weird self-deprecating crush where I allow myself to be treated like shit out of guilt for the bad things I've done. At least that's what Linda, my shrink, says. And it sounds right. I am a self-deprecator.

He and I will never happen again.

NEVER AGAIN!

I have new rules about boys treating me like a whore and it never happens more than once.

But I see him everywhere since he moved here.

At the café.

At restaurants I like.

At the patisserie I enjoy the most.

At Chanel. What guy even goes to Chanel?

A guy who's dating someone, that's who.

And I hate that even more.

We had cheap sex in a moving car and out there is a girl who gets to be with him for real. Not in a moving car like she's being paid to be there.

The thought of it boils my blood.

"Oh shit, he's coming over. He totally sees us." She tightens her grip for a moment and then pretends to be browsing through the sweaters with me. "Yup, he sees us. Be cool. Laugh about something."

"Sami? Natalie? How are you?" His eyes dart to mine right away.

"Great," Nat answers as though she just got an avocado for Christmas like that kid in the video on YouTube.

"Good." I plaster the stupidest smile on my face. It's a phony "I'm fine" shining on my lips brightly as I nod.

Matt Brimley looks amazing. I wish he didn't.

It's sighting number eleven and he looks better, if that's even possible. I'm a sucker for dark-green eyes and perfect lips, especially when I know they are also the deepest eyes you'll ever gaze into and the lips contain the best kiss you'll ever have.

He's got a peacoat on over a suit, like the one he wore when we met, because why not? Why not torture me with a tailored suit and a pale blue dress shirt? He's clearly just starting the night; he's still pressed and clean and doesn't have a lipstick stain on him, not yet.

He and Nat natter on about Christmas while I suffer through the image of him kissing me in the very suit he's wearing.

Nat turns, smiling. "Yeah, she and I are both just chilling this year. Her dad wanted to go to London but I'm trying to convince her to stay with me at my mom's in Greenwich." She gives me a knowing gesture to snap out of it, like I've missed something important.

I force myself to connect him with the memory of my being nothing more than a backseat bang for him. It makes me feel like shit. He makes me feel like shit.

"No London this year, huh?" He tries to smile like we might be friends. It pisses me off more.

"Nope. I don't know that I'll ever go back to London. Bad memories."

"Yeah?" His eyebrows knit for a millisecond. "Well, I should go. You guys have a great Christmas." He gives me that lazy grin, the one that melts me out of my clothes. "I'm glad I ran into you again."

My traitorous vagina twinges with my stomach, but I shut that shit down. I'm not a backseat bang. I almost give him the "Bye, Felicia," but I don't. I just turn back to my sweaters, though I don't see them. I see him, and the smile, and the way he makes me feel nauseated.

"Oh my God, he's hot. Why are you always so mean to him or avoiding him?" Her eyes fix on mine as if she's trying to read my mind. "And I don't want to hear the bullshit story you gave me when he came by in the middle of the night looking for Carson. I wanna know what is going on with you two."

"It's nothing. I just don't like him. He's a player. Dirty hockey pig. They're gross." I shrug and lift an argyle, pretending it might be an option for Nadia. It's not. I already have her gift and it's so much better than a sweater.

"But he's always so nice."

"Whatever. Do you think Nadia would like this?"

"Sure." She shrugs. "I guess. It's all right."

I put it down and continue to saunter, staring at everything. Nat gets stuck on some ugly-Christmas-sweater idea in the corner as I make my way to the gloves. I lift them, caressing the soft leather and putting them down. My heart isn't in shopping anymore.

Sensing I'm being watched, I lift my gaze to find him staring at me from across the rack.

I jump but he just smiles. "Hey."

"What are you doing?" I scowl.

"I was wondering if you wanted to hang out again?" He comes off as flustered and sweet, but I've seen this act before. Sitting across from me in the limo begging me to stay with him.

"No. I don't want to hang out. When have we ever hung out? If you mean hang out in your limo again, I'm good." I almost throw down finger quotations on the hang out. "I don't need another tour of the slummy parts of the city."

"Okay." He pauses like he's confused. "Guess I'll see ya around."

"Whatever." I call my shrink as I watch him walk away.

"Hello, Sami," Linda answers trying to sound happy to hear my voice.

"I just saw him and he booty called me. He like legit just asked if I wanna hang out again."

"I told you this before, you need to either be honest with him about your feelings or you need a power shift."

"I don't have feelings. Besides hate, I hate him."

"Why are we having this conversation about a guy you have no feelings for then? Why have we been having these conversations about him for years, if he's no one to you?"

"Continue." I sigh.

"If you want to be honest with him, yourself, and me, you'll tell him you like him and be a big girl and explain why you were angry and how his actions made you feel. Be vulnerable and put yourself out there. You never do that. You're miserable being single, but you never lower the guards and let guys in. You say you don't want to date but it's clear you do."

"And if I don't want to admit any of that?" There's no way I'm being vulnerable.

"Then you should think about the fact that you like to be in charge and you're not, he is. He played you last so he held the control last. There has to be a shift. You have to get the control back or you won't ever be relaxed with him. You're clearly bothered by this young man's ability to disassociate himself from you, even while engaging in sexual encounters. Most likely since you aren't able to do that yourself."

"I know all of this, Linda, but I don't know how to use it. I need practical application here."

"You ask him out, not for sex obviously. You choose the time and the place and the conditions with which you hang out with this young man, and the power will shift back into your hands. If he wants sex, you hold the cards. You choose no sex so you flirt but don't let him know that. You act sexy and make him think you might give him sex and then don't. You walk away and leave him wanting more and *bam!*—you're in control again."

“Genius.”

“Nope, worst advice I’ve given out all year but it’s the sad truth.” She sighs.

“No one cares about your conscience, Linda.” I hang up and tap my phone against my lip, watching him leave the store with his purchase as I come up with a plan.

Chapter Eleven

A sad boner and a heavy heart

Matt

Watching the game clip for the tenth time I still don't see what the assistant coach is talking about. The other team's defense has no holes or aggression. They skate fast and flawlessly, regardless of being beasts. They anticipate the pass, always being where they need to be. Half their damned team is Canadian so they probably all know each other. No wonder they play well together.

"A Miss Sami Ford is waiting for you in the parlor, sir." Benson enters the doorway, interrupting my thought process.

"What?" I pause the game, certain I misheard him. "Who?"

"Sami Ford." His old face mocks me more than any words ever could.

"Are you taking the piss? Did Charles put you up to this?"

"Possibly. You'll never know if you don't go to the parlor." He winks and leaves the room.

I swallow hard and drop the remote on the couch.

She's here?

Why?

"Shit!" I jump up, checking my armpits for at least a trace of deodorant and make a run for the parlor, skidding on the marble foyer and pausing, getting my game face on.

My stomach aches, reminding me that last time I saw this girl she acted like she might murder me.

Not that I blame her.

I'm an idiot.

I clear my throat and stand tall as I enter the doorway, trying too hard to be cool. I exhale as I see her and not some cruel prank by the evil Englishmen in my life.

I take several deep breaths, forcing my heart to slow down. "Hey." I hope I look confused and not constipated.

She raises an eyebrow from where she's sitting in my mother's favorite white Queen Anne chair in the corner. "Hey?"

"What's going on?"

"Nothing." She stands up, revealing a knee-length trench coat and some very fucking high-heeled boots. Only an inch of leg shows between the black boots and tan coat.

I almost tear my gaze from her and look up, just to thank God for this moment.

But her facial expression doesn't quite match the stripper outfit she's wearing. She walks toward me, getting close enough that I can smell the delicious scent of her perfume and skin.

"Are you okay?" My fingers tingle, desperate to hold her in my arms, but she still has that weird look on her face, the one indicating she might smile or murder me but hasn't decided yet.

"I wanted to ask you what you wanted to do"—she pauses and steps closer—"but I didn't have your cell phone number."

"What do you mean?" *I'm lost, so lost.* Does she want me to make the first move or is she not here for that? What did I want to do? I can't even think straight. I wanna fuck, is that an answer?

"You asked if I wanted to hang out, in Bloomindales. It was like three days ago, remember?"

"Yeah, I remember."

"So?" She smiles wider, her perfect smile. Her teeth glow, they're so white against her red lipstick. I've never seen her in red before. Her usually tanned skin is pale so the contrast is hot. I can totally imagine those red lips around my cock but I need to focus. "What do you want to do?"

"I don't know. I just was thinking maybe—" about fucking but I can't say that since I already messed that up. "Dinner or something?" It's the lamest thing I've ever said.

"Really?" She tilts her head disappointedly. "I mean, I guess." I'm praying she opens that jacket and tells me where dinner is, but she doesn't. She shrugs. "We could do pasta, that place over in Harlem. You obviously like it there, since I saw you there last month." She blinks innocently.

"You did?"

"Yeah, you were with some girl, a brunette."

"My cousin, Harriette. She's from Kentucky." I don't care who I was with, who was she with? Carson said she isn't seeing anyone.

"Cousin." She blushes and glances down. "I was there with Natalie, the blonde I'm always with. It's great pasta. Anyway, when should we go?" She looks sexy being sweet. But she looked sexy being crazy too. She's just sexy.

"Wednesday night? I play in LA Monday, but I'm home Tuesday."

"That's Christmas Eve." She laughs.

"Oh shit, it is." I'm a moron. "My parents are going to be in Italy for Christmas with my brother, Anthony. I keep forgetting."

"You'll be here alone?" Her tone changes.

"No, I'll have Benson. Charles has a wife so he'll be busy for a few days, but me and Benson will chill."

"Is that your staff?" Her sexy red lips toy with a grin.

"I don't think of them like that." I shake my head, hating that snobby way of being. "Anyway, Wednesday obviously doesn't work. What are you doing for New Year's?" I can't help but grin. "Maybe there's a—"

"Don't say it!" She cuts me off.

"What?"

"You were going to say wet tee shirt contest that I could win." Her face flushes.

"I wasn't, I swear." I can't fight the laugh. I was totally going to say wet tee shirt contest. "I was going to say maybe there's a movie or something." I laugh harder.

"A movie? Liar." Her eyes narrow, which is intense

because she has really smoky eyes. It's like being stared down by the devil herself.

"I swear, I never thought of it." I try to get ahold of myself. "Forget dinner and a movie. Let's do something else." I work at seeming serious.

"Okay. You think on that and let me know." She takes a step back, her eyes darting to the door. "I do actually need to get going though. I only came over to ask that." She pulls out a piece of paper. "Here's my number but only use it if you think of something more fun than dinner or a movie." She hands it to me but doesn't let go right away. "It's not to Bloomingdale's or Nordstrom, I swear."

Her tiny hand gets swallowed by mine as I reach over with my other and pull her to me. She jerks back, leaving the paper in my hand, and freeing herself from my grip.

"I'll talk to you later." She brushes past me, leaving her scent all over my mom's parlor.

"Wait!" I grab her arm and spin her around on her heels, and end up catching her as her ankles sort of twist in the huge boots.

"What are you doing?" She stumbles to her feet and pulls out of my arms.

"I'm sorry."

"For what?" She is different suddenly, there's an expression of worry in her eyes.

"Everything." I don't know where to start so I go right for the beginning. "I pretended I didn't know you in London. I didn't want to scare you, you were alone on the street, and when I saw you I was worried. I knew who you were from a mile away, and I knew you were dating Drew. When you didn't recognize me, I didn't want to make it weird. So I played your game of not telling names. And I didn't want to make it awkward in the club with everyone else there when we saw each other again. You didn't say hi to me or act like you knew me so I took my cue from you." Everything just blasts from me in the least cool way possible.

"You're making it weird now." She scowls but only for a second before she softens again. "But you're right. I want to make peace too. So I'm sorry for overreacting about it. It just felt sneaky like you were trying to trick me. And in the club you made it seem like you didn't know me, and I assumed it was because people were there."

"I wasn't, I swear."

"Okay." She bites her lip but something is definitely bugging her. "I really do have to go though."

"No." My eyes lower to the coat and I realize she didn't wear it here for me. She's meeting someone else. I take one stride closer, wrapping my arms around her waist and jerking her against my abs. "Stay."

"No." She doesn't lift her gaze to meet mine. She just shakes her blonde head. "I can't."

I slide a finger under her chin and tilt her face. "Please."

"No." She lifts onto her tiptoes and plants a mushy kiss with a heap of lip gloss on my cheek. "I'm not the person I accidentally led you to believe I am." She lowers herself and pulls out of my embrace, walking out of my parlor and sight. "Goodnight!" she shouts back.

I contemplate running after her and forcing her to stay but all my thoughts have a creepy hostage vibe to them. I want to make her stay so I can explain better—tell her I like her. I don't want her to meet the person she's going to meet, but I have no right to make her stay here.

She's probably going on a date with some fuck who gets to touch her. I can't even imagine what's under that trench coat. Actually, I can.

Shit!

I walk over and slump in the Queen Anne chair, lifting my phone to my ear as I press a name.

"Seriously, cuz, I'm winning *Pong.* What *do* you want?" Bev, Harriette's sister, answers the phone gruffly.

"She just showed up in a trench coat, bare legs, and stilettos. She asked me out on a date, kissed my cheek, but nothing else. I think she has another date after coming here."

"Who?"

"Sami Ford."

She pauses. "Sami Ford just showed up at your house unannounced?"

"Yes!"

"Was she dolled up in those high heels and trench coat?"

"As fuck." I can barely breath and my dick is so hard I'm scared for it. And not just because I'm talking to my cousin.

"Wow."

"What does that mean?" I'm lost.

"You just got the revenge play for the backseat bang. Did you try asking her out again but like a gentleman?"

"Yeah. I did as you said and asked her if she wanted to hang again."

Bev pauses again. "Hang? Again?"

"Yeah?" I don't like her tone.

"Like booty call *hang?"*

"No, like see if she wanted to hang out."

"Sweet Jesus," she groans into the phone. "Boys are so dumb. The last time you hung out with Sami she was your borrowed whore in the backseat. So if you say 'hang again,' of course that's where her brain is going. She thinks you just booty called her. What kind of gentleman booty calls?"

"A busy one!" I am getting defensive.

"Don't you snap at me. You called me, shithead. And me and Mike just lost at *Pong* because of it."

"I just need to know if it's good or bad that she showed up?"

"Good, if you want something with this girl. But she upped the ante, letting you know she's into it, but you're gonna have to work a lot harder for her. If you want some of that, it's gonna cost effort. She's a smart girl. She knows her worth. She just let you know it too."

"Great." I close my eyes and nod. "I have a game almost every second day of the season. I'm busy as balls for the next three months, longer if we make the playoffs. How much effort?"

"What am I psychic? I'm your cousin, not some gypsy. Take a cold shower and beat the Ducks into a pulp with all your horn-dog rage. Forget about girls, especially Sami-friggin'-Ford. She'll eat you alive." She laughs and hangs up on me.

I sit for a full five minutes, arguing with myself as best as

I can with the oatmeal I currently have residing in my head; all the blood in my body is stuck in my cock.

"Effort?" I whisper, knowing the answer to the question of how much time I have for girls.

I don't have time for effort.

I liked the easy bang.

Having no commitments is easy.

No commitments also means Sami's single, and the idea of her being single and other men touching her has me in a dark place. Not as dark as the place I went when I confronted Drew for making the video, but dark enough.

I don't have time to even stew on this. I have two more game clips to review a hundred times before I get on a plane tomorrow to fly to Anaheim and crush the Ducks.

I don't have time to chase Sami Ford, but I don't have the desire to walk away from her.

It's a predicament.

Chapter Twelve

Shrinkage

Sami

"If I could moonwalk in these heels, I super would," I gush into the phone to Linda on the elevator ride down.

"See, now as long as you control the aspects and the depth you allow yourself to become immersed in this pseudo relationship, you'll find a level of comfort."

"I know, right? He acted like he might die of a heart attack and he begged me to stay."

"Sami, I'm going to be brutally honest, just like you pay me to be. You should consider the fact you like torturing this boy so much. You sound like a married couple. You are clearly preoccupied with him a lot more than any other guy in the past. There's a reason for that."

"Thanks, Linda." I roll my eyes.

"Night, Sami." She ends the call, no doubt excited to be free of me. Paying her an extra hundred grand a year to tell me the brutally honest truth instead of trying to shrink my head has changed my life. She doesn't tell me what will fix me, just what the truth is. She's my go-to for everything and never tries to sound like a parent.

I used to confide in my friends—well, Nat—about boys but I found that girls say the right thing and not the honest thing when it comes to advice about boys. Linda doesn't give a shit about me. And she doesn't sugarcoat anything. I told her to think like a young woman who likes to get laid and tell me exactly what is smart. She doesn't always focus on smart though. She's the one who convinced me that meaningless sex wasn't making me feel good about myself. And she was right. Every now and then I like a boy more than he likes me, and I read more into the relationship than he does. No point in casual sex when one person can't be casual about it.

Like with Matt.

I can't be casual, not the way he is.

I wrote about him in my journal and have compared every kiss in the last couple of years to our kiss in the cab.

I'm glad I called Linda and didn't risk telling Nat about him. She's a romantic at heart. She would have us picking out china in a matter of hours.

Not that I want a boyfriend.

Well, maybe I do.

I don't know.

But even if I did, it wouldn't be a dumb hockey player who treats me like a whore.

And in the end, Linda is right, I do need to get over the hate I have for him. It's not doing me any good, and we clearly see each other a lot. I need to resolve the issue and take back the power. Then when I see him it's not me with the aching chest.

Having him pine for me is better than having me hate him.

In my head the theory means I'll look less crazy, but I'm not sure it's sound though.

I hurry down the street to the car and jump in, grinning at Vincenzo as he closes the door. "Can we stop quick and get a few things?" I ask as I lean forward, through the window.

"Of course. What is it you're looking for?"

"Nat is coming over in like an hour for a slumber party with a couple of girls from our grad class, so I just want to make sure I have everything."

"Citarella Gourmet?"

"Yes, please."

When we get to the apartment after shopping, Vincenzo carries the bags up for me. He goes to the kitchen as I head for the stairs.

"A Mr. Brimley is in the parlor." Nadia gives me a slight grin and follows Vincenzo into the kitchen to prepare the food I've brought.

"What?" I watch her walk, giving her a weird look as

butterflies try to escape my stomach.

"You heard me." She glances back and smiles wide, pointing at the parlor.

"No. That wasn't how it was supposed to work." I swallow hard, sensing all the power I've gained slipping through my fingers. Why is he here? What does that mean? Is he onto me?

Shit!

My feet take the steps my head isn't ready for, forcing me into the hallway. I gulp, slap a smug grin on my face, and saunter like I might just be half as confident as I hope he thinks I am.

My insides dance but I open the door, ignoring the nerves.

"Hey." I close the door and lean against it.

He's standing in the window with his back to me. "Hey." He says it without turning around.

"What are you doing here?"

"I needed to see you." He turns and leans against the window, not moving either. There's a large room between us but it feels small. "I was thinking, if you're alone because your parents are in London, and I'm alone because mine are in Italy, why don't we make Christmas Eve dinner together, like you and I each cook something? Then we could hang out on Christmas and go skating in the park and enjoy the quiet of the city."

"Uhhhh—I mean, yeah. Sure. We could do that." *What the ever-loving fackkkkk?* Christmas Eve dinner? Skating in the park? This is way more than dinner and him trying to screw me and me playing with his head a little.

Sweet Jesus.

"I thought it would be a good way to get to know each other. For real."

Why don't we just get married and call it a day?

Is he screwing with me?

I don't know the response I should have.

Do I laugh and say no so I don't look needy?

Or do I accept and play it off like it's no biggie?

Oh my God.

He's like a master of messing with me.

Why's he being so sweet?

I need Linda.

"And I also know what I want to do now."

"Why didn't you just call?" I'm scared of what he's going to say next. The whole skating in the park thing is tugging at the soft stupid parts of my heart.

"I needed to see you." He pushes off from the window and crosses the room, not quickly but too quickly for me to react. He puts his hands on the door, pinning me here. He lowers his face, speaking softly, so close to mine I feel his words on my lips. "I think I say and do the wrong things with you. I was worried I might not get the point across properly if I called. I want you to see I need to fix this."

The nervous feeling he creates in my stomach hits hard.

"And I hate the way you look at me after I say something I think is okay. So I was thinking we could hang out now, right now, and you could tell me exactly what I did to piss you off. From the very moment we met. And I could apologize properly and never do those things again."

"Did you do some drugs before you came here?" Not that there was time for drugs.

"No."

It's a weird request but it's also unpredictable. I never saw it coming. It's not dinner or drinks or just fucking again. Combining it with Christmas Eve and skating in the park makes me uncomfortable and panicky.

"Please, just tell me everything you hated so I know."

"I don't know what to say."

"Yes, you do. When was the first time I let you down?"

"When you didn't come and find me after the kiss in the cab. You just walked away and let it be." The words fall from my parted lips. Fortunately, I stop myself before I mention I still have his suit jacket in my closet, hanging up.

"I thought you were dating my friend." He looks so cute the way he says it, like he's some honorable guy and not a pervert who gets his driver to tour the city while he bangs chicks in the backseat.

Remembering that enrages me again. I take a break. "I

broke up with him. He was fucking my friend in London. I was single in the black cab."

"That wouldn't have changed anything." He wrinkles his forehead. "I had this rule: I didn't date girls my friends had already dated."

"That's stupid. What are you, seven? You can't share your toys, Beast?" I am unable to resist the urge to laugh bitterly.

"You're not the first person to tell me that," he concedes. "I'm sorry I'm a moron. I wish I could take it all back. All the stupid rules and thoughts and the times I let you down. All I can do now is be different."

"I forgive you." I truly mean it. How can I not after that?

"What else is there?" he asks with a smile.

"You really want this?" I can't believe he does.

"I do."

"Fine. You were a shit in the bar when you didn't even acknowledge me that night I got super trashed. You acted like we didn't know each other and we did. And I didn't understand. It hurt my feelings, like the kiss was some cheap shit you were ashamed of. And I didn't feel that way." I can't believe I've said it aloud. I'm being vulnerable. Linda would be so proud.

"I didn't know if you wanted to explain to anyone how we knew each other. I wondered if you felt awkward when you saw me in the bar, you kept giving me weird looks. So I thought we could start fresh and not be the people we were in London."

"I liked you in London." Again I'm stunned at the words leaving my mouth.

"And I have liked you for far longer than London, but every time I get a chance to see you, you have a boyfriend. And we run in the same circles so they're always guys I know."

"Who said anything about dating?" I cock an eyebrow. "You honestly seem like you're only into sex."

"I think I've given you the wrong impression about me too. I swear, I'm not like that either. Like I said, I've liked you far longer than London."

I almost lose the strength in my knees when he says that. “How long?”

“A while.” He looks down. “What else is there?”

I lower my head, fighting for the bravery I always act like I have. “I don’t have sex in cars while someone drives me around. Ever. I’m working on my—anyway, it wasn’t cool if you ever wanted to see me again. That’s something you do to someone you don’t want to see again.”

“And I treated you like you don’t mean anything?”

I lift my gaze to his, sensing the burn in my stare. “Uh, ya think? You threw the dirty condom on the ground and offered me a ride back to the bar. As if you were going to pick up again. You really think that was cool?”

“No. But I don’t really think when I’m around you.”

I swallow the lump that’s building in my throat. For whatever reason being honest with him is killing me. I’m on the edge of crying. “I’m sorry I called you blue collar and treated you so badly. You wounded my pride and I acted like a dick.”

“I’m sorry for everything from the moment I left you in the cab in London.” His eyes are lit with a form of green fire.

“Black cab.” I grin.

He laughs but it’s not real. There’s something else stopping him from laughing.

“What do you want, Matt? Why are you here? We barely know each other, and we’ve been nothing but mean to each other. If you truly think about it, we both think we know the other person but what do we know?”

“We have awesome sex.”

“Right. But what else is there? Is there a reason at all to try to make this be anything beyond that one time we had awesome sex?”

“I don’t know. I know I can’t stop thinking about you. It’s been years. But at the same time, I don’t have anything to offer. I work hard for eight months of the year and girls are the last thing on the schedule. And yet you have me undone, and I can’t seem to get it back together. You freak out so easily and the next thing I know I’m upside down.” He lifts a hand to my cheek. “But it seems like the last thing I want is to be right-side up."

"I want to know what you think. You're all up in my grill about why I was so angry with you, but I think the reason was that I didn't understand your motives. You act like I'm nothing to you, and yet here you are playing me again. Why?" I refuse to give up the hard-earned power shift between us.

"You're not nothing." He lowers his lips to mine, brushing one of those soft and delicious kisses I get lost in. "You're killing me, trust me."

"Good." I lift his face, separating us. "Now I have plans, so you have to go. We can both think about what the other person has said and talk about it over dinner."

He scowls. "But that's why I'm here. I don't want you to have plans."

"What?" My back straightens as I prepare for the war between us to refresh itself.

"This." He tugs at my trench, untying it to reveal a tee shirt and fuzzy shorts. "I did not see that as a possibility for what was under this jacket." He cocks his head, stepping back.

"Why?" I look down on the outfit. "I have a slumber party in ten minutes."

"Slumber." A stupid look crosses his face. "With other girls?"

"Of course. What exactly did you think was happening?" I know what it looked like. I'm not an idiot. I wore the coat on purpose, and I am loving the look on his face.

"I mean, it's a trench coat and boots, and you're you."

"A slut?" My humor fades rapidly. "This is why you can't have nice things, Beast!"

"No. You just always have someone you're stringing along." He says it and shakes his head, seeing the shocked expression on my face. "No. Wait. That's not what I mean." He steps back in, scooping me into his arms and pressing his face into my neck. "I mean, you're a girl who has fun and has no rules and just does what she wants. So when I see a girl like you in a trench coat with boots and bare legs I assume you're about to rock someone's world. I wanted it to be mine, and I was crushed when it wasn't." He kisses softly. "I don't want you to rock anyone's world. Just my world." He pulls back and winces. "That's too much, right? I sound like a needy chick, don't I? I swear I'm cooler than this."

"Oh, I know you're cooler. I got played in that limo by the cooler side of you. You're a player. That move with the limo was smooth; it was perfect. You've done that before, a lot. And I don't want to hear that you haven't. It was a precision effort."

His eyes lower as he bites his lip, the look of guilt.

"So you will have to excuse me if I don't believe you and the things you're saying. There's an old saying that warns when someone shows you who they are, you should believe them. You've shown me that when no one is looking you are all about me, but when anyone else is around I might as well not even be in the room. In the black cab you kissed me, in the bar you ignored me. In the bar we fought and ignored each other. In the car we fucked and you made it perfectly clear you were done caring about me from the moment you came in me."

"That's not true." His eyes widen. "You just got weird. You tensed and freaked out."

"Because you and I didn't seem to have the same—" I take a breath. "It doesn't matter."

"See, this is the problem." He lifts a hand. "I don't want to fight. I swear to the gods, we don't communicate at all. You're talking and I'm talking and nothing is being said. Let's just agree to have dinner on Christmas Eve. Leave it at that. I'll go now before your friends come over so you don't have to explain why I'm—"

"I'm not embarrassed to be seen with you. Yes, you're a stinky hockey player who's known for being the black sheep of his family—"

"You're doing that thing again, where you think I'm saying something that I'm not saying, but I'm not saying what I actually want to say the right way. I'll see you Saturday night." He nods once and walks to me, lifts me into his arms and kisses me. It's not passionate or intense and yet it is. There's no fire like we might rip each other's clothes off but there's something. He spins me, puts me down, opens the door, and flees from the house.

I don't know what just happened, but I'm blushing and standing in the same spot moments later when Nat comes in crying.

There's no way I can tell her about my weirdly arranged date when she's suddenly single again and everything is a hot mess.

Friggin' William Fairfield ruins everything.

Chapter Thirteen

A Seven Nation Army couldn't hold me back

Matt

Sami-fucking-Ford.

She's the kind of girl you fall in love with before you even know you've tripped. She's a problem.

And yet I don't bother dusting myself off when I feel myself falling. I just lay in the dust and confusing feelings, unsure of where this goes from here.

The last two days I've spent contemplating everything we said and didn't say.

And now I'm at the end of the game, thinking about her instead of focusing on beating the Ducks to a pulp.

Fortunately, the game is going well for us even if I feel like I'm stuck in slow-mo, with everyone moving at a snail's pace in my eyes.

I spin, collecting the puck and passing it along, listening to the sound of it scraping the ice.

My skates dig in as I push ahead of the player next to me to get the puck back.

But to me it looks like we're under water, floating across the ice.

When the pass is made the puck slaps my stick and I flick my wrist, shooting it at the top left corner as my eyes stare directly at the right. The goalie falls for the trick shot, his eyes meeting mine and he follows. He dives right and I swear I can hear the shift in his gear as he panics and tries to go left, but it's too late.

The puck lands in the net and the lights and sounds go

off, signaling a score.

But I hear nothing.

I see nothing.

I'm reliving the moment she finally smiled at me, just the once.

It ruined everything.

Ruined me.

Hands slap my back as Laramie embraces me, dry humping but only slightly so he doesn't get in shit from Coach. He hates it when we act like footballers.

I flash back into the game when I realize I've scored.

Coach gives me a nod. It's his version of patting me on the back. He's not showy with his love. Whereas our goalie is screaming that if I get one more of those he'll suck my dick himself. That makes me laugh and I blink Sami Ford outta my head and relish the moment. The stadium spins and I realize it's my second goal of the night.

"One more, big boy, and you got your first NHL hat trick!"

"All right. Well, let's make it happen." I'm back. I don't look at the scoreboard. I size up the team. They're everything in this moment.

We skate back to our positions for the puck drop. No more slow motion or moving like we're under water. I'm sharp and alert and ready.

The ref wipes his brow and centers himself as the sticks hit the ice. The stands are quiet, not silent; they never get quite there.

The captain's eyes dart to mine and then to the centerman's and then back to mine. It's a signal.

As the puck lands on the ice the sticks clash and slap, fighting for it already. The guys grunt, shoving each other just within the range the ref allows. The Ducks are an amazing team. But we seem to have God on our side tonight and our center gets the puck, shooting it through skates as it heads for Laramie and then the captain. I see it in my peripheral but I keep moving forward, not to cherry pick but just about there.

A flash of black covers the captain as he's hip-checked into the boards by a huge defenseman. I weave, receiving the pass and using my skates to ping-pong it through the two defensemen eyeing me like they might ask me to be their prom dates.

I spin and pass back to our captain who has just recovered from the dirty humping he took in the boards. He fakes a pass to the center but flicks it back to me as I pause to avoid a shoulder in the face. Ducking the first defenseman doesn't stop the second one from hitting me hard. I take the hit and spin, letting him slip off my shoulder so I can get the pass.

It's three on two and the defensemen aren't fast enough to keep up with the passing and zigzagging we are doing.

Me, the captain, and the center glide smoothly through the middle, taunting them until we're close enough. Then I whizz past the left side of the goal, staring straight in the goalie's eyes as I flick it to the right corner.

The lights flash and the buzzers scream as the team mauls me like a pack of wild animals.

Coach grins wide and holds his hand out for me to take my victory lap.

The crowd goes nuts. It's a mixed reaction. Some of them are screaming like they might riot any second, but the Ducks' fans are booing and calling for unsavory things.

I lift a hand, offering a gloved wave as I weave my way through the hats littering the ice. Our fans are waving their hats and shirts. One girl rips off her jersey and tosses it at me, jiggling her bare breasts as she jumps up and down in a frenzy.

The feeling of a hat trick in a regular game, in a regular league, is one that can't be described by a regular person with no poetic capabilities. But this is a whole other level of excitement and adrenaline.

Everyone skates around, clearing the ice of debris by flinging caps back over the glass, but when I make my way back to the center line, it seems like there are more than when I started my lap.

I do a slow circle, watching the stands still going crazy as the announcer tries desperately to explain this is my first NHL hat trick and seventh in my career since starting with the University of Michigan.

I don't know how to react to this moment.

So I don't.

I just watch them go berserk.

The captain skates over, slinging his arm over my shoulder and laughing. "What a way to make your mark, kid." He squeezes and skates back to hat cleanup.

It takes a full five minutes to get everyone back in their seats which is mostly done with insanely loud music.

"Seven Nation Army" blasts as we all get back into position.

There's a minute and a half left on the clock and the song pulsates through me.

We're leading by two, the last two goals I got.

It's an incredible feeling.

When the puck drops, the Ducks' centerman aggressively hits ours, taking the puck. Our defense comes to life. The captain heads that way while us wings wait for the pass. A Duck takes the puck along the boards, just close enough to enjoy the captain's elbow as his next meal. He drops like a sack as our team gets the puck and sends it sailing to middle ice. Our center grabs it fluidly, but before he can turn, the Ducks are on him, making the mistake Coach discussed with us. Under pressure they fall apart and start to get sloppy. They're known for going violent instead of skilled. I didn't see it in the videos but I see it here. Our center drops, losing the puck. The ref calls it.

They have a penalty for roughing and we have the advantage. Not much of one though. Our center grins through the pain but it's slowing him down.

I turn at the wrong moment, taking a hit as I pass. The ref calls the penalty, again roughing.

The stands are going nuts, Coach is screaming at us, and every Duck remaining looks like he might come at me.

We pass but it isn't graceful, it's painful. Captain takes a hit as the buzzer goes and the game is ours.

"Fuckers!" A glove flies at my face. I try to duck but someone hits me in the back, launching my face at the fist. It rings my head in my helmet.

Gloves drop to the ice and the benches clear.

My helmet's ripped off before I can see who I'm fighting. I take a bare knuckle to the cheek and a shot in the back. The crowd of players is a mix of blue and black jerseys, but it's almost impossible to make out faces.

A third shot to the face brings me to life, although I'm struggling to see through the stars and pain gripping my face and head.

It usually takes that many to get my blood pumping.

I start grabbing jerseys, flipping them down and forcing faces into the feeding of my fist. As a black jersey drops I grab another. A shot to the back of the head spins me, still holding the other jersey. I smash the two of them into each other, tearing jerseys off. Something grabs me just as I see red.

"I'll fucking kill you!" I point at the bleeding face of the nearly stripped guy in front of me. It takes a second for him to smile a bloody grin. "Brimstone!"

"McNulty!" A bitter chuckle leaves my lips as I nod. "Drink after the game?" I shout at my old center from Michigan.

"Fuck yeah, man!" He gives me a thumbs up as a fist flies at his jaw. I wince but lose him in the crowd.

Coach's red face is the next thing I see as I'm flung into the boards. "Nice fucking game, kid!" He nods once and stalks off.

It's chaos and reminds me a bit of a scene from a movie.

"Dude, you need some stitches." Laramie hands me a towel as he spits one of his teeth into his hand. "Fuck, I just got this one fixed." He glances up from the bucket he's bleeding into. "I think your nose is broken, eh?"

I lift a swollen finger to it, trembling as I make contact with the torn skin. "Yup."

When the chaos ends, getting down the hall to the locker room is hard but listening to the coach tear us a new one as he reads the suspensions for conduct is much worse.

"Half the team is bleeding and three guys are out for a game each. This is some shit!" He cracks a grin. "But what a game!" His eyes dart to the captain. "Merry Christmas! I expect to see all your pretty faces at my party on Boxing Day." He leaves the dressing room in the captain's capable hands.

He stands and smiles. "All right, ladies, that was a good game. Bad ending, but we didn't throw the first punch, so whatever." He glances behind him down the hallway we can't see as a cart filled with champagne comes around the corner, led by a girl dressed as an elf. She's drop-dead gorgeous. The kind where you almost start looking for flaws because otherwise she's a unicorn. "Tandy has a toast for us all!"

Of course her name is Tandy.

She lifts a bottle, pointing it in my direction. "To the first hat trick!" She shakes the bottle and uncorks, hosing my broken face in champagne. I close my eyes and open my mouth. The comments fill the air with Tandy squealing and everyone else cheering and clapping.

"He likes it when you shoot in his mouth!"

"Nice position, Brimstone! One you're used to no doubt."

"Bend over, Brimstone, show her where you really like it shot!"

I lift my middle fingers in the air, waving them back and forth as she attempts to drown me with cold booze.

When it stops, glasses are handed out and toasts are given. None of which dull the ache in my body, but they do dull my raging adrenaline.

I haven't been part of a rumble in a while.

"Have a merry Christmas. Like Coach said, we will all see each other Boxing Day at his place. Hope you have something nice under the tree." Captain winks at us and hugs Tandy into his gear. She giggles and rubs her giant boobs against his chest. Her tiny elf costume hides nothing. She clearly digs pucks.

We all take a drink.

"Rest well and enjoy your four days off with your families. January is going to be fucking brutal and it starts on the twenty-eighth of December with the Predators. See ya on Boxing Day!" He toasts again and we all drain our glasses.

No one wants to party with the team. We have four days to get home and be with family.

But I don't have family. I have Laramie and McNulty from the Ducks for drinks and then dinner with Sami.

The shower isn’t a relief. It hurts and burns the places I need to have taken care of by a doctor. I stay in extra long, trying to work out a couple of knots in my shoulders.

I’m shampooing for possibly the second time because I can’t recall if I already shampooed or not, when a girl’s voice whispers, “Somebody deserves an aftergame kiss.”

“What?” Before I can say anything else, my cock is lifted into a warm mouth. I open my eyes as shampoo slides into them. I blink and shout, backing up, but she stays with me. “Ow, shit. Stop!” I start rinsing my eyes, but they’re badly wounded from the fight.

“Oh fuck. What are you doing?” Whoever she is, she works the shaft, sliding her hands up and down in the steamy water. Her mouth expertly sucks the head and down to about the middle. She massages my balls, slipping her fingers close to my asshole.

I get my eyes clean enough and pull back, pushing her off of me. “Are you insane?”

“What?” Tandy, the fucking champagne elf, pulls back, wipes her mouth, and stands up. Her giant boobs are hanging out of her elf costume.

“Don't! What the fuck?” I’m sputtering and shaking my head. “Get out!” I shout at her, making her jump.

“Don't make it weird, Brimstone!” She leaves in a huff, ass swinging and all.

I grab the soap, massaging my still rock-hard cock with it, praying I’m dreaming and that I didn’t just almost have the greatest fantasy blow job ever with a PF. Every guy dreams of a shower surprise. Usually he hopes he knows the girl and can see out of both eyes.

The dirtiness doesn't quite wash away in the water as I look around, hoping no one saw that shit.

When I’m done in the shower I wince as I towel dry and pull on my clothes. Every bit of me, dick included, is sensitive.

"Lucky we don't need coats, eh?" Laramie strolls over and bends down to get his shoes on. He has a funny look in his eyes.

"Yeah, New York is gonna be brutal to go home to. But it might help to ice my face in the snowbanks though."

He laughs and grabs his bag of gear. "So, we still drinking after this?"

I lug my huge bag over my bruised shoulder and nod. "Yeah. McNulty is coming too. I texted him to meet us at the hotel bar."

"So Tandy offers the full service, eh? And here I thought you had a thing for Sami Ford."

"What?" I say it too loud and too fast.

"You and Tandy. I just assumed you had a thing with Sami." Laramie's shit-eating grin grows.

"It's not a thing, not really. We sort of—it's nothing." I hate the dirty feeling in my stomach that he knows about Tandy. He must have seen, something I'm not comfortable with.

"She's a hot little number, eh?" Laramie laughs.

"What?" My blood boils.

"Calm down, champ, I meant Tandy. She deep throats like a porn star. She's my favorite." He nudges me and laughs harder.

And there it is. The absolute grossest part of hockey. Pass around girls. "Yeah, I don't know." They're like the groupies of hockey, the girls who just want to fuck. She doesn't even want to have a conversation with me. She just wants to fuck and leave, like I'm a piece of meat. Fifteen-year-old me thought it was amazing. Now, not so much. I should have known Tandy was in the locker room for a reason. I never even thought about it.

"So you and Sami are sort of on or what?"

"I don't know. Sort of. We're hanging out over Christmas, rich orphans do that." I try desperately to change the subject. Discussing a girl deep throating us both makes me want to relive the shower scene from *Ace Ventura* with "The Crying Game" playing and all.

"She's won't like this new look you got going on. What

day do you see her?"

"Two days." I sigh.

"Oh shit." He laughs and holds the door for me. "That's not long enough to heal, bro. Your tux will match your eyes. They're swelling hard."

"Yeah, well getting soap in them didn't help," I mutter and change the subject, "She won't like seeing this. She's not a sporty girl." Thank God. I'll never have to worry about other hockey players nudging me and laughing about how tight that ass is. "I think that's one of the things I like most about her."

"And there it is, sports fans. He admits it!"

"Whatever, man. She's cool. It's nothing."

"Yeah, dude. Okay. Sell that somewhere else. You stare at her way too much. And last time we got drunk you bitched about her nonstop. Even Henrik noticed." Laramie nudges me. "Sami Ford. If you weren't a Brimley I'd tell you to be careful with that one."

"Rich girls only scare you 'cause you're Canadian. You're used to girls who fish and hunt and drive their own dogsled teams."

"I'm from Kamloops, bro. The girls from the Okanagan are well known for tans and plastic surgery. Especially in Kelowna. It's like little California."

"Sounds like a nice little inlet on the Arctic Circle."

"It's the desert, moron. It's hot as balls there. Summer is like eight months long and we barely see snow." He stops walking. "You know most of Canada isn't arctic, right?" He's completely serious.

"No. Every time we play in Canada I almost die. Vancouver is the only place that's not cold, and it's always raining there. The weather in Canada is shit."

"I won't argue that point, but not all of Canada. The Okanagan is actually quite nice. And Vancouver Island is nice in the summer. It doesn't always rain in Vancouver."

"You called it Raincouver last time we were there."

"I'm allowed to call it that." Laramie sighs and heads for the SUV waiting for us.

"So why do you think the Sami Ford thing is a bad idea?"

I can't believe he said that. He doesn't even know her. But Laramie is a smart guy, so I'm intrigued. There must be more to the story.

"Sorry, bro. But she comes across as a rich, snobby, fake, plastic toy. All the girls I know like that are as fake as they act. Even in their souls. They smile for the cameras and go to the right parties with all the right people. Everyone cares who she dates and who she screws. You'll be stalked nonstop by the paparazzi."

"You forget that's the world I grew up in. My parents are the same."

"Yeah, but she's been in rehab more than Nick Carter, bro. How many coke parties you going to before you're in rehab too?"

"Yeah, I guess. I don't know if she does coke."

"Look, she seems like a hot mess and your career is just starting. You have fought harder than anyone I know to get here. You're on your own, man. Your family is the only one in the world who couldn't give a shit about their son's hockey, and they're always trying to get you back to being a rich dick. You want a girl to drag you back into that world too?" His face becomes solemn. "I'm sorry for the harsh honesty, but I don't like bullshit. If I were you, I'd have fun with that girl somewhere no one can see you, and call it a weekend. Or have her be the dish on the side. But I wouldn't publicly date her. She'll ruin you before you even arrive. The first thing I had to learn when I got here three years ago was that there are wives and there are girls like Sami and Tandy. PFs are fun for the night or the weekend when your wife isn't looking. But don't get caught slumming." He says it in the nicest way he can, which is pretty nice since he's from Canada. But it still hurts like a knife slice in the ribs, especially when he calls Sami a PF. My face is pounding, my stomach is killing me, my back is throbbing, and now, because of what he's said, my heart seems to take the lead in what stings the most.

But he's right. I know it deep down. I've always known it. The Sami Ford the world knows is trouble. But I swear there's something there no one else sees.

And that is what's most intriguing about her.

I don't discount his words. I take them to heart and let them be the counter opinion to what the rest of me is saying.

Later that night when I get back to my room, high on scotch and a couple of doses of anti-inflammatory meds, I press on her name in my Messenger. Even her name tightens my stomach.

I type a message, telling her I need to reschedule our date.

Made-up lies flow from my fingers, spinning a tale of injuries so bad I can't face her. They're true, technically. I'm battered and bruised, but my heart whispers that nothing could keep me away from her. I could crawl from the airport to her door if my legs didn't work.

Our past picks at me, combined with Laramie's words.

She's a train wreck, but she's also an enigma.

Nothing about her is typical.

Yes, she's spoiled. She's rotten in so many ways. She's petulant and rude when she wants to be. She can be a diva.

But she's also vulnerable and weak at times. Her best friend is down-to-earth and calm, which speaks volumes for Sami. You are what you hang with.

Every bit of me is tired of the Upper East Side and the fake lives we live there.

But I feel it in my bones that she is the same, she wants something else.

I delete the message.

I have to know.

Even if she's the devil and everything she's shown me has been an act, I have to know.

I've never felt this way about anyone, ever.

And she's already broken all my rules.

So if I'm going to hell for ruining my career over a girl, I might as well go all the way.

Instead of messaging her, I call Bev.

"Nice game, cuz. Hat trick and all. I bet there were a team of hookers waiting to soap you up after the game." She laughs, not knowing how close to the truth she is.

"Yeah, it was a gooder," I mutter and then sit up. "The

game, not the hookers. I mean the hookers—*fuck.* Never mind. I called for a reason." I have to speak louder because she's howling with laughter.

"You're such a moron. I'm telling Gran you let whores touch your ding-a-ling."

"You're a ding-a-ling." I try to joke but honestly fear her telling Gran that. No one is scarier than Gran.

"What do you want, beefcake?" She snickers even more.

"I'm having dinner with Sami on Christmas Eve. We're both alone, no family in New York. Do I try to have sex with her?"

"I would play that one safe. It's Christmas Eve, you're a horny jock. Showing some self-control might be a nice little gift you could get her. Drinks and dinner and talking is about as far as I would let that go. Plus, she likes games and control, so—"

"You think this is a game?"

"She's a girl, everything is a game. Don't be daft. Anyway, she's not going to put out. She's going to want you to try, not actively, but let it be known you want her. But don't try to score. It puts the control in her hands, in her mind. But in reality the control is yours. You could have seduced her but you didn't."

"You're kind of scary." She really is.

"Jedi mind trick. Have a good sleep, you earned it. And word of advice: girls don't like to find out the guy pursuing them has whores playing with his ding-a-ling. It lessens the odds of *her* playing with his ding-a-ling. Ding-a-ling." She laughs and ends the call.

I hate that I can't argue and say there are no more whores in my ding-a-ling's diet. Whore-free since first year of college. I can't say that after tonight.

Chapter Fourteen

The cheeseball platter for one

Sami

I pace back and forth again, glancing at my outfit as I pass the mirror. I last three minutes before I do the thing I promised myself I wouldn't until after New Year's. I tap in the number and press the phone against my face as I take up pacing again.

"Sami?" Linda answers.

"Hey, I need to ask something quick." I hate that I couldn't make it a week without calling.

"Okay. But it's Christmas Eve. You know that, right?" she asks quietly. It sounds like she's getting up to go into another room.

"Yes, that's why I'm calling."

"Did your parents go to London again?"

"Oh probably." I brush it off. "But that's not why I'm calling."

"Do you remember what we talked about last Christmas, and the one before that?"

"Yeah, Linda. I'm not calling to talk about that. Seriously." I hate it when she tries to shrink me. I'm comfortable with the level of dysfunction I have with my parents. "We're having dinner tonight, together. Me and Matt. Alone. Like a date. Help." I squeeze my eyes shut and take a deep breath.

"I see." She sounds confused. "So after that whole ambush we planned like teenagers would have, he asked you to have Christmas Eve dinner with him? Just the two of you?"

"Yeah."

"Oh shit. No more games, Sami. This guy likes you. A lot. Guys don't do Christmas unless they like you. Ever. So if you don't genuinely like him, abort. Now. There are real feelings at stake here."

"You think?"

"I know. It's what I get paid the big bucks for. To know this kind of stuff. You need to call him and cancel if you aren't ready to completely let your guard down and try to have a real relationship. Not one of your boy toys, where you string them along because you need a date for an event."

I don't want to tell her I like him too. I don't want to jinx it. "Just tell me what to do."

"I can't do that. I have to tell you the truth, that's our deal. How do you feel about him? Be honest. No Sami Ford bullshit."

"I don't know. I mean, he's just different. I've been watching his hockey games and he's really—"

"You watched his games? Jesus, Sami. This is serious." Her tone is funny again.

"I don't know."

"Let's focus on the important stuff. You watched his game; you clearly like him more than the other guys you've dated. And honestly, he's the first one I've seen you act like this with. We've been talking about him for years. You dated that last guy for a while, and I can't so much as recall his name, but Matt has been the one constant since you left high school. You need to think about that."

"I am. That's why I'm calling. This is important."

"Well, Christmas Eve is a whole other ball of wax. This will be a pinnacle moment at the start or end of a possible relationship. Either this is the guy you finally let in or you will turn him away. The moment will present itself if he genuinely likes you and wants to know you. And in that instant you will have to decide if you want something more than the flirting and games."

"Be vulnerable," I blurt and almost throw up at the idea of it.

"No, Sami. Be brave and believe there is real love in the world. Your parents have never shown you real love, and you're a cold bitch because of it."

"Happy Christmas, Linda."

"Merry Christmas, Sami."

I hang up, attacked by self-doubt, but I close my eyes and replay her words until I can imagine it.

He's going to come to the door. I'll smile and he'll smile back.

He'll be beautiful in something casual but still proper dinner attire, not going full suit because he's technically still a caveman, but he won't go full barbarian either.

He's going to kiss my cheek and maybe linger for a second but not try anything else. Mostly because this is a night of talking and getting to know one another, being vulnerable and not sexual.

Then we eat and we laugh, in candlelight.

He reaches across the table and takes my hands in his and tells me he likes me a lot.

Maybe we kiss under the mistletoe before he leaves and when I open the door it's snowing.

I'm a cheeseball . . .

I exhale loudly and open my eyes again, terrified. But seeing my reflection gives me one more chance to double check the outfit.

The push-up bra beneath my blouse has just enough cleavage going on that the buttons look strained but not like they're going to burst, sending button shrapnel everywhere.

The skirt is short but still respectable. It's church short.

My heels are comfortable, in case he wants to do an after-dinner stroll in the park.

My hair is perfect. Nadia left my locks long, in soft beachy curls.

My makeup is natural. It appears as if I'm hardly wearing any, even though there's a cake on my face. And the glossy lips are pouty and swollen from the Buxom gloss. I have a mild allergy to the ingredients so it works even better.

Remembering everything Linda told me, I leave the room chanting, "Be brave."

"It's after seven." Nadia pokes her head around the corner as I click my way to the stairs.

"He's late? Shit. I didn't even look at the time. Is he fashionably late or *late* late?" I slump. "Oh my God, what if he's going to show up later, like *sleepover* later and just want sex? Is this another booty call?"

"That doesn't even make sense." Nadia doesn't bother with the usual formalities on this one. "He's coming for Christmas Eve dinner and asked you to make food. He wouldn't stand you up; that's a big request. Go wait in the parlor and we'll show him in when he arrives. The lasagna is likely ready. Wait five minutes and then take it out. Let it sit on the counter for fifteen minutes before you cut it or it will fall apart."

"I still can't believe I cooked it."

"You did great. It looks tasty." She smiles. "Repeat after me: take it out in five minutes, let it sit for fifteen, then cut."

"I got it."

"If you say so."

"If he doesn't come we'll be eating it for days," I grumble. "At least I learned something in all of this."

"What?"

"I hate cooking."

"Well, at least you won't have to do it again." She rolls her eyes and goes back to whatever she was doing. She's gotten a lot sassier in the last couple of years.

Every step I take down to the main floor has me more depressed.

When I make it to the parlor a knock at the door and men's voices in the hallway stop my heart.

I spin, staring at the doorway, waiting for him.

"She's in here, sir."

His footsteps sound loud, building my suspense. When he gets around the corner and into the doorway, my mouth hits the floor. "Sorry, I'm late." Matt grins but I can hardly tell if it's him or not. His eyes are tiny slits, his nose is bulbous and cut, his cheek has a gash, and his lips are both fat. The bruising and disfiguring swelling is disgusting actually. He looks hideous. Like really, *really* hideous. "Hey! Merry Christmas Eve."

"Oh my God!" I take a step back, shaking my head, lost in the sight before me. "What happened? Are you okay? Was there an accident?"

"No, a fight. You should see the other guy." He chuckles and saunters in.

"Uhhhhh, is the other guy a grizzly bear?" It takes me several heartbeats before I bounce back and speak again, "What the hell happened? Were you attacked by a gang? Who fights? Like you were mugged?"

"I'm fine, honestly. It's way better today. I can see out of this one now." He lifts his bruised finger up to the left eye. "Yesterday was nuts." He walks to me, trying to act like he hasn't just taken a shovel to the face, many, many times.

"I don't even know what to say. What kind of fight?"

"Hockey." He just shrugs. The fight at the end of the game flashes in my mind, but there's no way he was beaten like this in that. He won the fight. He went full savage on them. My nickname for him, Beast, made perfect sense in that moment.

"After the game?"

"No." He is seriously acting as if everything is normal. "How's it going here? Smells good."

"Fine," I answer blankly, still lost in the harshness of the wounds as he gets closer. "Can I get you anything? A plastic surgeon?" My great plan of how things would go ignites in flames. There won't be any kissing or laughing and talking unless it's at the emergency room.

"Really, I'm good. It was just the game. It got a bit rough. I got into a fight—"

"When the benches cleared I knew it was bad but the cameras didn't show these kinds of wounds—" I pause as his constricted eyes attempt to narrow more.

"You watched the game?" I don't like his tone. He sounds annoyed.

"No." I lie too fast. "I mean, I watched like a couple of

minutes. I was scrolling." I act like it's nothing. "Not like the whole game or anything."

"But you were watching hockey?" He leans against a pillar next to the baby grand piano. "Do you like hockey? Is this a thing for you? Hockey players? Is this something I should know about?" The way he asks it makes me uncomfortable, as if I shouldn't bring up the hat trick and how cool it was to see the ritual of everyone throwing their hats onto the ice. He sounds crazy. Maybe it's the brain damage from the beating of a lifetime he apparently took.

"God, no! I don't even understand it. I literally watched a few minutes at the end when the benches cleared." I lie like a rug. "I thought maybe if I caught the ending I could see you, like if there were awards or something at the end." I say the dumbest thing I can think of. It's an actual thought I had when his first game ended months ago.

"Oh." He laughs, mimicking a scary mafia thug. "No. No awards. Just one at the very end of the season but it's more of a trophy."

"Cool." I know what the Stanley Cup is, but the smug way he's talking now makes me think I need to keep that a secret, which is weird. I would have thought he'd be excited about playing, not ashamed. "Can I get you a drink?"

"No thanks. I'm on some meds and shouldn't have booze with them. I had some drinks the night it happened after the game and it was the wrong choice. I slept through my morning flight. I was really drowsy all day."

"Drugs for this?" I wave my hands in front of his face.

"Yeah. I need to bring the swelling down. We have another game on the twenty-eighth and I need to be in tip-top shape for it."

"Oh, so soon?" Like I don't know the entire schedule. I hate that I have to lie to him about this. I thought hockey might be something we could talk about, since it's an obvious passion for him.

"Yeah. A game every second day for the entire season. It's aggressive. It's why I don't date or have relationships with anyone but friends who understand they'll sometimes go the whole season without seeing me."

The last sentence hits me right in the gut. He's telling me he doesn't want a girlfriend, but he's asked me for Christmas Eve dinner. I can't even with him.

"Seriously." He turns and glances at the hall, changing the subject, "It smells great in here."

"Right!" I turn and hurry to the kitchen, trying not to focus on the comment about not having relationships. "The lasagna." I click along the wood floors to the oven, turning it off and opening the door.

"No smoke and no burnt smell. Must be all right." He mocks me.

"Otherwise we're getting takeout. Because if this tastes gross, I don't expect you to pretend it's fine. I'm not going to pretend yours is fine if it's not." I point at the weird-looking container on the counter. I can only assume it's his. It wasn't here when I made the lasagna.

"You don't have to be scared of mine. I'm actually not a bad cook." He strolls over to the oven and plucks the hot mitts from me, pulling the casserole dish out for me. He attempts a grin but it's terrifying.

"You look like the scary guy on that weird movie, *The Goonies.* Natalie made me watch it. She's a fan of eighties movies."

He wrinkles his puffy forehead. "I never saw that. Is it bad?"

"Yeah." I don't try to sugarcoat it. "Super bad. You look like you got hit by a car."

"No, just a couple of huge defensemen."

"I don't want to think about that. It must have been terrifying." I shudder and tilt my head, flashing back to the other thing he said. "Did you just say you can cook?"

"Yeah. My grandma is a great cook, and she loved to let me help her in the kitchen. She said it was so I could survive college, but I don't think she understood what college was like for me. I never cooked once."

"That's weird." I glance between the lasagna and him. "Why would she cook?"

"My dad's family isn't rich. They're farmers in Kentucky. Like real cattle farmers. As in, they shovel shit and grow their own food."

"Ohhhhhhh." I shudder. "When Carson said your dad's family had farms I imagined it was more like plantation farming where they have a mansion and lots of workers who sort of stay on their side of the fence and sometimes on Sundays they do those weird civil war revivals and shit."

"Not quite." He scowls and it's a bit disturbing with all the swelling and bruising. "Revival is more of a church thing. I think you mean reenactments."

"Right. Those."

"We do have them—reenactments that is." He pauses. "It's weird seeing it. I guess because my great-great-great-grandpa was one of the men who died in Kentucky during the war, forced to fight for the Union. He believed in equality for all men, but he wasn't a soldier."

"That's terrible. At least he wasn't a racist like everyone else in the South."

"They weren't all racist in the South. My mom's family in the North pretended they were Union, but they might as well have been from Alabama or Mississippi. They're still not opposed to slaves, and they don't care what color. Anyone beneath them should be licking their boots."

I want to tell him mine are better but they're not. "Yeah."

"Anyway, my grandpa tried to get out of fighting in the war, but it was made clear that if he wasn't with them he was against them. Kentucky took a beating being a border state. When he was killed, my great-great-great-grandma kept the farm going and the kids safe. A few years after it was all over, she remarried to a man who had lost his wife. They had a bunch of kids between them so they ended up with fifteen kids. Now the family is huge. Fifteen kids all having, on average, about five kids each is a lot of grandkids. Going down there is like being in a different world, and I'm related to half the town, and it's not a quaint village. It's not a bad size." He smiles.

"You go there?" I vaguely recall him telling me once he was from Kentucky.

"I try to go for a couple of weeks in the summers and help on the farm. Keeps me grounded."

"That's crazy."

"It's not so bad."

"I can't even imagine working on a farm."

"It's fun. We shoot shit and drive cool equipment and have spoiled-milk fights." He laughs like he's reliving a moment. "I can't wait to go again this summer, once playoffs are over." He lifts his bruised hands and turns them over. "Remember when you said my hands were rough?"

"No."

"It was the night I carried you guys home." He laughs.

"Oh God, I hoped we might never discuss that again." My face flushes.

"Well, you did, you said they're rough. That's why. Working the farm and playing hockey. It makes my dad crazy. He hates hockey almost as much as he hates that farm. And seeing my calluses drives him nuts."

"Your dad hates hockey?" I play dumb but a conversation between him and Carson vaguely rings in my head.

"Yeah, he's all about finance and business and making money on the markets and rubbing elbows with the right people. He thinks he did me and my brother a solid by marrying into my mom's family and getting their name to mix with his fortune. He doesn't see that I could have been a Kentucky farm boy just as easily. I probably still would have played hockey though."

"Wait, so you did actually live in Kentucky?" His life is fascinating in the most average way.

"Can we finish this conversation over food? I'm starved."

"Sure."

"I have to ask you a serious question first." He lifts his brows and steps in close, trying to intimidate me with his size. "Tell me the truth, I won't judge you at all." He sounds serious.

"What?" I giggle nervously.

"Did you really make the lasagna?—because it smells amazing."

"Yeah! Oh my God!" My face heats up again as I peek down at the pan. "I can't lie, I used Rao's sauce for the tomato part, but I put the whole thing together. Nadia supervised. The chef refused to be in the kitchen with me. She was mad I was even in there at all." My gaze darts to the dish he brought in, still with the lid on it. "Why? Did you cheat?"

"No." He sounds offended. "Of course not. I made it, beaten and battered and bloody and all. It's called 'sex in a pan.' It's amazing." He doesn't sound like he's messing around.

"Sex in a pan? Is there sex involved?" I almost wrinkle my nose staring at his face, but I manage to keep that in check.

"No. Just trust me."

"Okay." I peer back to the pan of lasagna, not sure if it's been fifteen minutes or not.

"You have to cut it and put it on the plates."

"Thanks." I tilt my head to the side, hoping he's joking but annoyed he might think I'm that dumb. "I know that much. I was wondering which knife I would need to cut it with because it's so cheesy." The smell is impressive, which is likely attributed to Rao's sauce and not me at all, but I don't care. It's pretty much perfection.

"A big one."

"Okay." I turn, grabbing a knife from the cutting block, and hover it over the lasagna, a bit worried about doing it.

"Let me help you." He walks over, sliding his body up behind me, placing his puffy hand over mine, and controlling where I cut.

He leans over me, slicing in tiny jerks, pressing his warmth into my back and arms.

I slide my hand out from under his, letting him keep the knife, and spin, staring up at him. Wincing at the closeness of the injuries and possibly even forcing myself, I lift my hands to his puffy face, tracing the wounds. "They look really painful." I want to kiss him but this is a bit much.

Under it all he grins, leaning into me more. "They're getting less painful by the second."

"Really?" I cock an eyebrow and consider just doing it as I'm starting to see him again behind the mask of mayhem.

"Are you sure you're okay?" Deciding I do want a kiss but not if it hurts him more.

"I'm fine."

Taking his word for it, I lift myself onto my tiptoes and brush my mouth against his, kissing cautiously until he drops the knife and wraps himself around me, lifting me in the air. I take it as permission to kiss more, pulling his face down.

He steps to the side, setting me on the counter next to the warm lasagna pan as his lips crash down on mine. He winces after a second, pulling back. "Not fine. Not even a little." He steps away from me, lifting a trembling hand to his nose. "Oh shit. That hurt." He grunts.

"Oh my God, did I bump it?"

"There was bumping." He nods, squinting as water fills his pained eyes.

"Oh my God, I'm so sorry." I can't help but laugh. We're ridiculous.

"You sound like it." Even his words sound painful.

"No, I am. I just can't believe I nudged your broken nose. You're a hot mess."

"I hit my nose on you, not the other way around." Matt groans, "Fuck, that hurt." He shivers like he's cold, but I think it's the pain.

"Why do you do this to yourself?" I mutter.

"Love of the game?" he asks and laughs, blinking and nodding. "Okay, let's eat."

"Maybe this is God's way of making us talk."

"Maybe." He grabs the lasagna and carries it to the table that Nadia has set for me.

When he gets to his seat he wipes his eyes with his napkin. "I didn't even cry when it happened, but man, that smarted."

"Smarted?" I laugh harder, pouring him some of the wine Nadia corked earlier for us.

"Yes. Sometimes I revert back to a hillbilly. There's no actual fixing what being in the South breaks." He serves me some piping hot pasta. I take the cue and dish him up some salad. It's Cecilia's Caesar with Parmesan wisps. I love them.

He breaks off some garlic bread and puts it on my plate before he gets his own.

Chapter Fifteen

Confessional Christmas

Matt

"Why were you in the South?" Sami asks like she doesn't get it. Probably because she knows who my mom and dad are; they're no different than her parents. They wouldn't be caught dead in the South. "Were your parents there?"

"I was there with Dad's family, but my parents didn't come. My mom would die in the South. The heat alone would be a personal insult to her."

"You went alone?"

"Yeah, Mom and Dad wanted me to homeschool so we could travel a lot when I was a kid. Then they wanted us to go to boarding school, which I wasn't into. My brother was all over it, but I wanted to play hockey. My grandpa took me to a game when I was six, and I wanted to play from then on. So they let me stay with them for my schooling until I was thirteen. Then I billeted out in the Northern schools or stayed at houses my parents bought and staffed."

"No way."

"Yeah. Benson and Charles came with me everywhere I went from thirteen on, and they took care of me when I was in the city before that." I shrug, pretending it doesn't bother me. It doesn't really anymore, but I do wish my younger years had been spent with different parents. At least I always had Gran. I lift my water glass, not wanting to feel sorry for myself. "Happy Christmas Eve, Sami Ford." I attempt the grin but my face hurts. "I can't think of a single place I'd rather be than here." It's the God's honest truth.

"I'm glad you're here." She flushes with color. "Thanks

for taking me out of my comfort zone."

"I'm enjoying you being out of the comfort zone. I think I'll try to keep you on your toes so you're just always there." I pray to the gods of all the holy things she didn't notice that lame comment I made about why I never have girlfriends. She makes me uncomfortable and I sound like a moron, constantly. I wish just for once I could be the strong silent type. Those guys have it so easy.

"Funny." She sips her wine as I put my glass down and cut into the lasagna. I lift the first bite, a little scared. She's wrestling with a grin, making the whole experience scarier. There's a slight chance this is all a ploy, a game, and she agreed to dinner just so she can poison me.

I gulp and close my eyes, taking the bite in my lips. I chew woodenly for a moment. My throat refuses to swallow, it's closed and not opening. The flavors burst in my mouth and after a minute I force the masticated food down my esophagus. "Good." I try to smile.

"Really?" She takes her bite as though she waited for me to eat. "Oh my God, thank you, Jesus. It is good."

I relax and take another bite, actually enjoying it.

The sauce is perfect, the cheese is salty and crisp on top, and the noodles are cooked just right. I nod after a moment and grin, certain I have spinach teeth. "It's perfect. And excellent choice on Rao's sauce." I drag the bread through the sauce that's spilling onto the plate and moan as I take the next bite. "So tell me about you. What don't I know about the infamous Sami Ford? What isn't in the papers or being whispered at all the ridiculous parties we attend?" I need to crack this can open.

She takes another bite, contemplating the question. "I like scary movies."

"I knew that."

"I like cats."

"Okay, we're going to have to dig a little deeper. Everyone knows you like to drink but not do drugs and you like cats and you're perfect. Show me the cracks. Get uncomfortable." I say exactly the thing I've wanted to since we met, "I need to see behind the curtain."

"Behind the curtain?" Sami swallows hard, maybe contemplating what is actually behind her curtain. "I don't know where to start. You know when you were a kid and you had a personality and every time you showed it to your parents or friends you were punished, until you finally sort of fit into the void they wanted?"

"I do."

"That's what I'm trying to overcome. There's a smartass bad girl in me who rebels against everything, but only the things I know I'll bounce back from. I don't do drugs or take anything too far. Not anymore. But that person is my armor. She's the wall." She gives me a look. "Does that make sense?"

"Perfect." I don't want to say too much, this is like striking oil.

"I never knew our way of living, with our parents ignoring us and having servants take care of us and being alone all the time surrounded by stuff instead of love, was wrong. I thought everyone lived the way we do. It was my normal." Her words punch me in the gut.

I don't want to interrupt this so I sit back, listening, maybe more intently than I ever have.

"Until I went to Nat's house for a slumber party when I was little and saw how normal people live. It's little things like her dad whistling while he made waffles. Or how he asked us questions like he wanted to know what we liked and what we wanted to be when we grew up. He wanted to know us and see us. He knew all her favorites. I had no idea life was like that for some people until that moment. And then I kind of wanted it."

She laughs and glances at her plate, shaking her head and sounding bitter when she speaks, "I still wanted a Fendi bag and a yacht but I wanted that too. So I stayed with her all the time. We had movie nights and we snuck things, stole from her parents because there were rules about things she was allowed. Like sugar after ten at night and movies that were rated R. Her parents say no, still. And she listens."

"It's insane seeing it, isn't it? Normalcy. No one understands how relaxing normal is to us, just like how we won't ever understand how stressful it is for them. They don't have money all the time. Sometimes they have to go without something because they're short on cash. Mostly, they only buy the things they truly need. They look at every price and calculate before buying. It's like an alien planet."

"I know." She gets excited. "Nat's mom talks to herself when she's at the store, adding up prices and putting things back. Sometimes she would drive us so far to buy food from obscure markets that I thought we were going on a trip. Then I'd see the market and be disappointed. Money is such a big deal to them, but if you try to give it to them they won't take it. They'd rather suffer. Like our money isn't any good." Her voice trails off there.

I almost laugh at that. "Oh God, no. Middle-income people don't take charity. My grandpa had to sell some land a couple of years ago to pay something off and my dad ended up buying it in secret because Gramps wouldn't take the cash from him. And Dad didn't want to see the land separated."

"Yeah, I've paid for things Nat and her parents have no idea about. They think they got a deal but I paid most of it."

"What's your favorite part of being around them?" I chuckle as I take a huge bite of bread coated in sauce.

"Conversation at parties. When they honestly don't know who I am and they're just talking, it's real. They talk about crazy stuff, not trying to impress anyone or compare lives or fortunes. They have real topics: death and birth and pain and joy. You can just sit and listen and wonder how hard it must be to always worry about things. But at the same time, how cool it is to have worries that aren't shallow and selfish? I actually stress about being seen in public doing anything beyond looking like a statue because I hate the paparazzi. I worry about people following me and about being kidnapped for ransom ever since I got rid of the bodyguards. But at the same time, I doubt I did get rid of them; I think he just has them hidden better, my dad I mean. He worries about me being taken because of how it'll affect my public persona, not 'cause I'll get hurt. He's always worried about how I look to everyone, even though he's not looking at me himself. He doesn't see me. And he doesn't want to. They want the shell, the mold they gave me to fit into. They hate it when I get all teenage girl on them." She takes a small bite, obviously as uncomfortable as hell.

I'm uncomfortable too so I don't say anything, hoping she'll continue to wow me with her depth.

"We're spoiled and snobby and shallow and vain. And that's how we're supposed to appear. No one wants us to be anything else. We have to date right, marry right, live in the right areas, and have the right jobs. We need to hang with the right people having fun, but not reckless fun. Borderline reckless fun. We want people to talk about us but not too much. My dad has shares in clubs and bars and clothing and handbag lines, which he expects me to promote. He makes a fortune off the lip gloss I use when everyone's watching. He thinks I don't know but I do. He leaves lists and samples of products for me to Instagram and assumes I'm clueless as to why. I know he has a financial interest in them. I don't even care, I just wish he'd talk about it instead of acting like he's doing someone else a favor."

She puts down the fork and grabs her wine, biting her lip for a second as if fighting the tears in her eyes. "That's as real as I get, Matt. I don't have secrets. My life is all out there in the world, plus the mistakes I haven't made. Everyone knows all about what's under the rocks; they don't even need to lift them."

"Like rehab," I say after I take a big gulp of wine for bravery.

"Right. I've never stepped into a rehab clinic except to see a friend once. I've never been. But the magazines all say I've been so many times. Same as the abortion scandal two years ago that didn't happen."

"I didn't hear about that one." I can't believe she never went to rehab. It makes me wonder what else is bullshit.

"They make up shit all the time and that girl is the only one my dad cares about. Whatever she's doing makes or breaks it for me."

"To be totally honest, I thought you were in rehab." I drop it, hoping she understands some of my apprehension about her.

"Nope. Not even once."

"I'm sorry for believing that."

"Oh, I make it easy for everyone to believe everything they hear about me."

"Watching your life in the news makes me nervous. For us both." I feel sick that I've judged this girl so harshly. She's not any different than I am. She's alone for Christmas too. And this isn't the first time.

We eat and laugh and talk and it's real. Just like I prayed it would be.

When we finish the meal and I contemplate kissing her, she gives me a funny look from across the table.

"Stay." She isn't asking.

"Where?" I can't imagine she means stay the night here.

"Here, with me. We can sleep in separate rooms, but stay and do Christmas morning with me." She blinks a couple of times.

I have no defense for her pleading stare. "Are you serious?" I don't know if she's thinking this through. My eyes flicker on the wine bottle to see how much she's had. "Christmas morning?" I ask when I see it's still almost full.

"I got you a present. So it won't just be crap under the tree for me and nothing for you."

"Oh shit, I don't have anything for you." Now I feel like a jerk.

"It's fine." She shakes her head and gets up, walking out of the dining room. "Just stay. I can send a car for your gifts."

"I won't have any." I laugh and follow. "My family is in Italy. They'll Facetime and say happy Christmas and tell me they sent me some chocolate or something. Honestly. We don't do the gift exchange anymore. It stopped when I was about fourteen. It was too hard being away from everyone for hockey and school and none of us hung out. So we canceled the gift exchange. Now we send each other chocolates from wherever we are."

"Smart," she says as she fights a yawn. The eating and talking and joking have worn us both out. I'm bagged from the last couple of months of constant playing and in need of a few days off. “Please, just stay. I hate being alone on Christmas.” She hits me with the eyes again. I can’t fight her when she gives me that look.

“I hate being alone for it too. I’m assuming you have a guest room?” It’s not that I don’t want to sleep with her. I honestly just need sleep. Her lying next to me will send mixed signals to my cock about what my body is capable of doing. And there is no exhaustion enough to stop me from wanting to fuck her, broken face or not. Tandy already proved my dick isn’t broken. I shudder thinking about it.

“Yeah. I’m scared of hurting your face again.” She’s been giving me the same pitying look for hours.

“Me too.” I offer up a sheepish grin. “If you don’t mind showing me the way to my room, I’m going to hit the hay now before I pass out. I have to ice my face and take a shwack of drugs too.”

“Okay.” She turns and walks for the stairs.

I can’t believe she wants me to stay. I can’t believe we just had a civil meal filled with warmth and conversation and realness. She is exactly what I thought she was. The expression on her face in London came back a hundred times tonight as we discussed our lives. We carry the same wounds and fears. Abandonment, mixed with a lack of compassion and love, leaves scars, even on the rich and famous. It’s hard to know who to trust.

“So we didn’t kill each other.” I nudge her.

She glances over, flashing a grin. “No. We used our big people manners and everything.” Her smile dies. “And we got very uncomfortable. I hope you won’t tell anyone what I told you. I haven’t even said those things to Nat.”

“I’ll keep your secrets with my own.” I don’t tell her I hate who she is to the world. “I like the quietly vulnerable side of you.” I try to keep it positive.

Her eyes widen. “I don’t know about quiet. I’ve never talked this much, not even to Linda.”

“Who’s Linda?”

“My shrink. She’s rooting for you.” She giggles and takes the first step, hurrying like she wants to escape the conversation. Halfway up she turns back with her lips parted like she might say something, but her eyes narrow. "Are you staring at my ass?"

"Yes. Yes, I am."

"Really? I thought we just made a pleasant friendship down there, and you're degrading it?"

"Yes." I smile wide. "It's a nice ass. It pairs nicely with that wine and our new friendship."

"No." She glares and turns back around to take the stairs. I continue to stare at her ass as she climbs.

"Still a great ass."

Her answer comes over her shoulder as double middle fingers followed by a subject change, "No one ever sleeps in here. I hope the bedding isn't stale and the bed isn't shit." She takes me to the obvious guest room, opening it for me. It resembles a suite in a fine hotel.

"I sleep in different hotels so many times a month I forget what my bed feels like. Trust me, this will be fine even if it's shit. I'm used to it." I step to her, brushing my abs against hers. I savor the feel of her chest pressing against me. "Thanks for dinner."

"Thanks for dessert. It was delicious and I'm going to get that recipe for the chef."

I reach up and tuck a curl behind her ear. "I like you. The real you. Not the shell. I like who you are when no one else is here."

Her lips part and her eyes shine but she says nothing.

"Goodnight, Sami."

"Goodnight." She swallows hard and steps back. She's so pretty I can barely take it.

She turns and walks down the hall and I can't help but say one more thing, "Where's your room?"

"Why?" She glances back and scowls.

"In case I decide I can't stay away."

"But we just got to the friendship zone. Why ruin it with sex?" She flashes me that smile, the one that makes my stomach tighten. I swear, staring at her lips hits me in the dick every time.

"We can do both."

"Then I guess you'll have to come find me."

"I might."

"Maybe I'll be ready for you, Beast." She saunters off with a wave. "Have a good sleep." There's extra swagger in her hips as she rounds the corner.

I almost follow her but the throbbing in my nose suggests I won't keep up with the promises I'm making myself.

It's hard to close the door and get ready for bed. It's harder to get into the bed. I want to be charming in the pursuit of her but I'm in agony. Kissing was such a mistake.

Chapter Sixteen

Methy Christmas

Sami

When I was a kid sleeping in on Christmas was impossible. I would lie awake and wonder what Santa had brought Nat. Her gifts were never as expensive as mine but they were more personal. She got things like a telescope or a keyboard. They were fun. When my parents told me about Santa it made so much sense. He'd always given me expensive gifts, whereas Nat always got cool things.

But even after they told me, I continued to be excited about Christmas. I was still pretty young when my parents spent their first Christmas away. That was when I stopped caring so much.

But because Nat grew up this way, her gift giving is also thoughtful. One year she gave me a painting she did herself. It was digital art that had taken her six months to perfect. It didn't cost anything but time.

My parents never gave gifts like that. They paid to relinquish themselves of having to spend the time. My mom used a personal shopper. She didn't even pick out my presents.

That was when I learned the value of someone's time over the value of a dollar.

Time last night with Matt was amazing.

I regret everything I said, not because I was my usual ass self, but because I gave everything of myself away. He makes me uncomfortably naked without taking a stitch of clothing off, and I have never been more proud of myself.

I couldn't sleep because of it all, tossing and turning all night, and when I did finally sleep, the dreams weren't the sort you walked away from.

I wake in the morning wanting more of Matt. A lot more.

At seven in the morning, I throw in the towel and get up, flinging my robe over pajamas and sauntering down the stairs.

His gift is already under the tree. I put it there the day after he asked me to have Christmas Eve dinner with him. I had the gift flown over the moment I knew we'd be spending Christmas together.

The thought of that stops me on the stairs.

After everything we've discussed, I can admit it.

I like him. I more than like him. I want to see the normal side of his family and date him and be me around him because he's comfortable now, like Nat.

Nat!

It's finally my turn to wake her up on Christmas morning.

I grab my phone and call her, hoping she's not awake. This can be my gift from her.

"Hello?" she groans into the phone.

"Merry Christmas." A smile spreads across my lips as I sit on the stairs and wait for it.

"Why are you calling so early? It's still dark out."

"Get up and go see your gift." She is the person who taught me that giving is better than receiving. Watching or even listening to her get a gift is the best.

"No. Sami, it's like seven in the morning, on a holiday. Are you just getting home from your date with that Matt guy?" The smile on her lips is obvious when she speaks.

"Nadia! She told you?" I gasp.

"It was my Christmas present from her." She giggles.

"You're a dick!" I'm so relieved she knows I can't even be angry.

"Why didn't you tell me?"

"Because you were sad, I didn't want to rub my possible happiness in your face."

"You better stop, Sami Ford, or people will see you're not the evil little princess you try so hard to be."

"Shut up. I'm still an evil princess."

"I guess so, since you've gotten creative this time, girl." She stretches and yawns and makes me wish I were there so we could slumber-party gossip about it.

"Creative with what?"

"Ways to piss your dad off."

"This isn't like that. I don't want anyone to know about this until we figure out what we are to each other. I slipped the staff an extra five grand for Christmas to ensure discretion."

"You don't think Daddy Dearest suspected you might do that and offered them ten grand to spy?" She moans. "My gift to you is a warning: he knows. They're telling him everything, I guarantee it."

"That's all you got me?" I pout. My dad likely did do that. At least the staff got an extra fifteen thousand dollars.

"No. Go look under the tree, there's something else. I'll throw on my robe and go look at mine."

"Hurry up!" I stand and walk downstairs to the tree we left on after dinner.

There's something magical about a lit tree on Christmas morning with presents underneath. Even though the presents are few and far between. One from Nadia, one from Vincenzo, one from Nat, one from Carson, and a card from my parents. The rest of them are for friends who I'll see during the holidays and a few family friend ones I have yet to deliver with my winning Ford family smile. The tiny package for Matt stands out. Nadia wrapped all the gifts for my friends with expertise I don't have, so the fact I wrapped his shows.

Grabbing Nat's gift, I am lost on the contents of the box. It weighs a ton for the size. "Are you in the living room yet?" I ask impatiently.

"No. God! I barely have my robe on. I need some speed to catch up to you."

"Hurry up!"

"Good morning." Nadia strolls into the room with a large mug as I listen to Nat grumbling about her house. Nadia smiles wide. “Merry Christmas, Sami.” It’s so much better since she dropped the “miss.” It only took a year of me forcing my name on her.

“Merry Christmas, Nadia!” I jump up and give her a hug as she sets the mug down. Her hug is wooden but her smile is warm. I quickly hand her the gift I got for her. She opens it and beams at the Chanel purse. I’ve seen her eyeing up mine tons. “You shouldn’t have. This is too expensive.”

“I’m glad you like it. But look inside.”

“There’s more?” She scowls and opens it. Her jaw drops and tears fill her eyes. “No!”

“Yes!” And there it is, the reason for the season. I love Christmas like a giant fucking cheeseball and this is why. I love seeing this exact look on someone’s face.

Her lip trembles as she lifts the ticket to France with the full itinerary of destinations and prepaid hotel rooms and tours.

“You are a very naughty girl.”

“You were so bummed when you couldn’t go to France last year.”

“Thank you.”

“Merry Christmas.”

“You’re still a bad girl.” She wipes her eyes and exhales one quick breath. “Anyway, Mr. Brimley stayed the night?” She cocks a dark eyebrow, her eyes still glistening.

“He did.”

“Interesting.” She grins, clutching the new purse. “I’ll tell Cecilia we have an extra guest.”

“Thanks,” I say to Nadia as she leaves the room, but continue to listen intently into the phone for the moment Nat has her gift. I lift the mug of coffee, catching the hint of Baileys in my first sip. Our tradition since I turned fifteen.

“Okay, I have it. Why’s it so light? Jesus, did you just give me cash this year?”

“You’re an ass. I’m opening mine now.” I tear into the package she placed under my tree at some point in the last couple of weeks since we decorated it.

A wide smile spreads across my face as I see the very thing I have always wanted: a glass chess and checkers set done in pale pink and light turquoise. "Oh my God, where did you get this?"

"Do you like it?"

"I love it!" She is the only person in the world who knows me. "It's perfect. Did you get someone to make it?" I lift the tiny pieces and inspect the carving, noticing they appear to be made from sea glass.

"Yeah, this guy at my school carves with glass and makes it look like sea glass. He frosts it and rounds the edges. He makes the awesomest wind chimes. When I saw them I asked if he made other stuff and he said he could create anything. So I got him to make it." She sounds so proud.

"Best gift ever, Nat. I need a hug after this one. Can't you just come out? I'll send the helicopter. We could play a couple of games of checkers."

"No, crazy pants. I have to have dinner with the herd. I can't believe you won't be here. And because of a boy. I am shocked. You and Brimstone. I've only suspected forever.

"I wonder why they call him that?" I change the subject.

"I don't know." She laughs. "I'm opening mine now." The paper tears delicately. I can hear the tape slowly being pried away. She always unwraps like she might reuse it. It's annoying. "Oh my God, Sami! What the shit?"

"What?"

"This is way too much, for God's sake." She protests but the excitement is in her voice when she sees the invitation. "A Lumineers private concert? Are you kidding me right now?"

"No." I need to see her face. "Switching to Facetime." I press it and wait for the connection.

She holds the invitation up, beaming. "You're a shit. Why can't you give normal gifts?"

"This is a normal gift."

"No, normal is a scarf or a sweater or a chess set—"

"Anyway," I cut her off with a groan. "I talked to their manager and he says they won't be touring for another couple of years. So I arranged a little something. Apparently, the band has always sort of dreamed of playing at the

Musikverein in Vienna because of acoustics. So I got them the hall and arranged for the stage and sound to be handled if they just show up. They'll meet us there on New Year's. I've sent out private invites to a thousand of our closest friends, and the band had to be allowed to invite a hundred people, which I said was cool. So now it's all arranged. We're all staying at the Hotel Imperial. It's right next door to the Musikverein, and they have the best butler service in all of Vienna."

"You mean the most discreet butler service." She rolls her eyes.

"That too."

"I actually thought I had you beat this year." She sighs and stares at the gift. "But this is a top-notch gift. Not only do you have the money to pull off big gifts, you also have the connections to make the impossible happen. But the most important part of a perfect gift is the heart. And believe it or not, Sami Ford, you have the heart. Thank you."

Blinking away the tears that are forming, I wave my hand. "It's not nearly as good as yours. And it's a selfish gift. I wanna see the Lumineers too." I smile. "The chess and checkers set is perfect. I really love it."

"I know you do. We're both incredibly thoughtful." She sighs sarcastically. "Now tell me about the important stuff like Brimstone and how this happened and why you kept it secret for so long."

"No. Maybe another time."

"I can't believe he slept over in another room. Are you guys saving it for marriage?"

"Seriously! How good are your connections in this house?" I turn and glare at the doorway even though no one is there. I don't want her to see my face. She'll see through the lies and know we've already done it. And I can't tell her that part; she'll hate him. And as odd as it is, I don't want her to.

"I have the whole house bugged. Come for dinner."

"I can't. I promised him we'd hang out. It's confusing enough just being the two of us."

"Have you eaten a PB&J with him yet?"

"No." I feign a shocked look. "I only do that with you."

"Whatever, we'll see. It'll be midnight and you'll be jonesing, and he'll find you with the spoon in the pantry, licking peanut butter from it."

We both laugh.

"Oh, and don't do that weird thing where you order for him and try to guess what he's in the mood to eat. No one likes that but you."

"You love it." I pretend to sulk.

"Would you like a coffee, Mr. Brimley?" Nadia says his name pointedly.

"Yes, please. Black." His voice makes my back straighten.

Nat winces and I nod. "I'll talk to you later."

"Right. Merry Christmas, Brimstone!" She sniggers and the connection dies.

"Merry Christmas." He smiles, looking much better than the night before. The bruising and swelling are down a lot. He almost looks like himself, but tired maybe. With cuts. And a bit of a drug problem. Like those meth before-and-after photos. Okay, he looks bad but at least he's on the better side of bad.

"Hi." I hold up the phone. "How long were you there?"

"PB&J?" He glances at Nadia. "Thanks." He takes the coffee in the fancy mug and sits. It's funny; to see it in his huge hands it looks like a teacup.

"Merry Christmas," I offer as I sip my coffee too.

"I didn't take you as an early morning Christmas girl. I figured we'd be noon or better."

"No," I lie. Nadia tilts her head, mocking me for a second before vanishing from the room.

"So from the stairs I thought I heard you talk about New Year's. What are you doing?" He sips his coffee.

"Going to Vienna to watch The Lumineers play at the Musikverein."

"Bless you."

"You're a dork. Don't act like you don't know what the Musikverein is."

His green eyes dazzle me with mocking humor. "The

better question is, how did you get the Lumineers there?"

"Charm?" I wink but he scoffs. "Fine, I used my name and connections and bribed people."

"That's more like it." He chuckles.

"You don't think I'm charming?"

"No." He offers a cheeky grin. "I imagine you can turn it on if you need to, but I want to believe you're above charming people."

"I'm charming, buddy." I act insulted.

"Then pretend it was a compliment." He stretches his neck and rolls his shoulders.

"Mmhmm." Still acting insulted I put down the coffee and get on my knees at the tree, plucking my small gift for him from beneath. "Merry Christmas, ass." I turn and toss it at him.

"What?" He laughs and eyeballs the little present. "How the hell did you have time to get me a present? Or did you know I would ask you out for Christmas? Are you psychic?"

"Just open it and stop worrying about my abilities."

He tears the paper like a normal person; it warms my heart. His lips, still swollen with the injuries, lose their cheeky grin. "Seriously?" He peers up through his thick lashes, dangling the keychain with the Oxford Circus tube station button and a small black cab.

I don't know if he likes it or not. "I just thought maybe it would remind you of me and—"

"It's perfect." He shakes his head. "It was the best ending to the worst night for us both, I think."

"You were covered in lipstick. I didn't think you had a bad night. You looked pretty happy when we met."

"I was happy when I saw you." He gets up and walks to me, getting down on his knees too. He's so big. It's weird for me to feel this small next to someone.

"I'd literally just escaped with my life. My buddy's girlfriend attacked me because she caught him with some girl. She thought I would be down for some revenge sex. I was trashed and pretty much passed out, and when I came to I realized we were kissing and she had my pants undone. Of course he came in at that moment. He flipped out. I flipped out. He wanted to fight me so I left and wandered the streets alone. Worst New Year's I've ever had, until I saw you."

"That's it? That's your worst? Wow. Lucky." I roll my eyes.

"What was so shitty about yours, Highness?"

"Well, let's see. Boxing day I caught my dad having an affair, one that involves real feelings, not some call girl or a socialite. No, this one has clearly been going on for a long time. She's a lady I found pictures of once, old pictures. So I confronted my mom and she gave me the worst smile I have ever seen. It was hollow. Her eyes were like staring into black glass, no life. She said she knew about the affair, of course, and it was high time I grew up and stopped thinking the world was so black and white."

"Oh shit." He cringes.

"Right. Of course we fought, so she left and went to the South of France. I stayed in London. I hated her more than him, I don't know why. But I couldn't look into her eyes again. I was scared of them, of the way she had detached." I laugh bitterly. "Then I went to meet up with Drew. I'd told him I was going to be late, I was seeing another friend first. But I arrived earlier than I'd planned at the New Year's party and caught him in an awkward moment with an old family friend of mine. I pretended I didn't see anything and got drunk. Finally, right before midnight I was pretty loaded and ended up confronting them about being together and their faces were pathetic. He didn't even really try to lie. I left the party, pissed in every way. Ended up at a pub with a wet tee shirt contest about to start. Drew followed me there. He tried to tell me it meant nothing and he and I were the right sort of couple, and we had to allow for a few indiscretions while we were young. That dating me was a social requirement and banging her was just plain lust. I could have killed him. Instead, I said I would never be that kind of girl, fuck society. I jumped on stage and won the wet tee shirt contest, humiliating myself to spite him and my family."

"Jesus. You win. Way worse New Year's."

"Oh, that's just one of them. And the worst part is that I

always manage to sabotage my own happiness to spite them. Like in my pea-sized brain I somehow believe that hurting myself will hurt them. It's dumb." I shrug it off, hoping we can change the subject.

"I know what you mean." He reaches forward, lifting my chin.

"You don't have to agree with everything I say like you always understand my point. It doesn't matter if you don't." I don't think he does.

"My parents are the same. My dad has affairs and my mom shops and buys houses and decorates them. She's distracted and he's always sleeping with someone else. One time, when I was about fifteen I saw him at a hotel. I didn't see the lady with him. She was behind a pillar in a lobby. I waved, about to run over, and he looked me right in the eyes and turned around. He told me later he didn't see me, but I saw him flinch when his eyes met mine."

"I'm sorry."

Matt nods. "Me too. But I think if we see it, there's a better chance we won't become like them."

"Do you honestly think that? 'Cause I don't. I worry that they were once young and saying the same things we are. They swore they'd never be like their parents and now they're worse."

"Yeah. I'll admit that worries me. I can see it in my mom. Maybe at one point she was rebellious and strong and the obligations and expectations wore her down. And that's where the fear is from. If it wore her down, maybe it'll wear me down."

"At least you have hockey." I can't believe how much I've lowered the guards around my heart, but he has too. "It's a career and a life separate from your family."

"Hockey is a joke to my family. It's like me standing in the middle of a British pub with my dress down, pouring ale on my boobs." He chuckles. "I might as well dance for the man for bananas like a monkey. I'm no different than an actor or a singer. It's not someone they'd have at their house for dinner; it's someone they'd pay to have at their house to impress their friends. Like a piece of jewelry or art."

"Oh, that's how my dad thinks of it too. Celebrities are on the hard limit list."

"Yours too?"

"Yeah, but my dad didn't grow up on a farm. I can't believe yours is such a hypocrite."

His eyes soften. "I can't either. My dad's life was an honest one. I always wonder what he would have been like, had he just married a girl from Henderson and continued being a farmer, instead of going into investment banking."

"My parents were born doomed." I say it fully knowing I'm doomed too.

He looks at me, his eyes piercing my soul. "We're different. We're not doomed."

I want to believe him more than anything in the world, but he's sitting next to a tree filled with lights where I used to believe a kind elf left me gifts. I don't believe in fairy tales anymore. I daydream about them and they never come true.

Chapter Seventeen

I'll tell ya what

Matt

Calling Bev as I cross the road to my place, I can't shake the uncertainty that I'm in over my head before any of this has even started. Laramie's words of warning still flicker in my mind, attached to the self-doubt that I'll ever be happy.

"Merry Christmas, cuz." Her drawl makes me chuckle.

"Merry Christmas. How's the family? Have I missed any good fights?"

"Oh, they're wrestling over the right way to cook the bones for stock as we speak, so it's safe to say there's nothing new here."

"I hate missing turkey-bone wrestling."

"The first Christmas without you has been nice, but I'm missing having that one person I can torment and taunt without it being a form of animal cruelty. Eddie isn't the same. I mean, he's as dumb as a bag of shit so mocking him is easy, but it's like making fun of a chair. There's no joy in kicking something that doesn't know it's being kicked."

"Good to see you haven't changed at all in the six months since I last saw you. Still dating that knuckle dragger?"

"What's that, Mattie? You wanna talk to Gran about that new girl you're seeing? Okay," she says loudly and hands the phone off.

"Bev!" I shout, scared.

"Matthew Johnson Brimley, now why did I have to hear about this young lady you're spending Christmas with from your cousin? You best get your butt down here the moment the season's over and introduce her to your family like a gentleman. Or I'll be coming up there and you won't like what you see."

"Merry Christmas, Gran." I am going to kill Beverly.

"Don't you merry Christmas me, young man. I want a 'yes, ma'am' and a schedule for when I will meet this young girl."

"She's no one, just someone I've known for a while."

"I'll tell you what, you don't spend Christmas with someone unless it's serious. This better not be some puck fox—"

"Puck bunny."

"Foxes, bunnies, whatever. You know what I think of those girls. Ain't no self-respecting girl worth her weight in dog shit giving anything away for free because you play hockey well. You don't play *that* well, you hear me?"

"Yes, ma'am." I wince, not even sure I understand but I definitely hear her.

"Now, tell Granny what this girl's name is and who's her family? Is she in college too?"

"She's a Ford. Not the car company, the finance and development family. She's at Columbia University here in New York. We've known each other for a while."

"Ford? For God's sake, you're dating some rich girl from the city? Have you learned nothing about rich people, Matthew? You're gonna end up with some ditz like your brother. I still don't know if his wife speaks or not. I've never gotten one word from her. Is she even American? Because I tried Spanish on the off chance, but she still just blinks and smiles. Like talking to my dog, minus the winning personality." She says Matthew firmly as she borders on slightly racist but maybe it's more that she's untrusting of foreigners. She does say the word "foreigner" with a tone.

"She's different, she's not like that. She's American."

"She's from the North, you mean."

"Gran, hating Northerners is weird."

"I don't hate all Northerners. Canadians are actually very nice. None of that snooty self-entitled attitude."

"You can't label all Northerners that way. I'm a

Northerner," I say but she's not listening to me now that Beverly's laughing in the background and saying Sami's name. "Gran? What's Bev saying?"

"Beverly says she's got some video I have to see."

"Video?" I stop, mid sidewalk and shout, "Gran! No! Don't look at the video! It's fake! Sami was in a movie! It's not real!" My heart is leaping out of my chest with every beat and slamming back in-between beats.

"She's an actress?" She sounds sidetracked. "Must be a dull movie if all it has in it is her hiding from the reporters or posing. She's some pretty though. Not as pretty as that girl who's with her. That blonde girl, she looks nice. Why don't you try to date her instead? She looks humble."

"Seriously?"

"What?" She tries the innocent old lady act.

"It's nothing serious, I just like her. Can we just give her the benefit of the doubt?"

"Well, no shit, Sherlock. It's obvious you like her. You think I'm falling for the 'she's no one' spiel? You're spending Christmas with her instead of your granny. She must be something special. I certainly hope you're helping with dishes and being polite, showing her family that someone besides that Fifth Avenue nitwit taught you some real manners."

"Yes, ma'am." It's a lie but trying to explain that we have servants who would have a heart attack if we did the dishes isn't a fight I want.

"Are her parents nice people?"

I contemplate lying but just go with the truth, hoping for the best. "Not particularly. They're sort of like my mom's family—"

She cuts me off with a sigh but I smile.

"She's not though. She's different. Trust me, she's not like them. I have enough Brimley blood to know a nice girl from a skan—not nice girl." Saying skank to my grandma feels wrong.

"Well, all right then. Are you having a nice Christmas? We sure do miss you down here."

"It's been nice. Quiet. We're going out for dinner tonight

and maybe hanging out at a party for my team tomorrow night. Then I have a game on the twenty-eighth and thirty-first."

"A game on New Year's? That is ridiculous. Don't people have anything better to do than expect a hockey game every damned night of the week? Do you play Christmas Day for those savages too?"

"No." She makes me laugh.

"We'll be watching but I won't like it! You deserve some downtime too. Now I better get you back to Beverly. I have some people in my kitchen unsupervised." Her tone softens, "Miss you, brat!"

"Miss you too, Gran."

She's gone and it's silent for a moment before Bev comes back. "How far did your heart get out of your chest when I said video?"

"You're an asshole."

"Maybe. But it was like getting a second Christmas gift. I haven't been able to bug you in months. Now what do you want?" She knows me too well.

"So, we had Christmas at her house like friends—Sami's house. And by 'like friends' I mean no kissing or messing around. It was awesome to truly see the kind of person she is and there were no games. None I could see anyway. She was just cool. We really hit it off and I thought it was a romantic connection. We hung out and talked and then I realized she was treating me like one of her girlfriends. I followed your advice, leaving the hint about being interested in her. She didn't try to take the bait at all. She didn't even really flirt. So now I'm worried. I told her I liked her, out loud. She said nothing back."

"And?"

"And what? She's not giving me any signs. She got me a super thoughtful Christmas gift and then punched me in the arm as I was leaving this morning and called me Beast." While I rant an older woman gives me a dirty look as she passes by. I hurry to the house, waving at the doorman as I get inside. "I don't know what to do. Do I try to seduce her tonight or is she friend zoning me? When you said she was showing me her worth and this would take effort, I didn't know we were going all the way backward."

"She got you a super thoughtful gift and friend zoned you? That's weird." There's an air of bewilderment in her tone. "She didn't even try to kiss you?"

"Well, we did once but my broken nose—"

"You're hurt?"

"Well, yeah. You saw the game." I nod at Benson as he gets the door for me. "My face is a bit busted up—"

"You're an idiot. Girls don't have sex or even make out with boys who have broken faces. Dumbass. Maybe if you'd been dating for years and she loved you beyond the hideousness. But new relationships don't include you looking like you might ring a bell and scream for sanctuary any second. *Moron."*

"Girls are shallow."

"You kissed her looking like the last thing you made out with was a shovel and then she didn't want any more of that? *Duh!"*

"So you think she's still into me like that or are we friends now? Because I legit told her I liked her and now I'm second guessing whether I should've." I don't bother telling her I might have cried a little too when our noses touched.

"I think if you're really lucky she won't notice just how dumb you actually are. Keep getting hit in the head at work, champ, it's improving you." She laughs and ends the call.

"Glad I could amuse you," I mutter and put the phone down.

"Trouble in paradise, sir?" Benson sounds concerned.

"No, that was Bev. I mean, there's trouble but it's the normal sort. Bev was just grinding my gears."

"Ah yes. Miss Beverly is always the one to get you worked up. Can I get you a drink or something?"

"No, thanks. I'm exhausted. I'm going to crash for a couple of hours before I take Sami to dinner."

"Dinner, on Christmas night? In a restaurant?"

"Right. No Southern turkey this year. See ya in a few hours." I saunter off to my room to sleep for a bit.

Chapter Eighteen

Whores you can't borrow

Sami

"No, we didn't do anything, I swear. It was nice. We honestly hung out. It was weird to just sit around with a guy and talk like friends." I roll onto my back and stare at the ceiling as I chat with Nat for the third time today. "I mean, I wanted to do things, but his face"—I wrinkle my nose—"it was a mess. We tried kissing and he cried it hurt so much."

"Jesus, like what level of mess?"

"Broken bones and cuts and scabs. Like the kind of mess I didn't really want near me. When we woke up this morning he was less puffy, a lot less. But it was still a bit nasty. Yesterday though, when he showed up and his eyes were slits, I hardly recognized him."

"God just did you a solid. You hung out with a guy and didn't molest him and then send him away, used and abused."

"Right. We joked about that actually, that maybe it was just a good way to see if we even like each other before it becomes a one-night stand." I say this because Nat doesn't need to know the backstory.

"And do we?"

"We do." My cheeks heat up. "He's not what I thought at all. He's kind of like a poor person but not."

"Oh my God." Nat laughs. "You are such a snob. A poor person? Seriously? His family is one of the richest. His mom is related to the Rothschilds or something."

"No, but his dad is nouveau riche. I'm not even joking. And his mom's family are like the Vanderbilts, land rich and cash poor. So of course his dad being an independently wealthy billionaire was a perfect choice for her. He brought the money and she brought the name. It's the only way these old-money families are surviving. My dad is a billionaire so he'll be looking to fit me with someone from a good family."

"Your world is disturbing."

"It will be your world one day too."

"Speaking of that, William just called before you. We talked. He's going to try to be more flexible. I told him that the time constraints we both have can't get in the way of seeing each other." She doesn't sound excited the way she normally does. She sounds beaten down, like her mother's will is finally too much.

My stomach sinks. "No way." I don't have the energy to pretend I believe him.

"Yeah. I told him to pick me up and we could go for a walk in the cold and try to get to a happy place with our insane timetables."

As if that is the only problem in their relationship . . .

"Sometimes I think it's sucky that we're so far away from each other. It would be easier if we were closer."

I almost throw up but manage to keep my level of disgust to myself, which means I'm silent.

"I should go anyway, he's going to be here soon. Maybe we could all double date sometime. He and William know each other."

"Oh, we're not dating. It's a thing. It's nothing serious," I lie.

"You spent Christmas together."

"Christmas isn't real for people like us. It's just another day. Every day is Christmas when you're rich." I feel like the biggest knob in the world saying it, but I can't bear the thought of double dating with William-shit for brains-Fairfield.

"You're such a snob."

"I know. Love you."

"Love you too." She ends the call.

I shudder and roll over, switching out the light so I can get some shut-eye before we go out.

When I wake up Nadia is nudging me.

"Why are you nudging me?" I swat at her. "Stop!"

"You have fifteen minutes before he gets here. I texted you half an hour ago. You texted back some nonsense. I assumed you were awake."

"What?" I don't understand what she's saying.

"He'll be here in fifteen minutes!" She pulls back the covers and switches on the light.

"Who? OH MY GOD! PICK OUT CLOTHES!" I scream as I hop up, swaying slightly as a dizzy spell hits. But I don't let it stop me. I rush to the bathroom and leap into the shower. It's the fastest cleaning I've ever had.

I jump out and throw on my robe, blow-drying my hair as Nadia does my makeup. When she gets a natural look slathered on, she spritzes my face with makeup sealer and moves onto the hair. She does a twist so she can hide that the thick mess is still damp.

I look hot, as in kinda sweaty and red-faced, but it's better than groggy and half asleep.

She helps me drag on my clothes, careful of my makeup and hair. The outfit is perfect: a short black tutu-style skirt matched with thigh-high lace socks and ankle boots with buckles and a flashy steel toe. On top we have a push-up bra and a thin cable-knit cropped sweater with long sleeves. She loops on a red scarf and hands me a thick wool jacket.

I finish with the last touches as she hurries downstairs to make sure he hasn't fallen asleep waiting. We're closer to twenty-five minutes than fifteen, but it's still the fastest I've ever gotten dressed.

I spritz with my subtlest perfume and leave the room, phone in pocket next to a credit card. I'm going purse-less. I don't want to have too much shit in my hands in case he tries to hold them.

When I get downstairs he looks much—MUCH—better.

His swelling has come down remarkably and his green eyes are taking on a normal shape again. When he smiles he doesn't look like a hit man. He just looks like Matt and I'm glad I chose the outfit I did. I want him to touch me.

"Hey!" He gives me that sly grin. "Ready?"

"Just barely. I fell asleep and didn't wake up until half an hour ago."

"Me too. But getting ready is only a few seconds for me." He turns and looks at the door. "I think there's some paparazzi out front. I passed a couple guys I think I remember."

"Back door it is. I prefer it anyway." I say it without thinking until his eyebrows lift as a comical look lands on his face.

"If you insist."

"Shut it." I turn and head for the other side of the house.

We sneak out, hurrying to the car he has waiting. His driver gets the door, but I pause and give Matt a look. "Really?"

"What?" he asks but the driver appears as though he might know what's up. His weathered cheeks flush as his eyes lower.

"Nothing." I cringe as I climb in.

"What's wrong?" he asks again as he gets in and the door closes behind him. His eyes meet mine and then widen. "Oh shit." He glances around the limo. "Oh shit!"

I cross my arms and stare out the window.

"What are you thinking?"

I contemplate lying when our eyes meet but the truth slips out, "How disgusting the backseat of this limo must be and that I was one of a hundred chicks and nothing more." I know it's something we've already worked out, but I can't get over the fact he brought this fucking limo.

"I never thought of you as that. You were different—you are."

"Whatever." The horrid taste in my mouth won't go away so we sit in awkward silence as the driver takes us through Manhattan and across the Brooklyn Bridge.

The silence and the disgusted feeling don't work well for

me. I'm not someone who struggles to remain taciturn. I'm a runner or a person who puts on a loud show so the other person knows I won't be forced into submission.

In my struggle to stay quiet about just how fucked up what he did was, I start to sweat. Maybe it's me, maybe it's the warmth of the car. Whatever it is, I pull my scarf off and lay it on the seat next to me, fidgeting with my fingernails to the point I might rip my gel polish off.

His eyes dart from my hands to my face, nervously. "It was the wrong choice. I should have brought the Bentley," he mutters.

I glare, about to say the car isn't the problem.

"Okay, you're right. It's not just the car. It's me. I made the wrong choice." He reads my mind or my death stare perfectly. "I just wanted you so bad for so long and when I finally got you in my arms and you were single and I was single, I went for it. We both got so angry and it ignited, sending the hold I had on my attraction for you to a fiery death. I needed you right then and there. The car coming was the only thing that saved you from getting fucked in that dirty alley."

My nose wrinkles.

"I don't know how else to explain this." He jumps up and leans over me, lowering the partition between us and the driver. "Charles, who have I talked about nonstop since forever?"

"Please, keep me out of this." Charles shakes his head.

"No, just tell her. She's been everything for too long. Embarrassingly long."

"This entire experience is embarrassing, sir." He scoffs and closes the partition.

Matt sighs and sits back. "You're the first girl I've ever brought into this car that I imagined having sex with anywhere else but the car."

I don't say anything. Mostly because Linda told me it drives guys nuts when you don't talk, but also because I don't know what to say.

"I kissed you so romantically in that black cab and then I ruined it in this car. But it isn't about the car—it's just about you. I want you. Even right now, I want to do it in the car again, mostly because I just want to have sex again, but only with you." He pauses, out of breath and looking a little crazy. "Say something."

"Okay."

"Okay?" He gasps.

"Okay."

"You wanna fuck too or okay that story makes a little bit of sense?"

Mulling over everything I want to say, I pause and take a deep breath. I need to breathe out my emotion first. Another Linda gem. "I don't want to fuck. Not in this car. Ever again. I don't even want to ride in this car again. I want you to sell or demolish this particular car." I take another breath because I'm getting feisty. "Your story doesn't make sense. It's gross. The fact you had your poor driver take you on more than one trip so you could bang chicks in the back with him in the car is nasty. And I don't want to hear anything about being young—I poured ale on my boobs—I get young mistakes. Car sex is disgusting when you drive somewhere to do it alone, adding the driver is nasty. It's something you do with a hooker. It implies you don't have to take a girl on a date, respect them, take them home to your house and hang with them, suffer through going to their house, eat a meal with them, or even let them clean up. You can actually drop them off, like a whore, and go on your merry way. If that's just how you like to have sex, you have a ballpark worth of issues you need to address. And I'm not slut shaming you; I agree with one-night stands, but there's a classy way to do it and then there's this way."

He cringes. "It sounds bad when you say it like that."

"It is bad. It's a mean thing to do and makes me think you have no respect for women. Which is known in hockey. What are they called, those girls? The player girls? It's a thing. What is it?"

"Puck bunnies."

"No, that's the tame version. Carson called them something meaner." I lift my finger when it hits me. "Puck fucks."

"PFs. Please just say PFs."

"That right there is the exact opposite of women's rights. Like different teams completely. The women who let themselves be puck fucked might as well stop voting." I glance around. "Especially in the car. Do you drop them off on corners so they can continue working for the night?"

His eyes narrow. "I get it. Your okay was the nice way of saying I didn't actually want you to answer."

"You wanted to see behind the curtain. You wanted to get to know me and see what kind of person I am, like you're so much better than me, and I have to prove myself to you. As if you're some fucking high standard of human that I have to substantiate myself to you, because I'm a dumb, rich, blonde ditz." I lean into him, seething anger. "Well, let me tell you something, I am ten times the person you are. I wouldn't do something like this." I lower the partition and look at Charles. "Am I right or am I right?"

"For the love of all things holy, leave me out of it."

"Translation, I'm right." I pat Charles on the shoulder. "Just swing back to my place, I sort of lost my appetite."

"Yes, ma'am." He closes the partition and I go back to staring out the window.

"I'm an idiot. I literally don't think. Ever. Will an 'I'm sorry' even come close to covering this?" He sits back, looking a little defeated. It disappoints me to see him give up so easily. I liked it better when we were screaming at each other, but I'm guessing he truly has no defense for this.

"I don't want an apology. I want you to see that you're not so fucking perfect. You're just as high and mighty as I am. You treat girls like garbage and refuse to date. Oh, like dating you is so special. There's nothing special about you, you're just as rich and snobby as I am. You spend all your time looking down your nose at me, like I suck for being my father's daughter, but *you're* still judging me. You think I missed it all these years? I know the look on your face every time you see me out and about."

"I don't think I'm better than you." His nostrils flare. "I like you."

"You hate that you like me," I challenge him. He flinches

and doesn't answer. "How can you hate me for being a Ford when you're you? That's like me disliking you for not following in your father's footsteps."

"You called me blue collar." He lifts his eyebrows.

"I never said I wasn't an asshole, I just said you were one too."

He leans forward. "I know I'm an asshole. I am trying not to be. It's more than I can say for you." He wrinkles his nose angrily. "No. Scratch that. I don't mean that. You are trying to be nice and I am saying things in anger." All the hate slips away when he exhales. "I like you, Sami. I made a mistake. I've made a lot of mistakes. Millions. The one mistake I will forever hate myself for was not finding you after the cab ride." His eyes soften again. "I just want this to be more than two rich kids with no real future or freedom. I'm scared to let myself be with you and it's not fair. But trust me, Sami, I want you. Not in the car. Everywhere. All the time." A shitty grin lands on his lips. "I'm better in a bed anyway."

His admission is hot. Hotter than the fight sex we had.

He's being vulnerable and somehow still cheeky.

When the car stops and Charles gets the door, Matt grabs my hand, "Wait. Don't do this. Please."

Instead of struggling free, I clamp down on his hand and pull him from the car toward my house. A camera flash goes off but I don't care.

When we get in the building he stops me. "Can we take a walk?"

"No." I shake my head. "I want you too." When the door opens Nadia looks confused as we storm past her and the butler and head for my room.

Chapter Nineteen

Checkmate

Matt

There are moments, memories, in my mind that battle for the top ten as far as sex goes. But number one will forever be the moment we get back to her room and she leans her back against the door and lifts her skirt revealing her white underwear, muttering, "Why don't you show me how much better you are at everything in a bedroom and how much you want me?"

The next seconds are a blur.

I drop to my knees in front of her, trailing my thumb up her. She bites her lower lip, her dark-green eyes are lit with excitement as I lean in, inhaling her. Everything that had slowed pauses for a moment when I circle my nose against the thin fabric.

She groans, grinding against me, and from that moment on we speed up.

I lift her into my arms and carry her to the massive bed across the room. I toss her down, running my hands up the side of her thighs and hooking my fingers in her underwear, dragging them down, pulling each boot through the leg hole. Then I spread her legs open wide, to the point her fragrance owns all the air around me.

She smells sweet, like honey.

When I lower my face, brushing soft kisses on her inner thighs and soft lips, she moans, moving like she's trying to force me to lick the center but I don't. I torment her longer, running my hands up and down her legs, touching and grazing until she's writhing.

She lifts her head, her eyes fill with ferocity, and then I bury my mouth into the heat we've created.

She cries out, her chest arching and her stomach moving with the rhythm I work her to. I can't wait to be inside her but the moment she orgasms she's up, drawing me to my feet and hauling down my pants. She drops to her knees, ripping my boxers down to mine. She backs away from my cock as it bobs in her face. She glances up, raising an eyebrow.

"I ate my Wheaties when I was a kid," I offer weakly.

She wraps her hand around it, caressing to the base before flicking the tip with her tongue. Heat tingles the head as she leans in more, enclosing her lips around it and lowering as best she can. She gets half of me in her and strokes the other half, dragging her spit down until her hand is sliding easily.

My head falls back as my thighs clench and my hands find their way into her hair, tangling in the bun she's wearing.

We just get to a good place pace-wise when she pulls back, stands up and spins us, pushing me back on the bed.

"I thought you wanted me to show you how much better I am in a bed." I chuckle, a little surprised by the response, considering the conversation we had.

"Oh, this is your chance. The foreplay isn't where I want improvement." She climbs into my lap—tutu, sweater, and everything.

Sitting up, I drag the sweater off, cupping her bra with one hand and holding her in my lap with the other. She reaches up, pulling her hair from the bun and shaking her head to unleash her mane. The scent of shampoo tickles my nose as she lowers to kiss me. It's gentle and soft, maybe because of the bruising and cuts.

Her lips taste like gloss and her perfume. Everything about her smells sweet.

She wraps her hands around my head, gripping me. Mid exhale I reach down, toss on the condom and maneuver my cock between her legs, feeling for the right spot. When I hit it she lowers slowly, taking a deep breath consisting mostly of moans.

I reach around, cupping and squeezing her ass cheeks, helping her lift and lower. She starts slowly, taking long strides up and down me. We kiss, we lick, we bite, we fuck.

Her breasts heave and swell with her gasps as she arches her back, rotating her hips and riding me.

I want to come the moment I get inside her, but thank the gods I'm wearing a condom so I won't look like I have no staying power.

She starts to bob, quickening and biting her lip as she bounces on my balls.

I ignore the agony of holding my balls back from wanting to finish the job, and just watch her. A look of pleasure mixes with torment as she gets close to orgasm. She wants it. The sweat on her brow glistens like sparkles and I believe she is the sort of girl who actually perspires glitter.

Her lush lips purse when she tightens on me, forcing my orgasm with hers. I can't believe I'm coming so soon but watching her orgasm is amazing. She finishes, slumping on me as she fights for her breath. Her forehead leans against my cheek, pushing on a bruise from my broken nose but I don't care.

I grip her, jerking everything I have into the last couple of strokes.

We're messy and the condom is slipping off, but I don't move or say a thing. She lifts her face, smirking. "You have a great penis."

"It's a fan of yours."

"Yeah?" She smiles wide.

"Yeah."

"Wanna play checkers?" She raises an eyebrow.

"I can't think of another thing I'd rather do."

"Okay, let's get cleaned up and I'll get the board." She climbs off and hurries away, leaving me to pinch myself through the surreal moment.

Chapter Twenty

The Wizard of Lies

Sami

He kings his man, giving me the shitty grin I adore.

"Whatever, I'm rusty. We haven't played in a while." I roll my eyes.

"You lose poorly, just in case you were ever wondering."

"I beat you at chess, that's the harder game."

"If that helps you sleep at night." He laughs and makes his move.

"It does." I reach forward and pinch his arm, pulling the hair a bit.

"Ow!" He chuckles harder.

"Are you hungry?" I ask as my stomach rumbles for the tenth time.

"I bet there's lasagna, isn't there?"

"I don't know." I get up, pulling on my robe over the shorts and tee shirt in case anyone is still up downstairs.

"Well, let's go see." He lifts me into his arms and flings me over his shoulder as I squeal.

"Put me down!"

He slaps me on the butt once hard and places me down, spinning me like we're dancing. "You're prettier like this," he says when I stop spinning.

"Like what?"

"You barely have any makeup on and your hair's all messy and your clothes are frumpy." He lowers his lips to mine. "And you're smiling."

I squeeze his hand and turn back for the bedroom.

"Round two already? You don't want food first?" He jokes but I drag him to the bathroom. When I flick on the light he grimaces. "That's bright."

"I want you to get the full behind-the-curtain effect." I snicker, pulling my hair up into a messy bun. I grab a cotton pad and pump it into the top of the makeup remover. "You boys are so gullible." I run the pad over my entire face, dirtying it and getting a new one. I leave it face up on the counter so he can see the horror show. I scrub the mascara, peeling my false lashes off.

"Jesus!" He jumps back.

"Right." I fling the eyelash on the counter next to the black-and-blue streaked pad, next to the foundation-covered one. On pad three it starts coming up clear so I rinse my face, wash it, and spritz with toner. I finish with lotion and a sigh. "That feels better."

His expression is a mix of horror and confusion. "Oh my God."

"Still think I'm prettier like this?" I laugh, glancing at the red blotchy skin I have due to the scrubbing.

"Uhhh, yeah?" It comes out as more of a question. "I'm seriously feeling tricked, not just by you, but every girl I've ever met."

"The girls who look like they're wearing the least are wearing the most." I wink. "Now you've seen behind the curtain. There's no wizard, it's all fake."

"I feel sick." He jokes and swings an arm over my shoulders. "Now I really need some lasagna."

"No, Beast, you need me to do your makeup tomorrow so you look regular."

"What is with this 'Beast' nonsense?" He nudges me.

"You're a beast, we both know it."

"I know no such thing." He pulls me in tighter. "Unless that means you're Belle, then I guess it makes sense."

"Honestly, if anyone was going to be Belle it would be Nat. She's such a nerd."

"She is kind of a Belle, isn't she?" He chuckles. "You're

my Belle though."

"I'm more of a Rapunzel, but like the one from *Tangled."*

"You hit people with frying pans?"

"No. I'm always worried about my parents and their reactions, and then I do irrational things to spite and vex them and later worry about winning them back. It's confusing for me to want to rebel but want their approval at the same time."

"Do I ever know this story." He leads me to the kitchen and spins me again, this time so I land in a seat at the bar.

"Okay, let's see what we have to munch on." He opens the fridge, nodding. "Impressive." He pulls out the lasagna, the weird sex cheesecake dessert he made that was delicious, and a large slab-of-wood cheeseboard.

"Your fridge must look the same?"

"It does, but it's more like party food in case my parents surprise attack the house. Caviar and champagne and weird buffalo cheese."

"Gross. I hate buffalo cheese. It's so slimy."

"Me too. My gran, the fan of fridges that are stocked to the point of disgusting, would like this one. She'd approve. Her pantry is terrifying. But she never has to worry about not having food. It doesn't matter if the entire state shows up for a meal, she's got it." He puts the pasta in the microwave and then places the cheese board next to me with the box of crackers Cecilia left on the counter. "Why do I get the impression you don't know where the food is?" He lifts a hand. "Wait. I think I'm good at this. Your chef leaves the crackers out for you when she makes a cheeseboard, so of course you never have to look for them. No wait—normally she gets up and makes you the food at all hours of the night, and this board of food was just a convenience for her, not you. You don't even heat up your own leftovers, do you?"

I lift an eyebrow, forcing a sneer.

"So she gets up, rifles the fridge for the premade snacks, feeds you, and then Nadia tucks you into bed?" He gives me the grin I love. "How right am I?"

"Whatever." I snap my eyelids down and look to the right.

"You are a princess, we both know it."

"And you're a beast." I grin back, batting my eyelashes.

"And if I'm being totally honest, I can't believe the difference in your face without makeup." He looks stunned.

"Oh my God, that's rude."

"Maybe, but it's true. You're still pretty, just a different kind. Usually, you're like an Austen Powers Fembot. Very Stepford-pretty. A little too perfect is what I mean. So this is a better look. You look like someone I could be friends with. Actually, your friendship with Natalie makes more sense now. You're a human being."

"Wow!" I sit back on the barstool.

"Even Christmas morning you had makeup on." He tilts his head. "I mean, that is some hardcore makeup-ing."

"You're a dick. You don't get any cheeseboard now." I pull it to me, and point at the fridge. "Grab the red pepper jelly though please. Cecilia must have forgotten that."

He narrows his gaze. "I'm not getting the jelly."

I get up and walk to the fridge, watching him the entire time. He reaches for the cheese and meat. I swat at him.

He turns, grabbing me and forcing a stinky kiss on my cheek.

"I hate you!" I fake cry, wiping my face.

He pins my arms, kissing the other side, breathing the prosciutto on me in exaggerated words, "Whaaaaaat? Are you okayyyyyyy?"

"You're the meanest boy in the whole world."

"Oh, you mean *beast-like?"* He laughs and kisses my pouting lip.

"No. I take it back. Beasts are nice. You're a Gaston." I struggle to get free and grab the red pepper jelly.

"Admit it, you always had a small Gaston fantasy." He snickers as he gets the lasagna out and passes me a fork. We eat from the dish like I do at Nat's. Me, sitting on the counter in my shorts, tee shirt, and robe; and him, in his pajama pants but bare chested. He brought an overnight bag this time. He tells me stories about normal-people things, his cheeks puffed up with food as he waves his arms around and his still mildly puffy eyes widen.

It's the best date night ever.

The fight in the limo is forgotten in the admission we both sort of suck sometimes.

When we head back upstairs he clings to me, kissing my neck and whispering, "I'm sorry about the limo. I never thought about it the way you do. It makes me sick to think about it."

"It's not okay, but I forgive you."

"And although it's also not okay, I forgive you for basically lying with your Christmas morning makeup. So we're good then?"

I slug him in the stomach, getting a grunt from him. "Not even close."

Chapter Twenty-One

Boxing Day party, literally

Matt

"Mr. Brady is here, sir. You were aware he was arriving this evening for the hockey party tonight?"

"Shit! I completely forgot. Is he in the guestroom?" I smack myself in the forehead. I'm exhausted from having sex multiple times and I still smell like Sami. I'm not ready for Brady, but luckily he's the easiest guest ever.

"He is. He's taking a nap."

"Perfect. I'm going to do the same. We have that party tonight. If he wakes up before me just tell him I said, 'mi casa es su casa.'"

"Very good, sir," Benson mutters drolly and leaves the room. "And you might consider a shower. The sparkles may be a bit much for a hockey party."

I scowl. "Sparkles?" But Benson is gone. When I get to my room I sigh, seeing the glitter all through my hair. *"I washed it all off,"* I mock her and move my hair around to find half of me drag queened in there.

But I'm too tired for a shower and head for my bed.

It's massive without her here. It's cold and empty. Last night was amazing and filled with chess and checkers and sex and laughs and snacks. Razzing her about the makeup got me a full makeover. She drag queened me like RuPaul, even doing my hair, hence the glitter.

It started as her saying she could get rid of the bruising so I would appear normal. I accepted her challenge and ended up a woman. A not-so-attractive woman. She laughed and told me I looked like Wesley Snipes in *To Wong Foo.* She offered dresses but I took the high road, knowing nothing she had would fit and I'd end up a sausage in a casing.

If I was going to be in drag I was going to be hot. Wesley Snipes or not.

I close my eyes, grinning and remembering the entirety of what we squeezed into such a small amount of time.

She isn't at all what I thought and everything I had hoped. And in the end I was the bigger disappointment. I always assumed the Southern influence in my life made me a better person than the East Siders. But I was wrong. And she was the better person by forgiving me of that foolishness.

Seeing her face in the limo nearly killed me. I hadn't thought about it, even when Charles recommended the Bentley. I told him no because the tint isn't dark enough. I'm still kicking myself for it all. I sigh and realize that if I don't get any sleep during my nap it'll be because of guilt.

But I do sleep, and dream.

When I wake up to the alarm on my phone, I'm more exhausted than when I started.

"Brimley!" Brady's voice echoes in the room, but I don't see him, making me blink a couple of times to ensure he's really calling me. "Brimley!"

"Yeah?" My throat is scratchy and my voice groggy.

"You alone?"

"Yeah."

He comes in, flicking on the light like a dick. "Of course you're alone. Benson told me about your slumber party. Is it your turn to wear the Secret Sisterhood pants or did you actually nail that chick?" He winces. "Dude, your face."

"You're the only Secret Sister I have." I lift my fists in the air and bump the sides of them at him, like Ross on *Friends.*

"The fight didn't look that serious on TV. Are you getting more delicate in your old age?"

"Yes. I am."

He laughs at the admission and heads back out the door. "I'll be downstairs with Benson, getting more dirt while you get the glitter out of your hair, Nancy."

"Save me some tea," I shout after him, swinging my legs over the edge of the bed and stretching my neck and arms. Brady is about the only person who can hang with Benson and get conversation out of him. He's humble and funny and easygoing. He doesn't have a chip on his shoulder, and he absolutely refuses to be waited on by Benson. If he makes a mess, he cleans it up. If he needs a ride he borrows a car and refuses to allow Charles to drive him anywhere, something Charles isn't a fan of. Brady's the true definition of salt of the earth. Typical Providence boy.

He loves hockey, but like me, he knows he needs to finish his degree. When we played at Michigan together, I thought he'd draft before I did. He's not rich and he needs the money. But his focus is more on finishing his schooling. He's a smart guy.

If Benson knew about the Clinton though, that would be the end of the friendship. He was a big Clinton supporter back in the day. And he honestly believed the whole dress thing was a setup.

When I'm dressed, I head downstairs, sending Sami a quick text to tell her I'm going to just hang with Brady tonight, and she and I can hang tomorrow. I beg her forgiveness on the matter and explain that I will miss her all night long.

Brady is mid story when I walk into the kitchen, his arms are flailing and Benson is laughing, actually laughing. It's a quiet, reserved laugh but funny nonetheless.

"So the fish jumps in the boat and my brother falls in the water," Brady says half in tears.

I've clearly missed something key to the story but the two of them are dying.

"Oh"—Benson wipes his eyes—"that's an amusing story. I would have paid good money to see that."

"It was one of those moments where if you hadn't seen it, you wouldn't believe it." Brady stands up, finishes the last of his tea and carries his cup to the dishwasher like a good boy. When he turns around he smiles wide. "Sleeping beauty, you're awake!"

Benson turns around, greeting me pretty much the

same. "Up from your nap and ready to go to your party, sleepyhead?"

"No. I don't even want to go. I love the coach and the team but I'm sacked. I just want to sit around and eat chocolate and watch movies."

"Pull your tampon out, man!" Brady makes a face of disgust. "Let's go before your ball gown turns back into a pumpkin."

"That doesn't even make sense."

"Whatever." He rolls his eyes at me. "Thanks for tea, Benson."

"No, thank you. The conversation was stimulating, as usual." He stands and nods politely. "Enjoy the evening."

"Thanks. Don't wait up."

"I never do." He lies with a chuckle as we head to the foyer.

"It's a team Christmas gathering. We won't be late, bro," I say it as more of a wish than a fact.

"Please." Brady scoffs. "Clearly, you don't remember the parties in Michigan. I slept at Coach's house for two days trying to recover. My liver felt bruised. I haven't even drank much since that night."

"You're a lightweight and you banged Coach's sister. The liver bruising might have been from the punch to the guts you got."

"She got the Clinton, and she liked it. And it wasn't my fault. I woke up to her smoking my peace pipe. I had to let her finish. It's bad for the ducts to stop part way."

"You're an animal, Blow Job."

"It's science."

"Keep telling yourself that." I shake my head at him as he gets the door.

We jump, finding Sami behind it with her hand up to knock. "Oh hey." She glances back and forth from me to Brady, like she's confused. "Hi."

"Hey." My cheeks flush so I glance down, not really sure if I'm ready for the Sami thing to be common knowledge and just a fact of life. Me and Sami Ford. The cameramen who caught us the day before got a shitty shot of me with my head down and a lot of swelling. My own grandmother wouldn't have known me in that photo.

But if my friends start seeing this—friends like Brady or Carson—it will get around fast.

"I'm Sami." She awkwardly offers her hand to Brady after a moment of me pondering if I did send the text telling her I was busy tonight or if she ignored it.

"Shithead here seems to have forgotten his manners. I'm Brady Coldwell. Nice to meet you, Sami." He doesn't make it weird at all. "You coming to the party with us?"

"Us?" She continues to stare at me. "I don't think I am." She stares at me for a second and then turns to leave. "It was nice meeting you, Brady."

"Wait!" I finally spring to life, not sure how I should be or what we are. I give Brady the look. He nods back at the door and steps inside, closing it.

"What?" she snaps, pressing her lips together right after, like she is regretting her reaction.

"Didn't you get the message I sent, telling you I was busy tonight?"

Her brows furrow and the blank stare in her eyes suggests she might not have seen it.

"I sent a text that Brady showed up and I forgot." I pull my phone out, cringing when I realize I sent Laramie the text and not her at all. And his response was that I needed to get my dick back from her, strap it back on, and get my sexy ass to the party. "Shit! I didn't send you that message."

"Getting girls mixed up?" She doesn't sound like she's joking even though she's smiling.

"No, I was just waking up and I thought you were the last person I texted but it was a different friend. And now he thinks I'm not coming and has sent a couple of messages and a weird picture of the coach's red face." I step toward her, putting my phone away. "Anyway, I'm so sorry. I invited Brady before you and I agreed to dinner, and I forgot about him completely because we were having such a great time and then he showed up and now—"

"What are you doing?" She steps back, cutting me off with her words and her body. Her face is hardened in a way I don't think I like. Whatever she's thinking is bad, for both of us. She has the self-destruct face on full blast.

"Explaining." I tread carefully.

"Why?" She scoffs. "We're just friends, Matt. That's all. We aren't exclusive and we don't explain ourselves, not to friends. It's fine. Have fun." She turns and walks away.

"Don't do that. Don't make it like it isn't something more than friends. I don't want to be friends."

"So you want to date, like in the real world?"

"No. I just thought—"

"Well, I wouldn't call us much more than fuck buddies." She laughs bitterly. "Or rather, *puck buddies."* She shakes her head and steps into the elevator. "It's cool. Text me next week some time, and if I have a chance we can hang out where no one can see either of us." She says it just as the door closes.

"Shit!" I shout.

Brady opens the door. "She hates you. And you handled that piss poor, bro. She was testing you when she asked if you wanted to date. My brother's girl did that to him. It was a test. You failed."

"Do you know who that is?"

"Sami?"

"She's not just Sami. She's Sami-fucking-Ford. She's American royalty. She's a blue blood, the real kind. Her family is like my mom's family but worse."

"So?" He closes the door and strolls over to the elevator. "It's not quite *The Prince and The Pauper.* You're not exactly hurting for cash."

"No. I know that. It's just—" I pause, thinking about what exactly it is. "I have to be really sure I want to ride this train publically before I get on. There's no going back. Everyone in the world will care I'm dating her. We will be stalked, constantly. People probably followed her here tonight. I don't know how much I want that this early in my career. Laramie had a good point about it, and I don't need the extra attention."

"Oh, bro." He laughs, slapping me on the arm hard. "You don't have to worry about that, not now. That girl is never going to date you. Ever. I hope you had extra fun the last time, like played the back nine and everything, because you are never getting on that train again. Never," he says as we step off.

I am the biggest jerk. I wish I'd said the right thing but I never do. I look at my phone but decide I should wait and text, I likely won't get that right either.

When we get in the car out front every single bit of me wants to tell Charles to go to her house but I don't. I do the wrong thing.

Maybe it's my pride. Maybe it's my way of making an easy decision that cleans up the whole mess of what to do. Maybe I'm just a coward and I have no idea how to be with a girl.

When Brady and I get to the party, the house explodes with excitement to see him. He's like a little brother to a lot of people. All the college guys are. I was that last year.

Coach gives me a swat on the arm and nods. It's equivalent to a hug. "Merry Christmas, Brimley. Go somewhere exotic for your days off?"

"No, sir. Stayed here and slept a lot."

"Your face looks like you might need a bit more sleep." He lifts his drink and moseys off to socialize, if you can call it that.

His wife hugs me and offers me drinks and food quickly before scurrying off after another person to ensure they're comfortable and being taken care of.

"Opposites attract, eh?" Laramie grins wide.

"She's like some kind of saint, I suspect." That's about as far as I'll ever go into bad-mouthing the coach.

"Gold standard for hockey wives, across the board." He settles in next to me at the large bar in the kitchen and grins. "Did you solve that Sami Ford problem?"

"There's no problem." I don't want to discuss it with him. She is who I thought, and he has no idea who that is.

"I saw the photo on *TMZ* and assumed you must have released your inner demons on her, but then I got the text." He takes a swig of beer from the bottle, typical Canadian. "I sort of hoped you got it out of your system."

"Like I said, there's no problem." I change the subject, "What'd you do for Christmas?"

"Went home to the Prairies and froze my balls off. I actually left them back at the farm, no hope in getting them back till the thaw."

"I like how you Canadians say the thaw, like it's some great event. You never say spring."

"Spring can be a relative term in Canada. We always have snow in the spring so it doesn't feel like winter has ended."

"Because it's the Arctic."

"Whatever. So did you happen to see Tandy again over the holiday?" Laramie chuckles. "She'll be at the afterparty, and I sort of thought she had a bit of a thing for you."

"I don't think I'm in for the afterparty. I'm still kinda tired." I avoid the Tandy talk completely. I understand that guys enjoy bragging about their conquests, but I don't think of shower rape as a conquest.

He rolls his eyes. "You're a rookie. That's not a choice, my friend. Afterparty is at your house."

"What?" I laugh but he doesn't.

"Dude, it's tradition. It's always at the rookie's house."

"I'm not the only rookie." My stomach tightens.

"You're the only rich one who can house this shitshow." He turns and looks at the crowd. "Brimstone's in boys! His house afterwards."

Coach winces but lifts his glass at me as everyone else cheers.

Brady laughs at me from the corner.

All the humor falls away as I send a fast text to Benson, preparing him for the onslaught. It's something my parents do regularly so the house is always prepared.

I had planned on pleading with Sami to come over or going there and begging her to forgive me for sending the text to the wrong person, and for freezing when it came time to introduce her. And for being me. Whatever we were doing, it involves begging for her forgiveness and hoping possibly sex or chess or something pleasant follows.

And instead I'm stuck with a night of shenanigans.

I tilt the drink in my hand back and decide I need to loosen up if we're going back to my place. There's not much I can do to solve the Sami thing right now anyway, and I'm not getting rid of the team.

Many drinks later I change my mind on that. After multiple texts I probably shouldn't have sent to Sami have gone through and Coach is tired of us, we load up into cars and get driven back to my place. Coach stays with his wife. Both are grateful to see us all going.

I suspect it'll be the same look on Benson's face when we're done at my place.

The elevators don't hold us all so it's a few trips up until we're all in. The place is set up for a night of fun. Drinks and snacks, and not the caviar or the usual fixings, are laid out with proper serving ware, red solo cups and paper plates.

"Did you buy those today?" I nod at the dishes.

"I did. I figured your friends would feel more at home. If you need anything I'll be retiring to the study. I've taken the liberty to lock the doors we don't want open." He turns and leaves.

He remembers how it was when I was a teenager.

Brady is dropping his pants and headed for my hot tub, naked with a couple of girls in his arms. He's not alone. The group with loose morals and no love life, to speak of, head outside to the huge deck.

It's become a full-fledged PF party out there.

The wives have been dropped off and the side dishes have come out to play.

The guys who don't partake in the lifestyle are in the living room with the big screen going and the fireplace lit. What happens at the party, will stay here. No one shares or shits on their fellow teammates.

The boys on the couches are laughing and talking, eating chips and ignoring the half-naked girls squealing. There are two very different camps in hockey.

For every guy who loves his wife or girlfriend, there's one or two players who don't mind a little something-something from a girl who has no interest in being with you after her ten minutes are up.

I head in the direction of the fire and chips, taking a seat with a beer.

The fire's warm, my beer is cold, and my team is laughing and loving life. It's a pretty awesome night.

Laramie grabs us both another beer and sits down next to me. He stretches out on the large sofa and nods. "So your parents have a lot of money, don't they?"

"Yeah." I laugh.

"No, bro. I mean like a scary amount that you couldn't spend in a lifetime."

"Wellllllll." I grimace. "My mom might be able to, but my dad wouldn't ever let her. She's bad."

"This is fucked. I had no idea. I mean, I knew you were rich but not like *rich* rich. This is some next-level rich."

"I'm not *rich* rich. I'm normal rich." I don't know how to say that. "My dad is the billionaire. I'm not." I chuckle. "I won't ever be."

"Your family is disgustingly rich. You'll always be this."

"No, my brother is the shining star of the family. He'll inherit everything and take over from Dad. I'll be the one who has to scrape by, barely making ends meet on the interest from my trust fund." I wink at one of the guys across from me who's laughing at Laramie.

"Fuck off." He shoves me as the group of us laugh.

"Who wants shots?" a familiar voice asks from behind us. My spine straightens as I turn slightly, cringing at the sight of Tandy in my house. She's smiling wide with her long hair in pigtails and a dress so short I'm pretty sure I just saw some ass cheek when she spun.

She's dressed as a waitress from the fifties in a short dress and she's on rubber roller skates. She sails in, spinning and dazzling all the guys. Everyone laughs with her, nudging each other and making faces.

Her long tanned legs flex as she stops with the tray, not spilling a drop. She is a smooth operator.

"Time to double stuff the cookie, dude." Laramie nudges me, muttering as he ogles her in the tiny white dress that came with a nametag and everything. Something tells me she's like a mascot and everyone in the room has had a little

Tandy on them once or twice, whether they wanted it or not.

"I don't like crossing swords, brother," I turn him down politely and offer a viable solution just in case that's his thing, "But Blow J—Brady out in the hot tub will certainly. He's got zero standards." Throwing Brady under the whore bus would be cruel, if he were anyone but Brady.

"Sounds like my kind of guy." He slaps me on the back and reaches for our shots. No one refuses her shots. We all get one.

"To you, boys!" She lifts her shot in the air with us. I can't guess her age, but if I did I'd have to say early to mid-thirties. Not because of looks but because of confidence and craziness. She doesn't have that twenties look to her. She's been doing this a long time. It shows in the way she is with the team.

We drink and she skates off, winking at me before she goes.

Shots and drinks and laughs are had. Tandy plays bartender waitress, but like the slutty Barbie-doll version. She gets snacks and refills and switches up the music.

She leaves us alone in the living room for the most part and ends up catering to the guys in the hot tub.

But that doesn't mean we don't see our share of random shots.

The room spins as I jolt awake, not even realizing I fell asleep. I wipe the drool off my mouth, feeling stuck and hot and sweaty.

The TV is fuzzy and apparently I've slept on the couch for a couple of hours.

The captain is leaning on me, sleeping like a baby. I don't know how long I've been breathing his snores in but the air around me is too warm.

Shuddering, I get up, seeing that not many people have left. They're mostly still here, passed out on the sofas and the floor. I need my bed and maybe to throw up a little. I don't know which first.

When I stagger to the stairs I shudder again, sure I'm going to puke just as a voice whispers from the kitchen, "Brimstone."

I turn, not sure if I heard it or imagined it or if the place is haunted.

"Brimstone. Come here." They call again, still not raising their voice enough for me to guess who it is. It sounds like a chick.

When I round the corner I stop, scared of what I see, not because it's bad but because it's good. Very, *very* good in the creepiest way.

Tandy, still in her roller skates, is standing in my kitchen, leaning against the bar with her dress unbuttoned and her huge tits bursting through the gap.

She slides a finger between them, tit-fucking herself. "Come here. Let me finish what I started in the shower."

"Uhhhh, no thanks." I don't move, I sway back and forth trying to shake my head but end up moving my entire body. Fortunately, I'm so drunk my feet actually refuse to move. My cock ignores all of that as she lifts her white dress up and flashes her bare pussy. She slides back on the counter, spreading her legs and dipping a finger into herself.

It takes all of the strength I have in me to take a step back, lifting a hand like I'm signaling traffic to stop. "I gotta go. Sorry."

As I turn away, the roller skates come after me. "No you don't. Stay." She skates to me as I make it to the stairs and am almost fleeing in a drunken way.

"Don't be scared, Brimstone." She grabs the back of my shirt, wrapping her arms around me and shoving her hand down the front of my pants. "Let me make you feel good."

"No." I slip and fall, catching myself on all fours and lifting her off the ground. She's on my back, clinging to me but still undoing my pants like a crazy monkey. "Seriously. No. We can't," I mutter, trying to be quiet so the others won't wake up. My hands are on the stairs just above my knees and she's got me out of my pants before I can really resist. I manage to climb several steps to the floor above where everyone is sleeping with her piggybacking and jerking me off.

"I'm gonna fuck that meat stick, big boy," she whispers in my ear, but I ignore her as I fight not to get sick. The floor is coming at me fast and then backing off with a jerk. I feel a bit sick and shudder again. Three shudders. I'm going to throw up.

She swings to the side of me, still stroking my cock. She slides underneath me, sweet-talking me. "You'll like this, my pussy feels so good."

"No. I'm seeing someone. I can't."

"Come on, big boy." She bucks me forward and instantly shivers run through my body as a cold sweat comes over me. I burp again but throw up. I try to hold it in but a little bit comes out. It lands smack on her face. She gags and I gag and I leap up, running for the bathroom with my pants falling down.

I barely make the toilet before I unleash all the nasty shots she fed us, mixed with beer and chips and whatever the fuck else I've eaten in the last few days. I puke so much my broke nose hurts again.

I puke until there's nothing left, and even then my body still tries to find something. Eventually, everything goes dark and I'm pretty sure I'm dying.

Chapter Twenty-Two

Not quite the right Brimley

Sami

The seat in the Garden is cold. Way colder than I expected.

I've never seen a hockey game live before, and I should be in a box but when I got up to the one my dad has, I couldn't see shit. There's a huge TV screen and I did sort of have a bird's-eye view over the ice, but at the end of the day, it's no different than sitting in my living room, forcing Nadia to watch it with me.

She glances at me from her seat, offering a weak smile. Her eyes don't have any of the joy her lips are faking.

"Don't judge me."

"I wasn't." Nadia laughs. "I was actually just thinking how brave this is of you. I mean, you're out in public. With these people." She turns and offers the stands above us a horrified grimace. "And you're dressed like you're homeless. This is different for you."

"Do you want to attract attention? Don't glare at them." I swat her and take the plastic cup of soda from her.

"It's not diet," she warns. "The diet looked funny, thicker. The lady in front of me got it."

"Oh, whatever. I'll drink regular. At this point I've thrown all caution to the wind anyway. If he sees me here he's going to think I missed him and then he'll think I'm the weaker one and then I'll lose."

"Lose what?"

"Whatever the fuck we're doing with each other." I sigh and give her my attempt at an annoyed face. "I mean, he was a twat on Boxing Day. We were supposed to hang and then he changes his mind and goes with Brady because he doesn't want anyone to know about us. I don't even know why I still like him."

"Because that's all speculation and there's a good chance he just forgot about that guy, like he said. And he didn't want to make it awkward with his friend." She scowls as if the answer should have been obvious to me.

"I guess. And he did text all night long with weird messages about missing me but being scared to talk to me because he would say the wrong thing." I stare out at the ice, plastic straw in my mouth and all.

The game takes forever to start.

There's an ice show with some crap from the past Rangers games. Everyone in the stands goes crazy over that. They bring up the years the Rangers won the cup, which all seem like a billion years ago, and flash fancy images and movies on the ice. I suck back the entire drink before that's even over. Nadia huffs about leaving to get me another one, not quite under duress but clearly she's digging the whole preshow more than I am.

Finally, the teams come flying out onto the ice, banging sticks and skating around like they coordinated where they were all going. Some guy shouts over the speaker, introducing them and getting everyone else fired up. They don't need firing up. They're already going insane. At home I can fast-forward all this crap to the moment the puck drops.

When Nadia gets back, the guy adding the extra bit of soul to the national anthem is just hitting the last note, praise all that is holy.

Stats and names are flashing, lights are flickering, music is pumping. It's some shit song I've never heard before, about a crazy train. I want for death.

The people in the stands are not my people.

The people watching quietly in their houses, fast-forwarding, are my people.

"I got you a hot dog." Nadia hands me a paper wrapper with a disgusting-looking thing in the middle of it. I had one once when I was at Nat's. I remember not liking it.

"Thanks?" I question the whole choice she made but force myself to agree that it's the thought that counts, as Nat would say.

"I got one for me too." She sits and positions it like she might give it a blow job, and then puts it in her mouth. It's by far the most seductive thing she's ever done in front of me.

She squishes her lips down, pressing them into the bun. She takes the bite after a second of processing or foreplay, I don't even know. She moves the food around, but I don't know if she's chewing or just assessing.

Finally, she makes a crazy face and bites down again, cringing for two seconds and then moving her mouth like she's adapting to the thing in there. Her eyes dart to the side, again she's processing. I wonder if she'll be completely insulted if I dump mine under the seat.

She smiles finally, chewing normally. "It's good. Weird, but good." She nods and speaks with her mouth full. She sips the soda she brought for herself and sits back, clearly content.

After the longest, most drawn-out procedure, the players get situated on the ice.

"Thank God I don't have to watch all this crap on the TV! I never would have made it through the first game. This preshow shit is nuts. Remind me if I ever decide to come to a live game again to skip this and just show up when they're getting on the ice. My God." I say it to her but stare at the ice. Not because I'm desperate to see the game, but because he's starting. That's really good. He never starts and here he is, starting. "The hat trick must have helped, he's starting," I shout over the stupid organ.

"That's our boy!" She sounds excited. It's adorable.

The puck drops and the game begins—fast. I swear it's faster than in real life.

The Predators' centerman flicks it to the left wing as he drives hard for the Ranger's goal. The puck hits the boards, the centerman takes a blow, and the Rangers have the puck. Ice slicing and sticks smacking and guys shouting are the only sounds for a few seconds before the next song starts.

Matt has the puck. He skates like a ballerina. It's so fluid and poetic for such a beast of a guy. He gets hit and the next thing I know the hot dog is in my mouth. I'm chewing, watching, and nervous.

The game is real here.

The wounds aren't like they are on TV. At the end of the first period someone has already left the ice injured.

They start the music up again and I cover my ears. I can only take so much. Nadia is covering her ears too. "Why's it so loud?" she shouts.

"I don't know. It's annoying."

"I know." She grins through it, annoyed or not.

I hate doing stuff like this but I need to. I hold back my pride and speak softly, genuinely. "Thanks for coming. I know I made you come, but I'm just not ready for Nat to hate him with me." I always hate William so much for the shit he puts her through, and I don't want her to hate Matt. Not yet anyway. Not until I know if I hate him or not.

"I'm excited to be here. It was on my list of things I had to try once." She doesn't sound like she'll be back.

I'm still not sold on coming back.

The second period starts and when the ref makes a bad call minutes in, something comes over me. I'm shouting and waving my hands like a crazy person. I'm unaware of my behavior until the guy next to me offers me a high five after we both tell the ref to fuck himself.

By the end of the period I'm frothy and spicy and flustered. It's the greatest and most confusing feeling ever.

The third period starts and I'm eating a second hot dog. It tastes better with the grilled onions and beer, a recommendation from my neighbor. He's eating one too. He's older and looks like he knows a lot about hot dogs.

We eat and shout, and when the Rangers score, all my calm is gone. I'm in a haze. I might as well be skating and shooting and scoring. I'm off my seat, hugging strangers and screaming. Each boy, man, guy on that team is my brother.

My fellow warrior. We are the Rangers.

The game ends with a win and everyone in the stadium is beside themselves with joy. The true New Yorkers are emotional people, good and bad. They're huggers and lovers and fighters and savages.

A win means we all hug and cheer and some even cry.

Nadia looks lost as she's mauled by the lady next to her.

Waving goodbye to the old man, I grab Nadia by the hand and lead her out while everyone is still excited. It was the one thing Vincenzo made me promise, that I would leave before everyone else.

When we get to the hallway that's filling up with smart people like us, she tugs at my hand. "Why are we leaving so soon?"

"I need to beat the crowds so Vincenzo can pick us up."

We make it outside into the cold, damp air and the lights and camera flashes hit. "Guys! It's Sami Ford!" Voices come out of nowhere.

"That's not Sami Ford!"

"Holy shit, Sami Ford!"

"Look over here, Sami!"

"Where's the guy you were with?" Men rush toward me.

"Sami! Just one smile for us, Sami!"

They crowd us but I grip to Nadia and pull her through, brushing them off. One reporter grabs my arm, a major no-no. I want to turn and clock him one but I don't. I keep my head down, hood up, and press on through the crowd.

"Come on, Sami! Be a sport!" I lift a finger, flipping them all off as I hurry away.

Nadia is already texting Vincenzo for a pickup.

We break into a run, heading for West Thirty-Sixth Street, hauling ass two blocks before the limo pulls up. Vincenzo doesn't even get the door for us. We dive in and he speeds away before the downtown area becomes crazier than normal.

I'm sucking wind when I finally settle into my seat and start to calm down. My body isn't calming down though.

I'm on edge.

The game was thrilling.

I had no idea it would be like that. I expected fun and I like hockey games. But I didn't think I would almost die from feeling more emotion than I've ever felt all at once.

I get it now. The love of sports and the exhilaration of watching your team win.

We barely get home before my mother calls.

"Hello?" I don't know why she would be calling me this late France time.

"A hockey game, Sami? Really? Were you drinking?"

"No." *How the hell could she know that I was there so fast?*

"It's all over *TMZ.* The publicist called and woke me up to let me know you were out dressed like a gang member, leaving a hockey game, hand and hand with a woman." Her voice has never gotten shrill in my life, but this is close.

"Uh no. I went to a hockey game with Nadia because I'm alone on Christmas. My family ditched me so Dad could fuck that old flame and you could get drunk in the South of France. Remember? And we ran holding hands because there were paparazzi. One of them grabbed me." My tone hits the dark place it can get with her.

"Don't you dare use that tone with me, young lady. You know the public won't care that you were out with your maid or the reporters got grabby," she snaps back. "It was only yesterday you had your picture taken with some beastly looking man outside of our building. If they assume you're seeing men and women now, they'll think you've gone off the deep end again."

"Don't *again* me, Mother. I have yet to do any deep-ending. And I'm done with 'they.' *Who is they?* The papers? I don't give a shit about them or what they write. I'm the only person in the world who has been to rehab three times according to public perception, but not once in reality. The media has an agenda. Nothing they ever write is true. So why start caring now?"

"Sami, it's all for your own good—"

"Let's not play this game again. Nothing you have ever done has been in my best interest. I'm old enough to know what is best for me. And you and Dad are the opposite of what's best for me."

"Who was the man then?"

"Matthew Brimley."

"Oh." Her tone softens. "Oh." She sounds genuinely shocked.

"I was at his hockey game. He plays for the Rangers, Mom."

"That can't be the same Brimley." She scoffs. "His father wouldn't still allow him to play hockey."

"It's him. His dad hates the hockey."

"Your father knows Matthew's father and grandfather on his mother's side quite well. The photo must have been taken in muted lighting. I've seen him, he's very handsome. Is he a nice boy? Does he go to college with you? His father is quite wealthy. Are you dating him? Is the hockey a permanent thing?"

"We're just friends alone in the city because our parents don't give a shit about us. It's nothing." I hate it when they do this.

"You know that's not true. We care deeply for you." Her attempt is pathetic as if she's trying to convince herself she's a good mother. "Now if you and this Matthew Brimley want to join us for dinner when we return after New Year's, your father would likely be quite interested in that. You might make him very proud with this news, Sami. It's too bad it isn't the eldest brother. But we can always work around that." Her words actually hurt.

"Okay, well Merry Christmas. Tell Shelly over in PR that I'm fine. Not switching teams and becoming a lesbian with the maid. And the beastly dude was actually the son of a family richer than ours. So we're cool. And I posted the lip gloss pic on Instagram, so no need to go cutting my allowance just yet." I couldn't be cheekier.

"Okay, dear. Have a good night." She hangs up, chipper from the billionaire's son I'm possibly bringing home. I slump, banging my phone against my head once.

"Sorry I called you the maid. That wasn't about you," I mutter to Nadia. I don't like hurting her feelings.

"I know." She doesn't add anything else. She's always

careful about what she says about my parents.

Chapter Twenty-Three

Players

Matt

"I don't understand." I sit in front of the TV watching *TMZ* as they make another shitty comment, guessing which member of One Direction Sami was dragging out of the Garden. It's almost better they think Nadia is a boy and not a girl and a maid. Personally, I wouldn't care if it were Harry Styles who went with her. I just want to know why she was there.

"Did you invite her to the game?"

"No, Jesus. I was texting her all night and all day after the party, but she said she was busy. I assumed it was my punishment. She answered some of my texts with lame shit little emojis that I couldn't decipher. You have to be a prehistorian or some shit to understand girls' messages nowadays. They're coded. I can't believe this. I just don't get it."

"Well, it appears she went to your game on her own, sir." Benson sighs, pointing with his long finger. "I don't want to assume but the hockey arena is right behind her and Fifth Avenue and—"

"No, I get that. I mean why? Why would she dress down like that, hide who she is, and drag her maid to a game? I've never even seen her dress down."

"I suspect the same reason all celebrities dress down, including you, sir. She didn't want anyone to know who she was."

"I really just don't get the hockey, Benson," I snap.

"I was being obtuse, sir," he says flatly.

"Oh good. Joke about the situation, that's excellent. The girl driving me crazy is a secret hockey fan. She likes the game? What the hell is that? Why did she lie? I flat out asked her and she said no. How long has she liked hockey? Is that why we're sort of seeing each other?"

His eyes don't change from the sardonic expression of a moment ago.

"You know I don't like it when girls like hockey. I don't want her and the team to have anything in common. Ever. I don't want her going to parties or knowing the guys." I don't want her to know what happens at the parties—or what happened at the party I was just at.

Benson stares at me for a moment before speaking, "Matt, I'm going to explain something to you. I shouldn't be the one, but I suspect I might be the only person who ever will."

He never calls me Matt unless it's something important so I don't say anything else.

"You have some very wrong ideas about love. You've never been shown what a trusting relationship is, where one person gives their heart to another completely, without restrictions or back doors. You just open your heart and allow the other person to take up space. I have experienced this type of love, in my younger years. So I can tell you with some authority, it exists. And I believe you are capable of having it in your life, but if you don't wake up and smell the white mocha latte brewing, you're going to miss it. That girl loves you, that much is clear as day to me. But she is like you, scared of getting hurt or being made a fool. I understand your apprehension—in your world being made a fool of happens on an unusually large scale. The whole world is looking when one of you trips and stumbles. But to live life terrified of that, is to live a half-life. You will never know the kind of love you are capable of feeling until you let her hurt you. You must give her all of your heart and offer it up for slaughter. And if she is worthy of your love, she will protect it. That is love. Sacrificing your heart for another person's." He gets up and leaves me alone to think on what he said.

I know he's right but I also know we're not there yet. We barely—fuck. No. We're there. I feel it. She's under my skin and in my blood and there's no getting rid of her.

But how do I face her after what just happened?

How do I tell her that I'm crazy about her when my dick was almost in another chick days before because I was recklessly drunk with my team?

I hate the feelings inside me.

Mostly I hate me.

Deciding I need to see her and possibly just tell her what happened and beg her to forgive me, I throw on my jacket and head out. I don't message Charles for a ride but walk to her place instead. I need the quiet time to sort my thoughts.

Having never been in any sort of relationship, as I walk I debate whether I man up and tell her what happened or if I just put it behind me—tell her I want a relationship and then move forward from here.

I want a relationship.

I don't want her to slip through my fingers or screw this up.

Not sure how to word it so I don't end up breaking things off instead, I walk for a long time, passing by her place a couple of laps before heading for the door. Only as I approach it, ready and certain of what I need to say, she comes bursting out, laughing and clinging to Nat. She pauses when she sees me, but her eyes dart to Nat for a moment. She offers a wave and says something to her friend who glances over at me and waves before climbing in the limo.

Sami saunters over, her lips pressed into a weird grin. It's not sexual or flirty or any of the normal smiles she has when she sees me.

"Hi." My insides are in knots.

Her lips spread wider and she gives me a much better version of her original greeting, "Hi." I can smell her in the soft breeze that's blowing her hair around her face. The scent makes me ache everywhere.

"Hi." I say it again like an idiot and then stumble through

the next part in a rush to avoid looking like an idiot. "How's—uh—how's it go-going?" Obviously not thinking before I speak is awesome.

"I'm leaving for Europe now. We're going to the Lumineers."

"Right, New Year's." I don't know why it's awkward. We were playing chess and sharing food and laughs only days ago. We were naked and touching each other and making noises I want to relive. I want to relive them now.

"How was the party?" She cocks an eyebrow. Does she know? Is that where the cool greeting is coming from? *Fuck.*

"Why were you at my game?" I never want to speak of the party. I don't want to lie to her and say it was great. "It was horrifying" will bring up other conversations.

"Oh." Her cheeks light up with flames. "I"—she glances down, shaking her head—"I just wanted to see what the fuss was all about."

"Do you like hockey?"

"Players." She answers too fast and grins, half looking back up at me. "I like hockey players." She pauses. "I guess just one player. I don't know any of the others. So it's singular."

My chest starts pounding. "You like me?" Her words cut and make my betrayal of her worse. I want to confess and clear the air, but I know that's not what will happen, especially after she's just told me she likes me. We're too new for me to explain it away and how do I really? I should have ran and fought harder. I shouldn't have gotten so drunk.

Jesus, I sound like a rape victim at a frat party.

"I have to go." She points at the limo. "We have a jet waiting. Talk about this when I get back?" Her smile is gone.

"Yeah." I step forward to kiss her but she offers me her cheek, lingering for a moment and letting me press into her. I want to smell her hair, but I'm terrified of being that guy. The one she spoke of in the cab, the one who leans in to smell the girl to trick her into thinking he likes her more than he does. That guy is an asshole who also almost bangs other girls at parties. He doesn't deserve this girl.

I don't smell her, I just hug and press the kiss and pull back. "I'll text you."

"See ya later!" She half smiles and walks away, climbing into the car. It drives away, and I feel the exact same as I did the day I walked away from her in the cab.

Chapter Twenty-Four
Stubborn Love

Sami

"The Musikverein is magnificent. And I don't know if any of you know this, but the architecture is due to actual luck. Not enough was known about acoustics, optimum vibration, and placement of stage at the time it was built. The science wasn't there yet. The designers got lucky and did it right. Needless to say, the band is thrilled to be part of this evening and this private show. Without further ado, here they are—" The man introducing them claps, so we all clap but nothing happens. "The Lumineers!"

The room goes dark and we stop clapping, we sit in silence.

Suspense builds until the lights flick on, creating a candlelit atmosphere in the space, a warm glow.

The five of them walk out as we clap loudly again.

They wave but don't speak, just stand in the middle of us, looking at one another. The lead singer, Wes, nods and they begin the show. When his guitar starts with the first song, "Submarine," the hall beats, vibrating into my body. I don't know the song too well.

The drummer joins in with him, before the cello or piano or base.

Nat screams, the loudest in the place, as the lead singer leans into the mic.

The piano hits and I can't take it. I'm up off my seat clapping and moving with Nat. It's hard to focus on them when I glance at her and watch her reaction to them. The joy on her face is remarkable. I've never seen it before.

She screams and jumps, singing every single word to the song. She knows them all.

They win back my stare, working so hard for it with "Flowers in Your Hair." I've never seen a band this perfect in my life. Even their use of cymbals and tambourines is art.

The love of music flows from them as raw talent. Every single movement and grunt and word is placed in a harmonious flow. Their talent is beyond musician or artist, they're something else. Something better.

I've seen hundreds of concerts and this is the best. The magic of the hall is as believable as a Christmas tree.

They don't need anything but a couple of instruments to be flawless. There's no show, there's love.

We could be around a campfire and I would be in awe.

Their hipster vibe is even perfect. It suits them.

The attraction I have for the lead singer is disturbing. I don't fangirl. I don't even say hello to singers. But him, I want to have his babies. He's a pied piper, I believe that. I would follow him off a cliff if he would just keep singing and playing that guitar. He shows us love, true love. He loves playing and singing and music and possibly his guitar, and he lets us see that. There isn't an actor in the world who could fake that kind of love.

When they play "Stubborn Love" I almost die.

Her cello in the beginning cuts right through me.

His words bring tears to my eyes.

I want that kind of love.

I want someone who will stand and scream outside my house and refuse to leave until I come down and see them.

If Matt loved me like this, our relationship would be this song.

It hurts to face the truth of us in this song.

It burns in my throat with tears and my own version of

"Stubborn Love."

They finish the show with "Ho Hey," Nat's favorite. The entire crowd sings along. My skin vibrates with the feel of his voice and the foot drum and the cello. But I can't bounce back from "Stubborn Love." I love the song. I love them. I love this show. But my heart is broken.

The countdown hits as they're done the last song. We scream the numbers with them and when the hour hits, the ceiling bursts with confetti. Champagne is passed out and they play us "Auld Lang Syne." I push down my pain, like always, as we kiss and toast and hug, all of us—girls and guys we've known since we were kids.

When it ends, the band thanks us and wishes us happy New Year's.

And although they've just made and ruined my entire life with one song, they're humble and grateful.

And I can't even. I just can't.

Carson is screaming next to me as loud as Nat.

We cheer until I don't have a voice left as they leave us wanting more and yet satiated.

Nat starts to cry. Sobs rip from her as she flings her arms around my neck and clings to me. I don't know why she's crying but it doesn't matter. I hold her, letting her release on me.

Carson slaps me on the back, whispering, "Absolutely amazing gift, Sami. Top-notch. I think I came at one point. You better be careful or people will start to see you're not such a vengeful slut."

"Whatever." I laugh as Nat sniffles and giggles.

"Which club next?" He tilts his head toward the door where everyone is milling about.

"You pick. I haven't been here in ages. The clubs I went to before would be different now."

"I just want to go back to the room." Nat wipes her eyes. "I'm done. That was better than anything I've ever seen. I feel a loss from the show ending but the jet-lag is also hurting. I wanna sleep and dream about Wesley and that's all." She closes her makeup-smudged eyes and sighs.

"Okay, bed it is."

Carson rolls his eyes. "I'm going dancing, ladies. Peace!" He heads for the crowd, inciting craziness into everyone as he shouts and takes them away.

"Over a thousand people just flooded into the streets to go clubbing." She winces.

"Right, but it's a holiday. The clubs must be ready for the party."

"Yikes." She links her arm into mine and starts us walking. "Thanks."

"Whatever." I scoff. She has no idea how much I love her. She wouldn't understand. She has no idea how much I am capable of loving.

When we get to the room, we crash hard, both exhausted and a little drunk.

We sleep until my phone wakes us up.

I slap along the bed to find it, hitting it until it shuts up.

"I hate jet-lag," Nat moans.

"Me too."

"Sami!" Carson shouts at me from somewhere. He sounds funny, like he's in a hallway.

"Carson?" I lift my head, groaning. "Is he here?"

"The phone, dollface," he says, laughing.

I pick it up, realizing he's Facetimed me and I answered. "Hey?"

"You look pretty."

"Shut up."

"Breakfast in an hour?"

"Sure," I grumble.

"Your room or downstairs?"

"Downstairs."

"I'll meet you in the lobby."

"Okay." I hang up and sigh. "I'm sleepy."

"Me too." Nat rolls over, giving me a smile. "So are you going to explain the hockey game and the hockey dude and what's going on with you two?"

"No. It's just a thing." I don't want to talk about it.

"Okay," she says like we're going to talk about it more later on. But we aren't. "Stubborn Love" is clinging to me and my heart hurts. He doesn't love me like that. He doesn't love me. It's been years of this bullshit and I'm sort of done.

Linda's right, she always was. I want to be loved. I want to be safe.

I'll never be that with him.

"What day do we fly back again?"

"This afternoon. We're picking Mom and Dad up on the way. Mom's in France and Dad's in England."

"As usual."

"Right. So we'll have the six hours across the pond with them both, which I intend to be sleepy or drunk for. I advise you to do the same."

"Your parents love me. I'm dating a Fairfield. That's huge. I'm in college to be what I want and am starting my new job this fall, if I can find one. I don't cost them anything or make headlines." She laughs and pokes me. "I'm the daughter they never had."

I laugh with her, poking her back, pretending her words don't hurt. They wouldn't normally, but my mom's little spiel about Matt is still picking at me. My whole life is.

I've never felt so alone.

In my heart the only people who understand me are the Lumineers. It's an intensely desperate feeling.

When we get downstairs my phone vibrates but I leave it in my purse. Someone's calling.

They call a second time. But I don't answer. Instead, I paste that winning Ford smile on my face and hug Carson.

"Who has a hangover?" He inspects us both.

"I do." Nat nods. "A Lumineers hangover. I knew it was going to be amazing, but I had no idea it would be like that. It was"—tears fill her eyes—"magic. Real magic."

"Hands down the best performance I've ever seen. And I saw Prince live in a friend's backyard. Last night has me sending my dad's assistant demands. I want the tour schedule, and I intend to be backstage at least half of their smaller performances."

"I'm in." Nat nods.

"You have school and your mom would never allow it. Carson barely shows up to class."

"I still manage good grades."

"Whatever." I don't want to talk about school or the Lumineers or anything. I don't want to talk. I want to explode as we stroll to breakfast.

I stick my bag under the table when I sit. It's vibrating again.

Carson's phone goes off at the same time. His eyes lift as he checks out the screen and then he winces, putting it back. He takes a breath and glances back at the menu. "I do love the buffets in places like this—I just hate getting my own food." He turns in that direction. It looks like the sort of spread Cecilia puts out. Fresh homemade yogurts, stewed fruits and seeds, and fresh handmade breads and jellies. There's an entire selection of meats and cheeses and cut-up fruit. And then another wall of cereal and milks.

I don't want to eat. Something is picking at me.

The server pours us coffee and adds cream for me. I stir and lift it to my lips, sighing. I love European coffee and cream. It's just better. I don't know why.

Nat is on her phone too. She seems distracted. She sighs. "All the Lumineers web page says is that they're in the studio. There's literally nothing."

"Sami said that. There's no tour for at least another year or two." Carson's voice is funny. I don't know what kind of funny, maybe tense. He avoids my eyes.

"Are you ready to order?" the server comes and asks softly.

"I'll have a smoothie. Bananas, berries, fresh yogurt, and coconut milk," I say as low as she did. It's not on the menu but I don't care. Sometimes being Sami Ford isn't bad.

"Yes, Miss Ford."

Carson wrinkles his nose and then nods. "I'll have the same. Add chia to mine please. Might as well stay on track."

"Wow. Divas." Nat scoffs at us both. "I'll have the French toast and can I get some sausage on the side of that?"

"Of course." She scurries away from us.

"Why do people always do that? Why do they scurry?"

"Because you can be a heartless skank and they're scared of you." Carson laughs, glancing down at his napkin. "Guess I'm putting my own napkin on my lap." He drags it across smoothly.

"I'm not rude to anyone in service. My dad never tolerated it." I defend myself, something I don't usually do either. But on this one, I have to.

"It's true. He has always said Sami and I won't have a single maid or cook if we can't be nice to them."

Carson rolls his eyes. "My dad's shagging half of them, I think. He hires a type. It's creepy. They all look the same. Young, brunette, busty, curvy, and short. The opposite of Mom. I think it burns her but he likes her feisty. It's like foreplay I don't want to think about." He chuckles.

"Gross." Nat shakes her head.

"You have to have sport in marriage, Nat. You can't get bored because divorce is only for the weak. And we don't have the regular battles to endure. Our lives can be extremely dull if we don't create drama."

She looks at Carson like she's asking if he's for real but he shrugs it off.

"You wait. You and Fairfield will have the same life. He said you guys are thinking about moving in together when he's done school. You wait and see." Carson lifts his coffee and winks at me.

I force myself to snap out of the haze I'm in, nodding along. "Life for rich people is easy and hard in the exact opposite way poor people's are."

"You people have a screwed way of thinking."

"No doubt about that." Carson sighs and glances at his phone again.

I just nod. I can't argue the fact and I don't want to discuss it.

When we leave Vienna for France, I check my phone on the plane as we land.

I have sixteen missed calls and over a hundred messages.

All the calls are from Matt, but I have messages from other people too. I start to get worried about all those calls but check the messages first.

Matt has sent most of them so I go to the one from the person I don't know.

I click on the conversation, my jaw dropping when I see the photo. Matt's in some industrial-looking shower, his face is beaten to shit like it just happened, as in at Christmas when we were hanging out. With him is a girl in a costume on her knees in front of his naked body. He's got his hands in his hair and his eyes closed and his head back. There's water pouring down on them and steam all around. There's no text with it, just the photo.

My insides tighten.

"What the ever-loving fuck is this?" I whisper.

Who sent this?

I check the number and press call, confused. I get up and walk to the bathroom as it rings. I sit on the toilet and wait.

"Hello?" a girl answers.

"Hi."

"Hi." She pauses. "Who is this?"

"Why did you send me that picture?"

"What picture? Who are you?"

"THE FUCKING PICTURE YOU SENT OF MATT!" Tears fill my eyes as rage overwhelms me.

"I never sent a picture, just a sec." She still sounds chipper. She pulls the phone back, there's a difference in her voice as she switches me to speakerphone, "Oh shit! I don't even know who sent that, sweetie. We were at a party last night and I wasn't paying much attention to my phone."

"Did you suck his dick? Is that real?"

"Now that's none of your business. What happens between me and Brimstone is our business."

"Who the fuck are you?"

"Tandy. Who is this?"

"No one." I hang up, collapsing into the wall of the bathroom to sob. My entire body heaves as I'm blinded by rage and hate and pain. With trembling hands, I turn my phone off. I don't care what he has to say.

My heart falls out of my chest, smashing everywhere.

Of course this is how it ends. Of course this is my life. Of course.

Because why not?

I'm cursed.
I'm worthless.
I'm undeserving.

Chapter Twenty-Five

Bros before hos

Matt

January 15, 2015

"She won't see you, bro. She's in Paris drinking with friends anyway." Carson's eyes narrow. He's judging me and I don't care.

"I have to see her." But I don't have time. I have a game tonight and then one in two days. It's like that for the next two months.

"She told me she never wants to see you again. She never wants to see you or hockey or any of it again. I don't know what you did to her, but that photo has sent her over the edge. My mom said Sami's even told her dad he can pick someone for her to marry when she graduates. I think you were on the list but the hockey thing is killing you."

"She's Sami, she won't let him pick her husband." I can't believe that.

"I don't know. She's also switching her major from art history to business."

"What?" The dull ache inside me has been going steady for the two weeks since she stopped talking to me.

"Your side dish sent her a fucking picture of you getting a blow job after the game, dude. What did you think would happen? Of course she's done. She's Sami Ford. She doesn't let guys treat her that way."

"Tandy didn't send the photo. I don't know who did. Trust

me, I must have looked like I was going to kill her when I asked her. She started crying and said it wasn't her." I want to slam things and kill people and destroy worlds. I want to fly to where she is. I don't want to board a plane for another city to play another game with someone who betrayed me. "I gotta go." I wave at Carson and walk off, headed for home.

I dial Bev.

"Hey, skid mark. What's going on?" She sounds distracted and hollow.

"Are you playing a video game?"

"Yeah." It takes her a second to answer. "Why?"

"Can you stop?"

"How serious are we talking?"

"Turn the game off, please."

"Yup." She's silent for a moment and then she's back. "What have you done?"

"Nothing. Everything. I'm fucked." I climb in the elevator at my building and close my eyes. "She saw a picture of me and another girl."

"A PF?"

"Yeah—"

"You fucking idiot." Bev says it quietly, like it's worse in a low tone. It kinda is. "What were you doing?"

"It was after the game where I got in the fight, and the girl was on her knees in front of me. Sami and I weren't dating. We still aren't. I don't know what we are, but she saw the photo and she won't talk to me. Nothing happened—"

"Oh my God! You are a fucking moron. If your dad saw that, you'd be disinherited. Are you that fucking stupid? Seriously? For a blow job? And then that pic goes to the one girl you've actually liked for years? Wow! You're a douche and I don't even know what to tell you." She's lost it now. I almost relish the lashing. I deserve every hit. "I can say you need to leave this girl the fuck alone. You're probably killing her. She might be a dipshit rich bitch but she doesn't deserve this. She deserves way better than you. You're a fucker." She hangs up on me.

I look at my phone, lost. When I get into the hallway it rings. It's Bev again.

"Hey." I assume the hang up was for effect. It worked.

"And another thing, jerkwad, I'm telling Gran what you did." She hangs up again.

I enter the house, certain everyone knows everything. Benson smiles and nods at my packed bag. He doesn't say anything. He won't. He gave me that speech and I had my chance to come clean to Sami before she found out on her own. I blew it and now I've blown this.

"I was just about to send the bag down to Charles. He's waiting in the car out front. Have a good game." Benson offers something resembling a smile.

"I blew it, Benson. I ruined everything with her. She won't even see me and let me explain."

"I knew you would, sir. But almost anything can be cleaned up with some effort."

Effort.

There's that word again.

Effort.

I never have time for effort. I met her at the wrong time.

My chest is aching. My entire body hurts as I grab the bag and head back to the elevator.

When we get to the airport, the team is there ready to board.

Coach gives me a look. His eyes narrow and he nods to the side of the large hallway we're in. I don't put my bag down with the others. I head for where he is.

"I heard some bullshit, Brimley. I need it to be cleared up that this event didn't happen. I don't allow for betrayal of one's brothers. Normally, I wouldn't ask you to tattle on someone, but this is the worst crime ever committed in my fucking locker room—you hear me?"

I nod, scared of what I've done.

He lifts his phone, flashing the photo. I grimace and look away.

"Did you ask someone to take this photo?" He asks the wrong question.

I pause and stare, not sure how to answer. "Fuck, no." Is that the crime, asking someone to take a photo of Tandy? "No, sir."

"Good enough for me." He shoos me off. "Go drop your bags and don't worry about it again.

"I don't understand, Coach."

"That's what's saving your bacon, kid," he growls and walks off.

Chapter Twenty-Six

Evil Canadians

Sami

"Were you dating?" Carson asks, spreading some clotted cream and lemon curd on the scone in his hand.

"No. It was just a thing. We were—I don't know." I hate that he's still asking me this a month later. I've avoided talking about it as much as I can but he's relentless. "It was like we were together but not exclusive. I guess."

"But you're pissed he got his—"

"Don't!" I wave my hands in his face. "I don't want to talk about this, Carson. Please. Just stop. I'm not mad he got it on with someone else. I'm mad he wanted to. Like I wasn't enough." I say it before I realize what I'm saying. We both look shocked that I've just shared something so intense and personal. Something I haven't even shared with Nat. I don't know why but I'm still protecting Matt from her hatred.

"That's fair." He brushes the confession off. "So did you hear it was the Canadian he always hung out with, Laramie, who took the pic?"

"No. Canadians are nice. He wouldn't have. It had to be someone else. Maybe Matt wanted the picture taken."

"No. It was him. Matt and Tandy had no idea he took it or shared it. He's the one who sent Tandy into the shower. I think he was trying to sabotage your relationship from the start."

"Why?" That doesn't make sense. "And it wasn't a relationship. Clearly. Matt was getting his—anyway. It doesn't matter."

"It matters if the picture was taken out of context. And there's no way Mattie did what the picture shows him doing." Carson's gaze flickers to me.

"I don't want to hear that shit. A picture is worth a thousand words."

"Okay. Anyway, I think that Laramie guy is crushing on Mattie. He's being traded. Their coach is pissed. Taking photos in the dressing rooms is a total thing."

"Wow, fuck Canadians."

"I know, right? He's lucky Matt doesn't sue."

"I don't know about that. It's just a picture and Matt is a dirty puck." I roll my eyes.

"It's not just a pic. Imagine if it were you. His dad doesn't like hockey any more than yours does. If he sees that pic, Matt's fucked. He'll be out of hockey or disinherited."

"Well, he should have thought of that." I'm still angry. We might not have been dating; we might not have been anything more than me standing on the road telling him I liked him. And maybe he doesn't know how hard that was for me to do. But I can't let it go. I wish I could let him go.

"I heard you told Daddy Dearest he can pick your future husband." Carson laughs.

"I never said that."

"Did you pick me together?" His eyes shine a little too much for there to be only humor in his words, but I have to assume he's joking.

"Stop, oh my God. No. I only said I understood the need for advantageous marriages and I wasn't against them anymore. I'm never going to fall in love. So who cares who I marry? And I only said it to appease him. He was all over me last week about Matt. I told him it was honestly nothing. He didn't believe me. I gave him that to end the conversation." I narrow my gaze. "And no, it wasn't you we were speaking about. You just want me to be your beard so you can swing every way possible."

"Better friends than forced, Sami. You should think on it. I'd be game if you were." He lifts his eyebrows. "Lord knows we're in the same boat. Neither of us is free to do what we want so why not control the game?"

"I guess." He has a point.

"I heard your dad had been talking to Zach Palfrey's parents about his future. He's way worse than I am."

"Doesn't he play hockey too?" I scowl, almost annoyed that Dad would allow Palfrey but not Brimley even though they both play hockey.

"Yeah. He plays college. And he might farm team out for fun. But he won't go to the NHL. Palfrey's agreed with his parents; he's finishing school and going into the family business. This is like sowing oats and nothing more."

"Yikes." I glance at the tray of sweets between us. We both love high tea and it always looks like we're on a date, which makes our parents happy. "Zach's hot but I don't know about anything else."

"If we're not married by thirty, we marry each other?" Carson lifts his tea, offering me a dazzling smile.

"I don't know." It's only a tea deal but it feels too mature and too far away to agree.

"You don't want to be alone for the rest of your life."

"Fine." I say it to shut him up. I won't ever marry him or anyone by force. I don't want to talk about this anymore. "Anyway, Nat and Will broke up again. I hate him."

"Huge shocker there. Even I'm getting tired of Will's antics. Nat is too nice. I don't know how to solve this issue." He glances at me through his lashes. "Or any of the issues we seem to have."

"Whatever." I take an entire tart and stuff it in my mouth, not caring who's watching. I close my eyes and chew. Food tastes so much better when you're shattered and broken and devastated. It's soothing. The sugary lemon curd melts on my tongue as I chew and moan.

"That was a touch erotic, watching you take that whole thing in your mouth. No wonder Mattie boy misses you."

I flip him off but the words "misses you" sting.

After tea we part ways. I go home with Vincenzo and

play chess with Nadia, sending texts back and forth with a bummed-out Nat, trying to cheer her up with random gossip and the positives of being single and how boys suck.

Eventually, she wants to nap, which actually means game and block out the world, so I head up to my room.

My phone rings as I reach the stairs.

"Hey, Linda," I answer, wondering if I've missed an appointment.

"I wanted to check on you. How are things?"

"Sucky. But whatever. How's it going with you?" I don't think I've asked her that before.

"I called to check in on you. I want to be sure you're okay." She ignores my question.

"I'm fine. I mean I'm sad. I am human." I think I have to remind her that just because I don't show my emotions doesn't mean I don't have them. Or maybe that's me I have to remind.

"Are you angry?" she asks carefully.

"I don't know. I guess." I sit on the stairs and really think about how it all makes me feel. Being honest with her hurts and makes me hate everything I've said aloud, but then I feel better. But it's always later, after I've said it. In the moment, it sucks.

"Can you talk about it? Like why you're angry."

"I think the thing that pisses me off the most is that I did what you said: I put myself out there. I was vulnerable. And it backfired. It didn't work at all. I told someone I have worth and they didn't agree with me." Tears build in my eyes as my voice turns to a whisper, "He broke my heart but the worst part is he took away the worth I showed him." I heave a little, unable to speak for a moment, disturbed at how fast the anger and pain hit. "I felt something I've never felt before."

"What's that?"

"Agony."

"I'm sorry this happened to you. You must know you are worth so much more than how he has treated you."

"No. I don't know that. I've never known that. You always say my cruelty and cockiness are armor because I don't know my worth. You're the one who says I don't believe in myself or value who I am." I sniffle, wiping my cheeks. "And now everything hurts because of it. The kind of hurt you can't get rid of. It aches all the time. You said he liked me back."

"I'm sorry, Sami. I really thought he did."

"I should have just kept playing with him. I was in control. I got him and I got to say how and when."

"I'm so sorry."

"When I saw that photo, my chest tightened and I couldn't breathe." Tears stream from my eyes, and I see everything I want to say, but I don't know how so I force the words out, "I think my heart fell out on the floor of my parents' jet. And when I picked up the pieces it didn't become whole again. It's a mosaic and not a normal heart. It's fractured like patchwork."

"Amazing imagery, Sami. You have a gift. I hope you're still writing these down."

"I don't care about the imagery. I don't care about anything. Can't you see that? You broke me! I was doing fine before." I finally lose it.

"No, Sami. You were miserable. You came to me and asked me to help you and I did. You're better. I like you better. You're crying for God's sake. You never cry."

I don't answer. I can't speak. I'm crying harder than I can keep up with while still breathing. I hate her. This is all her fault. She convinced me to play by rules I wasn't comfortable with. I didn't see it until this moment but I do now.

"The important part of this story is that you felt something for someone and you told them. It's a start, kid. Feeling something bad is better than not feeling. You live in the zombie world of prescription drugs and detachment. So feeling destroyed isn't entirely bad for people like you."

"It feels bad. This all feels bad."

"It feels terrible. But I have been there too. I was heartbroken once and my heart was in a patchwork of bad things. But over time I healed. I fell in love again. And I loved more because of it. I understood the value of love."

"I will never love someone, ever."

She sighs. "You'll get over this. You did the right thing, ending it. He clearly was still not as into you. But that doesn't mean there won't be a boy who is. There are a million fish in the sea who would consider themselves lucky to love you." She says all the things I've tried to point out to Nat, only I was subtler. "He hasn't even tried to see you, has he?" She goes for the gut with that one.

"He came by the house a couple of times, but I told the staff I was busy and I never wanted to see him again."

"Sami, if a guy needs to see you, your staff isn't going to scare him off. He'll sit outside your house. He'll camp in a car on your road. He'll stalk the places you go. This one mistake shouldn't have scared him off, not if he loves you. You need to cut the ties. Any further involvement is only going to hurt you. That's my opinion."

She has a point.

Where is he?

Why isn't he on the street below, screaming for me to see him?

Why is my curse "Stubborn Love"?

Chapter Twenty-Seven

Chance number two hundred and eleven

Matt

February 28, 2015

The cabin fever party, my annual party, is in full swing.

The team has joined us this year, so it's double in size, but I made a rule that only wives are invited, so it's not trashy at least. My mom would burn the house to the ground if a PF were in it.

I stumble down the stairs, leaning on Brady, laughing as we head to the main house. The cold ocean air is horrid. It started as refreshing after the hours spent in the hot tub but now I'm freezing.

We stagger along the path, both of us cooling off quickly in the frigid wind. His teeth start to chatter.

"Good game tonight, Brimstone." Fairfield nods at me as he passes us, leading some brunette back to the boathouse at the bottom of the property. All I can hope is that he wasn't messing around in the house. My mom is home.

The girl he's with giggles and trips but he catches her, lifting her into the air and making noises like he's a car. He's such a douche. I don't understand what Nat sees in him.

I hate that Carson brought him to my house. We both dislike the asshole. But it's how society works. Had we slighted him on the invite there would have been parental issues. As in mine would have had a shit fit. It doesn't matter how old I get or removed from it I become, escaping this world is like getting out of Alcatraz. I invite the right people from the right families or in the right income bracket.

But it doesn't mean I have to like it.

"Did you see that dipshit?" I point behind us when I know Fairfield can't hear me.

"The brunette with the big boobs?" Brady spins, confusedly.

"No, the dick with the brunette." I chuckle. "Of course you only saw the girl."

"What?" Brady scowls. "What does that mean?"

"Nothing."

"What about the dick?"

"He's dating this girl—not the brunette—another girl. Anyway, he breaks up with her randomly so he can get with other girls. And then when he's done with them, he gets back with the girl afterward, so technically he didn't cheat."

"Bro." Brady lifts a swaying finger. "That's a legit play, bro. Don't hate the player, hate the game. That's a real way to get off scot-free. No drama."

"You're a moron."

"Whatever." He grabs his groin. "Men have needs." He laughs, leaving his hand there too long. His words hit me hard. He has no idea what it's like to love someone and wish you could be with them, but you can't because you don't deserve them.

"You mean to tell me if you met the one—the girl who just did it for you—you'd cheat on her if you could get away with it?" He can't understand the way I do. He's never been in love and he never will be. He's the ultimate manwhore. He started the club and handed out the first Wiserhood cards.

"Naw, man. Because that's a unicorn you're talking about. That girl doesn't exist. And if she does, I'm never going to be dumb enough to fall in love with her. Love's an inconvenient pain in the ass. My brother used to be cool. Now he's whipped as hell." He loses the cocky grin. "But for real, if I ever did fall in love, and I didn't kill myself, I wouldn't cheat. Cheating is something scum does. You get out if you're not happy. All those marriages we've seen in the hockey circuit with the playing around are gross." He says everything a little too loud.

"Right. And I enjoyed the kill yourself part of the story." I wrap an arm over his shoulder. "You're an idiot." I steer us toward the house, fighting the breeze the whole way.

"Girls aren't part of the schedule. Finish my degree and get to the pros, that's it."

"Good luck with that schedule." I chuckle, remembering how I'd had one too. I used to have all kinds of rules, but they didn't protect me. I would give up everything if she would just say she'd be with me.

"My dad never cheated on my mom. He was married for a pretty long time, and he never cheated before he died." He nods his head at the house casually, like he hasn't just dropped the dead-dad bomb that always makes me uneasy. "I think I need to take a piss. This isn't the kind of beach house where you piss on the grass, is it?"

"No. My mom will kill you." I point to the large door at the far side of the courtyard. "Go through there and go to the first door on the right. I'll meet you upstairs."

"Roger that." He lifts a thumb in the air and staggers for the wrong door. We've been friends for years but he rarely comes here. There's a good chance of my mom hitting on him here, whereas Mom is never in the city.

"He's going to piss in your mom's planters."

Spinning around I come face to face with the girl I was just talking about. "He probably is." I don't even turn back to check on him. I don't care and I can't look away from her. I have a terrible suspicion she won't be here if I do and this will be a drunk-induced hallucination. She looks so different. Maybe better looking but her eyes are sad.

She doesn't appear the way I would imagine her in this moment so I know it's not a delusion. She's different from everyone else at the party. She's in jeans, a parka, and a wooly hat—something the Canadians would call a toque. And she's carrying a bag of something. "It's a cabin fever party." I point at her jeans. "Bathing suits and flowery shirts." I glance down at my own bare legs and flip-flops.

"Yeah, I gathered."

"How are you?" I ask too quickly, desperate for her. It's the weirdest feeling, but I don't bother fighting it. I gave up on that the moment I lost her. The image of her receiving that photo of me and Tandy haunts me. I can see her reaction perfectly. I torture myself with it. I know her hands lifted to her mouth. Her eyes, that never tear, welled up and flooded her face. Her mascara ran and she sobbed, alone. Because she's Sami-fucking-Ford, and she doesn't show anyone what's behind the curtain. She suffers in silence, letting people underestimate her and abuse her. And I'm one of them.

"Good. I just came to bring a bunch of stuff you left at my place. I didn't think you were here. I just assumed you would want your stuff." She doesn't sound like she wants to hurt me, but her words and coldness toward me do. "I wouldn't have stopped in if I'd known there was a party."

"It's in the boathouse. Everyone's down there." I shiver slightly from the cold air on my bare arms and legs but fight looking cold. "Wanna come in?" She came to this house to be rid of me and my things, knowing I never come here. She wanted to avoid me. I deserve that.

"No." She says it breathy, in almost a whisper. Her face is filled with regret, but I don't know which part she's thinking about. Which acts she regrets. I suspect it's all the moments I wouldn't change, even if my life depended on it. They flash in the back of my mind, each one slicing me.

She bites her lip, maybe fighting saying something she'll also regret, maybe just to avoid talking until she mutters, "It was a good game tonight. Here's your stuff." She puts the bag down on the snow.

"I miss you." I ignore her small talk and lay my heart out there for her to reject. I'm already exposed to the elements; I might as well be naked in every way. She's the only person who has ever seen me vulnerable. Well, along with Charles and Benson, but they're like parents so they don't count. "I'm a fucking idiot."

"I know." Her expression changes for a second, possibly a twitch, but she doesn't say anything. She waves and turns. "I have to go."

"Wait." I jog over and spin her around. "Wait." I say it softer the second time. "Don't go." I step in closer, brushing her hair away from her face. "Stay with me. Let me explain what happened."

She lifts her gaze that hardens when her eyes meet mine. "Why?"

"Because I need you." I drop to my knees, in the snow. "Forgive me. I'm crazy about you and I fucked up."

Her lips toy with a smile but her eyes are flooded with emotions. She blinks, losing some of them down her cheeks. "Try not to get too drunk, Beast. You have a game in two days." She pulls out of my hands and turns away, leaving me there to freeze to death.

It's not the snow and the cold that will be the death of me.

It's my own stupidity.

"I need you." I decide it's time to do the thing Benson told me to do. "You're already in my heart, but I need you in my life. I lie awake at night, forcing myself to relive the moments. All the good ones. I don't think about the bad ones, they don't hurt as much. I know I broke your heart and hurt you and betrayed you. I know I underestimated you. I assumed the things everyone else sees in you were right, and when you showed me they weren't, I didn't protect that." My voice cracks and my body is stinging I'm so cold. "I force myself to relive the good stuff so I remember how good it felt. It makes the loneliness of you being gone worse. I relive it every day. I need you."

I offer her my heart to destroy. The same way she did me.

She parts her lips to respond and I prepare for the pain I gave her. But she doesn't do it. She holds my heart in the palm of her hands and she doesn't squeeze. She smiles softly and nods.

"I will give you a second chance."

"Oh, thank God. I thought you'd never—" I rush forward but she takes a step back.

"Don't thank me just yet." She looks down at my shorts. "The rules of engagement will arrive at your place in the city tomorrow. If you agree, you can let me know by text." She walks like she's coming to me but she passes me, filling the air with the scent of her shampoo. She bends and fishes my suit jacket out of the bag. It's the one I gave her when we were in England all those years ago. "And I'm taking this back."

She is breaking my heart, ripping it out.

I deserve that.

"I don't care what the conditions are. I accept. If it means I come close to a second chance, I don't want to wait. I miss you."

She holds the jacket tight to her chest and shrugs. "Okay. But there will be rules. And they won't be what you think."

"I don't care."

She stares at me for seconds, many of them. She looks like magic standing in the snow, clinging to a jacket I gave her years ago.

"Do you want to come inside?"

"No." She shakes her head. "I don't. I'll see ya around, Beast."

"What?" I step forward, confused. "I thought—"

"You thought I'd let you off that easily? Really? You believed I would let that all slide and invite you back into my life that fast?" She starts walking up the snow-covered hill. "I'll send the rules to your place when I get home. If you still want to try, I'll see you around." Her voice fades and she walks away.

I don't know what she means. I'm scared to know. But the fact she spoke to me is already a step in the right direction.

If it means I have to walk through fire to win her heart, I'll do it.

She's everything.

I don't even bother with the rest of the party. I head up to my room to change and get my things and go back to the city.

"Matthew!" my mother calls me from the hallway.

"Yeah?"

"Don't say 'yeah.' It's rude." She strolls into my room. "Was that Sami Ford here a moment ago in the parka?"

"Yeah." I say it again just to rub her the wrong way.

"Is there something going on with her?"

"Yeah." She actually cringes this time.

"What?" Her eyebrows arch.

"I don't know." I smile wide. "I hope a lot. I'm going back to the city though, so make sure you tell everyone I'm sorry and I'll see them in a couple of days at the game." I grab my bag and run out of the room.

"Matthew!" she shouts but I ignore her as I run for Brady and then Charles. I get a sense of freedom leaving everyone there. Freer than I've felt in a long time.

When we get to the city, I pace all the next day, waiting for the rules.

"Miss Sami Ford is here to see you." Benson says it with a tone.

I rush from the room to the parlor, not worrying about deodorant or how cool I look. When I get in the room she spins around, wearing jeans and boots and a coat. No bare legs and trench coat this time.

"Hi." I walk up to her, pulling her into my arms. I don't wait for permission. I can't. She's rigid. She doesn't melt into me, even when I try to squeeze her tighter.

But I don't push my luck with a kiss and just settle for a hug. I linger, taking a deep breath of her. She becomes my air.

"Here." She hands me a manila envelope, pushing her way out of my arms.

"Should we read it together? Is this like *Fifty Shades?* Is there a contract for some kinky stuff?" I laugh, taking it.

"No." She wrinkles her nose. "Wait—you read that book?"

"No. I saw the movie. It was hot."

"I read the book. It was hot." She agrees. "I have to go." A wide smile crosses her lips. "Let me know what you think."

She turns and walks to the door.

"Stay."

She spins and smiles. "The rules state I can't." She

waves and strolls out, leaving me wondering if I even want to open it.

That lasts a second before I have it torn open and am holding the paper in my trembling hands.

I swallow hard, not sure what I'm reading.

Rational thoughts leave me as I lift my cell phone up and press a name.

"I already apologized for calling you all those names. What could you possibly want now?" Bev snaps.

"Sending you a picture, tell me what you think. Sami Ford just dropped this off. If I want to be with her I have to adhere to these rules."

"Sami Ford? Are you insane? She's got revenge on her mind. This is a mistake. I don't need to see the rules. I can just tell you, mistake."

"Wait." I pull back the phone and snap a photo, send it as a message, and then lift the phone back to my face.

Her phone vibrates as it lands. "Okay, let's see what your punishment is for killing her emotions and breaking her heart." She pauses while she reads. I reread them too. "No sex. If you want to date me, you may date me. But we won't be having any sex. You may choose to date other people, that is your prerogative. No public dates. The pressure in our lives is enough and we don't need family involvement. No judging me for liking hockey, I like it. No telling anyone about the rules. No telling anyone we have anything beyond a thing. This expires on January 31, 2016. You already broke one of the rules."

"Yeah." I sigh, not sure what to say about it all.

"Wow." She sounds impressed. "She is the woman. Like I bow before her. So you will be allowed to spend the year with her, dating and hanging out. But you can't have sex and you can't tell anyone, and she's going to break up with you anyway. That's her conditions for playing her? This is genius. She's fucked. She's the Jedi of bitches. You're fucked too. You can't have her but this is the one way you can sort of have her?" Bev starts to laugh. "I guess you need to ask yourself if the juice is worth the squeeze?"

"Oh, she thinks she can play this one and I won't win her

over? I'm going to squeeze that berry until I get only the best juice. It's going to be worth it."

"You realize that part about dating other people is a test, right? You can't date anyone else. You're going to be sex-free for a year."

"I know that. I don't want anyone else." I sort of guessed it maybe. "That's a long time but that's only if she can hold out for the year."

"You're actually going to accept this challenge?"

"Yeah." I smile at the private joke the word is for me.

"Then I guess all I can say to that is welcome to being a man for the first time." She hangs up and I sit on the sofa, not sure how the hell to start this but certain I can use the next ten months to win over the girl I love.

Epilogue

Sami

"He agreed. He sent flowers with a note telling me he's cool with it all. He tried to deliver them himself, but he wasn't allowed in the building." I stare at the rules again. They seem strict.

"This is unhealthy. I don't agree. I think you're making a huge mistake. That's my honest opinion." Linda sounds tired.

"And that was the other thing; I'm going to go it alone from here on out, Linda. I think I'm done playing games. I don't need someone shrinking my head anymore."

"You're firing me?" She sounds worried.

"I am. You're the best, and I'll always recommend you. But I'm done. I feel good. I'm not depressed. I'm not worried. I'm carefree." I sit back and smile at the card he wrote to me.

"And what about when things are bad?"

"I might start talking to Nat. Or maybe Carson. I don't know. I'm not sure. But you've been an amazing sounding board. Thanks." I wait for her to spaz, but she just clicks the phone off.

I smile and put it down, hoping she's okay. She's spent a lot of her life worrying about mine with me. She might need a hobby to fill the time.

Flipping the card in my fingers, I wonder if I'm making the right decision. But that's the beauty of the whole thing: I don't know. It feels crazy and different. In my world different is almost always better.

I have no intention of giving my heart to Matt Brimley. I have no intention of giving my heart to anyone.

But I can have some fun and be young and stop worrying about the future. I've told my parents all the right things to buy me time. And now I'll have Matt Brimley without worrying about him hurting me.

It's the best of both worlds.

The End.

Obviously, not the end of Sami and Matt.

Want to read Roommates? You can find it here.

Tara Brown is an award winning, mystery writer. Sometimes she forgets which genre she writes, and these happy accidents bring an array of YA and NA and even some zombies to her list of books. If you look up the right titles, you'll also find the secret ones she writes under Sophie Starr.

She is known for plot twists and dark turns, so even her normal romance is a little off.

She lives in the PNW with her family of kids, husband, cats, and dogs.

79781352R00145

Made in the USA
Columbia, SC
08 November 2017